QUESTIONS FOR THE DEAD

"What are you going to ask your father?" she asked.

He handed her his list of questions. He had already memorized it. It said:

> What is this place where you are?
> Is there a certain length of time you can stay?
> What happens then?
> What should I do now?
> How much of the Pharmacopoeia doesn't work?

Janie finished reading and looked up, her eyebrows knitted together. "Can I go with you?" she asked.

He shook his head. "I need you to watch me, in case something goes wrong. And write down anything I say. I'll be dizzy and sick afterward, and might not remember."

"I don't know, Benjamin. This seems really dangerous."

"It's not," he said. "I've been there already."

"How long are you going to stay?"

"Until I get some answers," he said.

He picked up the glass of water and drank it down. Then he sat on his bed and closed his eyes, his feelings turbulent and strange. The After-room was the greatest scientific discovery in history—another dimension, a verifiable *afterworld*. And he had been there! And his father was there now, waiting for him.

OTHER BOOKS YOU MAY ENJOY

The After-Room

THE AFTER-ROOM

Maile Meloy

with illustrations by
IAN SCHOENHERR

PUFFIN BOOKS

PUFFIN BOOKS
An imprint of Penguin Random House LLC
375 Hudson Street
New York, New York 10014

First published in the United States of America by G. P. Putnam's Sons,
an imprint of Penguin Random House LLC, 2015
Published by Puffin Books, an imprint of Penguin Random House LLC, 2017

THE LIBRARY OF CONGRESS HAS CATALOGED THE G. P. PUTNAM'S SONS EDITION AS FOLLOWS:
Meloy, Maile.
The After-room / Maile Meloy ; with illustrations by Ian Schoenherr.
pages cm   Sequel to: The apprentices, The apothecary.
Summary: Teenagers Janie and Benjamin continue to explore the
secrets of the Pharmacopoeia while Benjamin risks
everything to find a way to connect with his father.
ISBN 9780399175442 (hardcover)
[1. Alchemy—Fiction. 2. Future life—Fiction.
3. Adventure and adventurers—Fiction.]
I. Schoenherr, Ian, illustrator.
II. Title.
PZ7.M516354Af 2015   [Fic]—dc23   2014046252

Puffin Books ISBN 9780147516947

Printed in the United States of America

The art was done in ink and acrylic paint on Strathmore Aquarius II paper.

1 3 5 7 9 10 8 6 4 2

For my grandparents,
Lou and Ed Montagne,
with love

PART ONE

CHAPTER 1

Skylark

Green and gold streamers hung from the ceiling of the gym, and the band glowed under the stage lights, against the folded bleachers. The singer had a shiny black sweep of hair and wore a narrow blue satin tie. It was late in the evening, and the punch bowl had been emptied many times.

The school dance had posed a problem for Janie Scott and Benjamin Burrows, because he was enrolled as her cousin, although he wasn't her cousin. They were not supposed to be a romantic couple. At Ann Arbor High, going to the spring formal together meant you were practically engaged. Janie wished they had spent more time thinking their cover story through.

Benjamin had wanted to just skip the dance.

"We have to try to have a normal life here," Janie had said.

The look on Benjamin's face said that he would never have a normal life. Ever. He lived underwater with grief.

Finally, Janie asked the Doyle twins to go with them. Nat Doyle was an excellent dancer, and had spun Janie all over the floor. His sister, Valentina, wore a pale blue strapless dress, her arms brown and strong from tennis, but Benjamin didn't seem to have noticed.

As a schoolboy in London, Benjamin had taken dancing lessons, and he could waltz and foxtrot in an automatic way, but he steered Valentina with only a small corner of his mind, as he did everything now. The best part of him wasn't there. He excused himself and wandered off toward the bathrooms.

The singer's face dripped with sweat under the lights, beneath his shiny helmet of hair. Janie and the twins went outside to cool off, and stood near the open door in a fresh breeze. Valentina had a complicated look on her face, and Janie knew a question was coming.

"Where are Benjamin's parents?" Valentina asked.

"His mother died when he was little," Janie said. "His father died last year."

"Oh," Valentina said. "How?"

The question had been bound to come up sometime, but Janie still struggled for an answer. The suffocating smell of smoke came back to her, and the dark of a deep mine. "In an accident," she said. "Smoke inhalation."

"Was he your father's brother?" Valentina asked.

This was another place the cover story broke down. Benjamin had an English accent, and Janie's father was clearly American. They should have thought this all through, but it had been a difficult time. "Um—" Janie said.

"He's not really your cousin, is he?" Valentina asked.

Janie shook her head.

"I didn't think so," Valentina said, smiling. "You don't seem like cousins. Your family took him in?"

Janie nodded.

"It's okay," Valentina said. "You don't have to explain."

Janie was grateful that she didn't push. The twins were private, too, and protective of each other. Their parents worked at the University of Michigan, like Janie's parents did, and their mother was black and their father was white. Most of the kids at Ann Arbor High in 1955 were just white. The twins played on the tennis team—they were unbeatable at mixed doubles—and they were careful with their friendship. They had been nicer to Janie and Benjamin, the lonely midyear arrivals, than anyone else at the school had, but they always had a kind of reserve.

Benjamin had just joined them when the backup singer took the microphone, and the band played the slow opening bars of "Skylark." It was Janie's favorite song, and she took Benjamin's hand. "We have to dance this one," she said. "Just one."

They walked out onto the dance floor, which had cleared for the slow song, and she stepped into Benjamin's well-trained dancing position. One of his hands touched her back and the other lifted her hand, but in no sense was she *in his arms*. At least someone was keeping the cover story intact: He danced like he was her cousin.

The girl sang, *"Skylark, have you anything to say to me? Won't you tell me where my love can be?"*

Benjamin looked over Janie's shoulder. Even his incorrigible hair seemed subdued. The stubborn waves had given up, and lay neatly down. As they moved across the floor, the girl sang, *"And in your lonely flight, haven't you heard the music in the night?"*

"This is your song," Janie said.

"It's not my song," he said. "It's someone talking *to* a skylark."

At least Benjamin still had his tendency to argue the smallest points. She would take that as a good sign. "All right, then it's *my* song," she said.

It was her song because Benjamin's father had disappeared in London, when she first met them, and had left behind a book full of strange instructions in Latin and Greek. An old gardener had helped Janie and Benjamin understand it, and made them an elixir that transformed people into birds. It all seemed unlikely and fantastical, now that they were in Michigan, surrounded by sensible Midwesterners with their feet planted firmly on the ground, but the avian elixir had really *worked*. Of all the things that had happened since Janie met Benjamin and his father, that moment of taking flight had been the most magical. To be suddenly free of the earth, to feel air currents in your outstretched wings, there was nothing else like it.

Janie had become an American robin: curious, a little proud, inconspicuous at home but noticeably out of place in England. Their friend Pip, a London pickpocket with acrobatic grace, had become a swallow with a long tail and a swooping dive. And Benjamin, with his shock of sandy hair, had become an English skylark, bright and quick and crowned with feathers.

Now he didn't seem anything like a skylark. He didn't take pleasure in anything. He was going through the motions of dancing, as he went through the motions at school. He hated doing algebra and identifying the metaphors in *Romeo and Juliet*, and did just enough work to keep the teachers off his back. He spent his spare time reading the Pharmacopoeia, his father's book, in his bedroom.

When Janie came downstairs before the dance in a dress the color of a lemon ice, with her hair up in time-consuming curls, Benjamin had barely looked up. She thought maybe living in the same house was a very bad idea, and they were going to end up like brother and sister. But she couldn't imagine being apart from him. There was no good answer.

The song ended and the band started a jangling fast number, to coax back the dancers who had wandered into the shadows. Janie dropped her arms and stood inside the cold fog of misery that Benjamin carried around with him.

"I know you miss your dad," she said. "I do, too."

He shook his head, staring at the parquet floor with its painted basketball markings. "You don't understand," he said.

"I do," she said. "I think about it all the time. I didn't want him to die."

"But he—" Benjamin stopped himself. There was a look of frustration and also of defiant challenge in his eyes. It was the look he'd had on his face the first time she ever saw him, when he refused to get under the table during a school bomb drill in London. It was a look that said *I am set apart*. Around them, people danced, swinging and twirling, skirts flying.

"He what?" she asked.

"He's still *here*," he said in a harsh whisper, the words catching in his throat.

Janie frowned. "You mean in dreams?"

Benjamin shook his head with impatience. A girl somersaulted over a boy's arm, behind him. "It's not a dream," he said. "I know it. My father's *still here*."

CHAPTER 2

Dreams

Janie took Benjamin's elbow and steered him off the dance floor, dodging flying legs and arms. The Doyle twins stood talking in the doorway, and Valentina gave Janie a questioning look.

"Just going to get some air," Janie said.

"We'll see you tomorrow?" Valentina asked.

"Of course!" Janie said. The Doyles were having an afternoon party. "Can't wait!"

The air outside was cool and fresh, and Janie sat beside Benjamin on the lamplit steps of the school. Her skirt made a bell around her knees. "Tell me everything," she said.

Benjamin took a deep breath and said, "It started after your parents sent me to that psychologist."

Benjamin had been unhappy in Ann Arbor, and Janie's parents had suggested that he talk to someone. His mother had died when he was three, so he had no one now that his father was gone. And living with Janie's parents seemed to remind him of what he'd lost. They tried to be kind and understanding, although her father still called Benjamin "Figment"

because of a forgotten, annoying joke. Benjamin had been reluctant to talk to the doctor.

"What did he say?" Janie asked.

"That it was normal for a kid to want to surpass his father, and replace him," Benjamin said. "But it's bad if your father actually dies. *Destabilizing*, he said. Because then it feels like your fantasy has come true, and you've defeated your own father, so you have all these feelings of guilt and responsibility."

"That makes sense," Janie said.

"No, it doesn't!" Benjamin said. "Because the doctor didn't know how *actually* guilty I am. He just knew that my father died in an accident. And what was I supposed to tell him? That my father was an international outlaw with quasi-magical

powers, who was interfering with nuclear tests, and I poisoned him trying to make a smoke screen, when we were held captive underground?"

Janie winced. "I guess not."

"So I skipped the second appointment," Benjamin said. "It was pointless, talking to that guy. Lying to him. And then the dreams started. I would be thinking about my father, about how I'd failed him, and how much I missed him, and then I would be in a dark place where I couldn't see anything. But I felt that he was there. When I came out of the dream each time, I felt dizzy. That should have tipped me off."

"To what?" she asked.

"You remember the powder I sent you. How it worked."

Benjamin had sent Janie a small glassine envelope of coarse

powder, when she was at school in New Hampshire. He'd told her, in a note, to dissolve a few grains in water, drink it down, and close her eyes. It was something he'd been working on while he was on the run with his father, so that they could communicate.

"You thought about the other person," Janie said. "And you could see where they were, through their eyes."

"Right," Benjamin said. "But it had a side effect."

"It made you dizzy afterward."

"Well, my father took the powder before he died," he said.

"Oh—" she said. The full importance of what he was saying began to dawn on her.

"You see?" he said, excited. "It hasn't worn off yet!"

"On you?" she asked.

"On either of us."

"But where is he?" she asked, looking around at the pale light cast by the streetlamp, and the dark beyond it. She felt a chill of fear, but of what, she wasn't sure—of ghosts? Of the possibility that Benjamin had lost his mind?

"I've been calling it the After-room," Benjamin said. "But it's not really a room. The walls aren't really walls, they're like—a screen, and beyond it is something else. Something farther. My father is there. I think he's keeping himself in that place, somehow. He's stalling, so he can communicate with me. Does that sound stupid?"

Janie shook her head. It sounded terrifying, but also somehow wonderful.

"The feeling is different from when we used the powder,"

he said. "It's not like being in someone else's body, because my father doesn't have a body. But he's *there*, I know he is. I know I'm not alone there."

Janie couldn't keep the hurt expression from her face.

"I don't mean that I'm alone *here*," he said. "I just—you know."

She nodded. "So what does he say?"

"That's the thing, I don't know. I can feel that he's there, but I can't get his voice. So I made some more of the mind-connection powder."

Janie felt a stinging jolt of surprise. "Without me?" she said. "When did you make it?"

"When you went to the movies with your parents."

"*What?*"

"I didn't know how to tell you."

"With *words!*" she said. "Like this!"

"I haven't used it yet," he said. "You came home before I could. And I was afraid to try it."

"You shouldn't do things like that alone!"

"But I think it might work," he said. His voice was eager and strained. "I think it might make the connection stronger."

A couple from the dance walked by, the girl's heels clicking on the concrete steps, and Benjamin waited until they'd passed. In her confusion, Janie was thinking about the fact that she'd been watching *Rear Window* in a movie theater with her parents while Benjamin was home making the powder in the kitchen. He'd said he had algebra to do. It wasn't right. She and Benjamin were supposed to work together.

"You believe me, don't you?" he asked. "About my father?"

The old gardener who had helped them decipher the Pharmacopoeia had told them that they shouldn't assume things were too far-fetched to be true. She nodded. "I do."

Relief transformed Benjamin's face, and his whole body relaxed. "I was afraid you would think I was crazy."

She smiled. "I didn't say I don't think you're crazy," she said. "I just said I believe you."

He smiled back, and she realized how close they were sitting in the lamplight. His knee was almost touching hers. He leaned toward her. They hadn't kissed since they'd arrived in Michigan. Her parents were always around at home, and at school she was supposed to be his cousin, and he'd been so unhappy and preoccupied. But now the steps were deserted, and his face drew near in the dark. She caught his familiar clean smell beneath her own borrowed perfume. She could feel his breath on her face, and the warmth radiating from his skin. Their lips were half an inch apart when the sound of a rattling engine broke the silence of the street, and then a beeping horn.

They both pulled away. A noisy, well-traveled brown Studebaker nosed up to the curb.

"Lord Figment!" her father called from the driver's seat. "Lady Jane! Your chariot awaits!"

CHAPTER 3

The Coastwatcher

In the dawn light, a body appeared on the island's northern beach. Ned Maddox spotted it from his observation platform in a banyan tree. He scanned the horizon through binoculars, but saw no boat, so he studied the body again. Thin, possibly a boy. Legs rocking in the shallow waves. It might be a trick to lure him down, a booby-trapped corpse. He tugged and scratched at his beard, thinking.

Finally curiosity got the better of him, and he climbed down the banyan tree and hiked through the brush to the beach. A wave gave the body another rolling push up onto the sand. The boy wore simple cotton clothes, sodden with seawater. As Ned approached, he saw a long black braid tucked under the shoulder. He circled slowly.

The castaway didn't leap up to attack him. He saw no wires or explosives. He grabbed a slender ankle and a wrist, rolled the body over, then jumped back, but nothing happened. It was a girl, Chinese, and her lips and eyelids were blue. He felt her wrist for a pulse. It was thready and weak. She started to cough and throw up seawater.

Still wary, he looked around, but no one appeared. So he picked the girl up and slung her over his shoulder. Water streamed down his legs as he carried her into the safety of the brush. His tiny island was theoretically under Communist control, but it was so inaccessible, surrounded by reefs and shoals, that no one ever came snooping. He didn't want them to start now.

Inside the camouflaged hut, there was only his own narrow cot, so he lowered the castaway onto it. Her eyes remained closed, and she shivered, soaking wet. He put a blanket over her. Her lips were chapped from the sun and the salt water.

He turned on the little kerosene stove to heat some broth. When it was ready, he poured it into a bowl and held it up so the steam would reach her nose. Her whole face contorted at the smell of food, and it seemed to drag her back to consciousness. She opened her eyes, blinking. He knew his beard was long and scraggly. He needed to conserve his fuel for cooking, so he didn't shave. The hair on his head was long, too. He owned a signaling mirror that he rarely looked into, but when he did, it gave him a start: A wild man looked back. Now the girl recoiled in fear.

"Don't be afraid," he said in Mandarin.

She watched him, waiting for more. She wasn't going to commit herself. But he knew she understood.

"Where did you come from?" he asked in Cantonese, just in case.

She was silent.

"My name is Ned Maddox," he said in English. "First lieutenant, U.S. Navy. Can you understand me?"

She gave a grave nod.

"Want some soup?"

She struggled to sit up, then winced and sank back, as if the movement hurt.

"Hang on," he said. "I'll help." He held her head and lifted it.

The girl took a few sips of soup and lay back against the pillow. She was young, no older than twenty-five, but there was something otherworldly about her. She looked around the hut and seemed to take everything in. He wasn't used to anyone witnessing his life. The Chinese runners who kept him supplied with food and fuel from the U.S. Navy ships were always in a hurry.

The hut had a narrow cot, a tiny table, a little stove, and a few shelves. His clothes hung on pegs. But it misrepresented his life. His realm was enormous: the black sky full of stars, the hidden platform in the banyan tree with a view to the horizon. He was lord of it all, listening and watching. He had been watching, this morning, for something in particular. An American naval officer had gone missing and was believed to be hiding in the islands. Ned had been looking for the officer, not for a Chinese girl. But could there be some connection?

"Who brought you here?" he asked. "Were you on a boat?"

"Long story," she said in Mandarin.

"Plenty of time," he said, in Mandarin also.

But the girl seemed to have no interest in recounting her story. She knew it already, so why should she tell it to him? Her eyes fell on a large yellow cloth, draped over a blocky shape at the foot of his cot. He hoped she would think it was a makeshift bureau: a crate, perhaps, where he kept his shorts and socks.

But she reached out and tugged the yellow cloth free, revealing his heavy suitcase radio and his headset. She turned to him, eyes shining.

He should be concerned, he knew, that he had exposed his listening station. She was a threat to his security and to his mission. But instead, he felt an unaccountable impulse to explain himself to her. That was just loneliness, of course. He'd been out here too long.

The girl spoke in English. "May I send a message?"

He shook his head. "It would give away our position."

She gave him an interested look. Why had he said *our*?

"*My* position," he said.

"Have you seen an Englishman?" she asked. "In a boat? A landing craft?"

He frowned. Were they looking for the same person? "Not an American?"

She shook her head, then winced at the movement.

"I haven't seen an Englishman," he said. "Is he a friend of yours?"

She frowned and closed her eyes, then lay back against the pillow again. He was left with the irrational feeling of having disappointed this intruder he didn't even know, and wishing he had the information she wanted.

He thought he should go through her things to find out who she was, but she had no things, just her simple clothes.

So he kept watch, in silence, while she slept.

CHAPTER 4

The Debriefing

J anie tried, in general, to understand her parents' point of view. They wanted her to be happy. They wanted Benjamin to be less depressed. They feared he would pull her down into his vortex of gloom, so they tried to combat it with their relentless cheerfulness.

But when her father had interrupted in his horrible noisy car, with his dumb jokes, just as Benjamin was about to kiss her, Janie thought she might scream. On the ride home, while her father asked if they'd enjoyed the ball, and talked about how difficult it was to get mice to pull a pumpkin, she seethed and said nothing. At the house, her father leaped out and opened the passenger door with an elaborate coachman's bow.

"Just stop it!" she hissed at him. "Please!"

Their house in Ann Arbor was a two-story Victorian with tall, narrow windows, which reminded Janie of a mournful face. Benjamin went straight inside without a word. He had finally started to talk to her—really *talk*, but her father's arrival had shut him back down. She went inside and watched Benjamin climb the stairs, and heard the decisive *thunk* of his bedroom door. She kicked off her shoes.

"How was it, honey?" her mother asked, curled up in her chair in the front parlor. She was grading student papers. Janie's father, aware he was in trouble, headed back toward the kitchen.

"It was fine," Janie said, in a voice that said it hadn't been.

"Your mascara's smeared," her mother said.

"Doesn't matter now." But Janie ran her fingers under her eyes.

"You looked so lovely tonight," her mother said. "Did Benjamin think so?"

"I have no idea."

Her mother frowned and patted the ottoman. "Is he thinking about his father?"

"Yes," Janie said, sitting down, because that was true.

Her parents knew about the apothecary's death. Count Vili, when he brought Janie and Benjamin home to Ann Arbor, would have given her parents drugged champagne to make them forget everything, but Janie had made him promise not to. Their memories had been taken from them once before, and it didn't seem fair to do it again. But Vili had given them *something*, some anti-worry herb or potion to make them calm and accepting when he told them that their daughter had been kidnapped and taken to Malaya. Benjamin and his father had gone to rescue her, and Benjamin's father had been killed. Her parents had been uncharacteristically mellow about the whole thing, and the story had faded, for them, into hazy background, like a fairy tale they'd nearly forgotten. That must have required some medicinal help. Her parents accepted Vili as a glamorous friend of Benjamin's father, a kind of godfather to Benjamin, who could fix things by nature of his aristocratic connections and his worldly skills. Janie curled and stretched her toes.

"What are you reading?" she asked.

"Oh, writing assignments," her mother said. "They were supposed to write a scene that takes place in a kitchen. I thought it might help them think about how people actually *talk*, in real life."

"Any good ones?"

"A couple, maybe," her mother said. "But two police officers just burst into the kitchen in this one, and said 'Hands up! You're coming with us!' For no reason, out of nowhere. I think next week we need to talk about how suspense works."

Janie's parents were screenwriters who had moved to London to avoid being forced to testify about their friends' political beliefs. But now America had grown tired of Senator McCarthy and his hunt for Communists. The senator had never produced a single spy for all his talk about having a whole *list* of them. Once, when a journalist asked him to produce the list, he'd said it was in his other pants. No one took him seriously anymore, and the Scotts were able to live in the United States without being followed by federal marshals. But there was no work at the Hollywood studios for them. The people who gave out jobs were still afraid, and moving away to London had given the Scotts the air of guilt. So they'd been teaching at the university in Ann Arbor, reading stacks of student work every night, for almost no money. Their savings were dwindling. It had been a stretch to buy the lemon-ice dress.

"I wish you could just *write* again," Janie said.

"You're telling me," her mother said. She wound her hair up in a knot, clipping it in place.

"Everyone knows you're not spies," Janie said.

"I know, but these things stick. Tell me about the dance, that's more interesting. What did the twins wear?"

"Nat wore a white tux. And Valentina wore a blue dress— sort of robin's-egg blue. And strapless."

"Mmm," her mother said. "They must've looked amazing."

Janie's mother was fascinated with Nat and Valentina, with their exotic looks and their tennis skills and their parents' bravery in marrying each other. Janie sometimes wanted to shield the twins from her mother's interest. "They did," she said cautiously.

"We're going to their party tomorrow, right?" her mother asked.

Janie nodded. She wished it were a party just for adults, or just for kids.

"Do you think Benjamin'll go?" her mother asked.

"I hope so."

"What else? Tell me more."

Janie tried to think of something besides the fact that Benjamin believed he had contacted his dead father. She could report that someone had spiked the punch early in the evening, but her mother wouldn't want to know that, and Janie hadn't drunk any, so it wasn't relevant. There had been a time when she could say anything to her mother. Not so long ago, she could say anything to *anyone*—to her teachers at Hollywood High, to her friends, to her parents' friends. Or at least there was nothing she wanted to say that she couldn't. Now there seemed to be conversational pitfalls everywhere. Was that what growing up was? An ever-mounting number of things you couldn't say? "The band played 'Skylark,'" she finally offered.

Her mother made a face. "Oh, that sappy thing. It drags so."

"It's my favorite song," Janie said.

"You're kidding."

Janie's eyes stung. She wanted not to cry. Her mother couldn't understand about skylarks, about flying over the streets of London with the wind in your feathers. Or about her extraordinary happiness when Benjamin had shown up to find her on that terrifying island, having been blown off course by storms and fallen from the sky. About how much she missed the old Benjamin.

"Honey, what is it?" her mother asked.

"Benjamin was finally talking to me about his father," she said. "He was *telling* me things. But then Dad pulled up and started making his stupid jokes, and now Benjamin's gone upstairs and closed the door." The tears spilled over, spotting the pale silk of her dress.

"Oh, sweetheart," her mother said.

"I'm so tired of his jokes!"

Her father appeared in the doorway, carrying a sandwich on a small plate. His shoulders hunched forward in apology, or maybe that was just his habitual posture, now that he was marginally employed. His curly dark hair was starting to retreat from his forehead. When he was anxious, he tugged at it, which didn't help. Janie found herself wishing that her parents were bad people so she could just be *angry* at them, without feeling terrible about it. Or at least that they would be consistently annoying, so she could stay annoyed.

"You chased Benjamin away," she said.

Her father set the plate beside her on the ottoman. The sandwich was cut diagonally, the way she liked it. She didn't want to accept the peace offering, but she was hungry, and it looked like an excellent sandwich. Turkey and Swiss cheese and crisp lettuce on toasted bread. She took a bite, and tasted tangy mustard.

Her father sat down on the couch, with his elbows on his knees. "I know I interrupted tonight," he said. "It's not easy for us, you know. Most parents don't have their sixteen-year-old daughters' boyfriends living in the house. I saw that he was about to kiss you as I drove up, and I went a little nuts."

Her mother smiled. "Oh, so there was a *kiss* at stake! I thought it was just about Benjamin telling you things."

"It *was*," Janie said. "I mean, that was the important part."

"It looked like a pretty important kiss," her father said.

Janie felt her face heat up. "It might've been, until you ruined it!"

"I'm sorry," he said. "It was an instinct. I felt protective. He lives under our roof. He sleeps upstairs."

"Believe me, *nothing* is going on," Janie said. "So you can relax."

But as she said it, she thought about what Benjamin had told her on the school steps. *Something* was going on under their roof; it just wasn't kissing. It was contacting the Underworld, or—what did Benjamin call it? The After-room. Benjamin didn't make things up, or let his imagination run away with him. He was practical; that was a core aspect of his personality. It was the first thing she'd seen in him, in London. He wasn't going to climb under the lunch table during an atomic bomb drill if it didn't make sense. And she didn't think he was crazy.

She put down the sandwich. "I'm going to bed."

"So was the dance fun, at least?" her mother asked.

"Sure," Janie said. "I don't know. It's hard to do normal kid stuff sometimes, I guess. Thanks for worrying about me." She brushed crumbs off her hands, over the plate.

Her parents looked helpless and forlorn, and she went upstairs so she wouldn't have to see them that way. The steps creaked and her silk skirt rustled as she climbed.

At Benjamin's door, she stopped and knocked quietly. "Benjamin?"

There wasn't any answer.

"I just want to say," she said through the door, "that I believe what you told me."

More silence. She was about to turn away when the door opened. Benjamin looked deranged, his eyes wild.

"I made a list of questions," he said, in an urgent whisper. "Tomorrow, when your parents go out—I need your help."

CHAPTER 5

The List

When Benjamin woke the next morning, he lay in bed listening to Janie's parents talking in hushed voices outside his door. "Shouldn't they be awake by now?" Mr. Scott asked.

"Oh, let them sleep," Mrs. Scott said. "The band played 'Skylark' last night. That'll put anyone down for a week."

They usually took a walk in the morning, and Benjamin waited. Finally he heard them go downstairs: *creak, creak, creak.* The house was old and the stairs complained. The front door opened and closed behind them. Then he jumped out of bed, got dressed, and padded in socks to Janie's door. She answered in pajamas, with black smudges beneath her eyes and her hair in flattened, messy curls.

"Now's our chance," he said.

She rubbed her eyes. "Just give me a minute."

When she came to his room, she was more recognizable, clean-faced and ponytailed, with a bathrobe tied over her pajamas. She looked prettier without the makeup. He remembered how they had almost kissed the night before, then pushed the thought aside. They had important things to do. His father was out there, he could feel it. He tapped a few grains of powder into a glass of water and swirled it to dissolve them. Janie watched.

"I can't believe you made that and didn't tell me," she said.

"Sorry," he said. And he was sorry. But he hadn't had the energy for teamwork lately, or for worrying about whether Janie would believe him. It would've shaken him too much if she hadn't, and he couldn't afford to be shaken. It took everything he had just to face her parents at breakfast, and get through school each day.

"What are you going to ask your father?" she asked.

He handed her his list of questions. He had already memorized it. It said:

> What is this place where you are?
> Is there a certain length of time you can stay?
> What happens then?
> What should I do now?
> How much of the Pharmacopoeia doesn't work?

Janie finished reading and looked up, her eyebrows knitted together. "Can I go with you?" she asked.

He shook his head. "I need you to watch me, in case

something goes wrong. And write down anything I say. I'll be dizzy and sick afterward, and might not remember."

"I don't know, Benjamin. This seems really dangerous."

"It's not," he said. "I've been there already."

"How long are you going to stay?"

"Until I get some answers," he said.

He picked up the glass of water and drank it down. Then he sat on his bed and closed his eyes, his feelings turbulent and strange. The After-room was the greatest scientific discovery in history—another dimension, a verifiable *afterworld*. And he had been there! And his father was there now, waiting for him. He tried to be calm.

He had to think about his father, to reach him. So he pictured the abstracted air his father used to get when he worked, the way he pushed his spectacles up on his nose and disappeared into his mind when he had an idea.

Then, unbidden, came the image of his father's agonized face, struggling for air, on the verge of death. Benjamin didn't want *that* memory—his heart began to race. His father had told him not to get caught up in grief, or anger, or bitterness. Because he was the vessel through which the work flowed, and the vessel couldn't be collapsed by guilt. But he couldn't help it.

He felt a twinge of uncertainty. Maybe Janie was right, and this was dangerous. He concentrated on the idea of his father healthy and well, in his shop back in London, and then the dark behind his closed eyelids opened up into the different, unearthly darkness of the After-room. He recognized it at once. It was both a place and not a place. A room and not a room.

"Dad?" he said—or thought. It was like speaking in a dream. "I'm here."

There was a silence that felt like disapproval. And why wouldn't his father disapprove? Benjamin had been responsible for his death.

He grimaced with the pain of remembering, and took a breath. "I have some questions," he said.

Still silence. The room had no corners—so was it circular? Not exactly. An ellipse, maybe. The walls were like a screen, and outside, he saw shimmering particles. Benjamin had always thought that he didn't remember anything specific about his mother, but now a memory came into his head. He was very small, and she was reaching down to pick him up. She was lifting him over her head, laughing—so young and happy—and then she brought him down out of the air and gathered him close.

His *mother*! He was prepared for his father to be here, but not for *her*. She had been gone so long. He felt that she was not in the After-room but outside it, in the place where the shimmering lights were, and he started to move toward them.

"Mother!" he called. "Are you there?" He pushed against the walls of the After-room. They were like gauze—no, they were like a thick, viscous fog. There was pressure mounting in his head, and he was getting very cold.

Then his father's voice came booming. "Benjamin—don't!" It sounded like the result of great effort: a gathering of strength to speak. His father was here!

But Benjamin was suddenly afraid of the things he would

have to say, if he spoke to his father. With his mother there would be no guilt, nothing for which he was responsible. He had been only three when she died. He moved toward her again.

"Benjamin!" his father called.

"She's out there!" Benjamin cried.

"You can't go to her."

"But I want to!" He sounded like a child. His careful list was forgotten. *How much of the Pharmacopoeia doesn't work?* What a stupid question! Why had he cared about that? He could go to his mother now, the mother he had never known. It was getting hard to breathe. "I want to see her!"

Someone else was calling his name, too, and he shook his head to make these distractions go away. Everything felt dense and slow. And so cold. To warm himself, he thought of his mother lifting him over her head again. Her smile, and her laughter. It was out there, if he could only get to it.

Something shadowy reached for him. Snakes. He pushed them away, but they weren't snakes, they were arms, hands, clutching and grabbing him. He tried to struggle free. Something was pulling him away from everything he wanted. Why would anyone do that? How dare they? The After-room began to disappear, the fog to disperse. He struggled.

"Benjamin, wake up!" Janie said.

He opened his eyes wide and he was back in a real room, a bedroom, *his* bedroom. Janie was there. It was her arms that had grabbed him. Her eyes were wide and terrified. He was lying on his bed and Janie was shaking him, shouting.

"Breathe!" she said.

He took a dragging breath that seemed to come through a tiny hole in his throat, with space for only a tiny sip of air. He gasped, the wheezing breath like sandpaper in his chest. It made a terrible noise. His lungs ached. It was so much easier *not* to breathe.

"Again!" Janie cried.

The room spun like a carnival ride. Benjamin closed his eyes and sank back into comfortable dimness. *Mother.*

Then a bright pain burst unexpectedly on his face, and he looked up at Janie. She had slapped him. He scowled at her. Slapped him!

"Stay awake!" she said furiously. "Breathe!"

His voice came out as a wheezing croak: *"I can't."*

"You have to!"

"Water."

"I'll get you water," she said. "But you have to keep your eyes open! And keep breathing! Okay?"

He managed to nod. She ran from the room. He watched the spinning ceiling but he couldn't stand it, he thought he would throw up, and he closed his eyes again, sinking into darkness.

"Benjamin!"

She was back, and shook him again. He opened his eyes, and she held a glass of water to his mouth. He drank, and his throat seemed to relax a little. He could take in more air now, and it didn't hurt so much.

"You stopped breathing," Janie said. "Your face turned purple, and you were so cold. You can't go back there again. Promise!"

"My mother," he whispered.

"You were dying, Benjamin."

"It was so beautiful. She was *there*."

"You can't go with her," Janie said. "I need you *here*. Okay?"

Downstairs, the front door opened and closed, Janie's parents back from their morning walk.

"Rise and shine!" her father called up the stairs, impossibly cheerful.

"It's so *gorgeous* out there, you two!" her mother said.

"I'm making eggs!" her father called.

Benjamin stared at Janie. "Don't tell them," he whispered.

She wiped tears off her face. "I think you should see a doctor," she said. "You weren't breathing."

"*Please* don't say anything."

"Do you think you can eat?" she asked.

Benjamin nodded.

"And talk to my parents?"

"As long as your dad doesn't call me Figment."

Janie smiled weakly. "I can't promise that." She picked up the glass jar of powder from his night table and slipped it into her bathrobe pocket. "I'll just keep this."

Benjamin watched the jar disappear. He said nothing, but he was surprised how painful it was to see it go, and how sharp his longing was to have it back.

CHAPTER 6

Traffic

The man who had found Jin Lo shared his food and water with her, and gave her his cot to sleep in, but she still wasn't strong enough to walk more than a few steps without support. She was annoyed at her own weakness, and irritated that Ned Maddox wouldn't let her send a message to her friends, or even listen to his radio, when that was the one thing she might easily do. He said it would drain the battery. So instead she slept, and thought.

He came in from his post in the banyan tree at noon, pulling a sun hat off his head. He had shaved his face and cut his hair since she arrived, and he looked less like a madman, but she missed the tangled beard of her rescuer. Now he seemed like a military officer, superior and insensible. She did not have good associations with soldiers. But she had an idea for him.

"With a bicycle," she said, "you could charge this radio."

His face broke into a wide smile, a smile that made her

think Americans were different. It didn't matter how much war this man had seen, or how long he'd been alone on a deserted island; his smile came from a place of innocence and excellent dentists. "You mean bring a bike in here, and wire it to the generator, and charge the battery?" he said.

She nodded.

"That's a good idea," he said. "You'll pedal?"

"Yes!" she said. Was he taking her seriously? "I will get stronger."

"Great, I'll requisition a bike," he said. "It should take about three years to get here."

She frowned.

Ned Maddox lifted his binocular strap over his head and hung it on a hook. He had quizzed her about her country's politics, wanting to determine that she had no love for Mao Tse-tung, and then he told her something about the work he did. He had been a coastwatcher in the war, hiding behind the Japanese lines, sending reports back to his commanders. Now the civil war in China went on and on, with the United States supporting Chiang Kai-shek against Mao's Communists. And Ned Maddox had been assigned here again to keep watch.

He was lonely, or he would not have told her so much. She thought she must seem like a magical being in a children's story, washing up on his beach. Maybe he believed she would grant him wishes. He made two sandwiches.

"So, you ready to tell me why you're here?" he asked.

She shook her head.

"People are on edge, you know," he said. "We almost had a nuclear situation. I'm supposed to report what I see."

She frowned. "What nuclear situation?"

He eyed her. "It was in the newspapers."

"I have seen no newspapers," she said.

So he told her that the two Chinese factions were fighting over the tiny islands of Quemoy and Matsu, close to the Chinese mainland. Chiang's Nationalists had been reinforcing the islands with guns from Taiwan, and Mao's army had bombarded them with shells from the mainland. President Eisenhower had considered a nuclear attack on China, but then had decided against it. The shelling went on, back and forth.

Jin Lo cursed herself, because it was exactly the sort of situation she was supposed to be watching for. Instead she had been lost at sea, barely keeping herself alive, with nothing to show for it: Danby and the supercharged uranium were gone. "I have nothing to do with that," she said, and it was sadly true.

Ned Maddox handed her one of the sandwiches. "So who's the Englishman you're looking for?" he asked.

"He stole something," she said.

"What?"

"Something I need back," she said. "He has an old landing craft, from the war, so he could be anywhere, hiding on any island."

"A boat like that needs fuel," Ned Maddox said.

"He is resourceful," she said.

"And did you ever run across an American officer?" Ned Maddox asked. "On his own, while you were out there?"

"Yes," she said.

He brightened. "Where?"

She pointed at him.

He smiled that wide smile again, with crinkles of amusement around eyes that were the color of the ocean. "A different American," he said. "He might be in a boat, like your Englishman."

"He is what you're looking for?"

"One of the things," Ned Maddox said.

She struggled to sit up. "I want to help," she said. "I can listen to your radio while you watch."

"You just want to find your Englishman," he said.

"I might find your American, too."

"I can't let you listen," he said. "It's against my orders."

"You have never done something not in your orders?" she asked. "Because you knew it was the best thing? The right thing?"

A muscle worked in Ned Maddox's jaw. "You can't use the radio," he said.

He took his sandwich and went back out to his tree. Jin Lo looked greedily at the boxy shape beneath the yellow cloth. She only had to wait now. He was changing his mind.

That evening, when he came in from his post, he said, "No transmissions. Or the Chinese navy will descend on us like hellfire. You understand?"

She nodded.

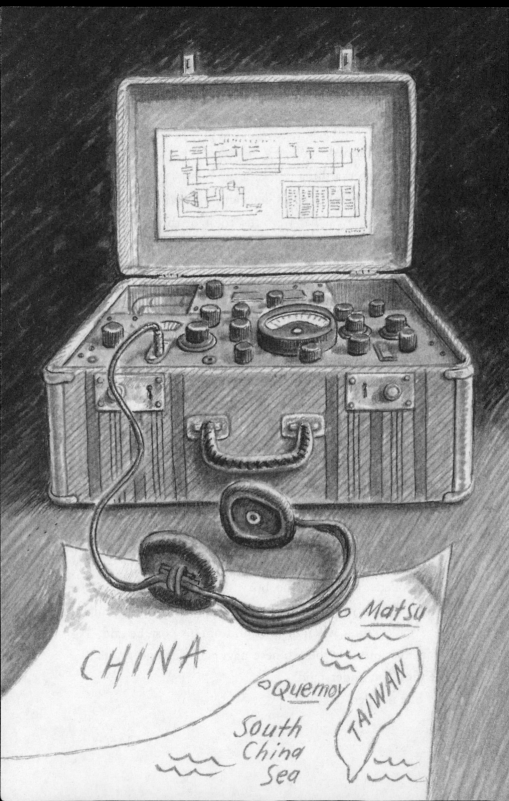

He uncovered the heavy radio and showed her how it worked, then handed over his padded earphones and started making up his bed on the floor of the hut. She put the earphones on and began to scan the dial. A thick cloud of radio traffic swirled around her, some in Chinese, some in English, some in code, back and forth among airplanes and towers, ships and ports and ground units. It was like dipping a cup into a vast river that kept flowing past her. How would she find what she needed?

Rotating the dial through a patch of static, she thought she heard the apothecary's voice, and her heart leaped. She turned the dial back, searching for it again. It had been kindly and firm, speaking English, a voice from the ether. What had he said? There was only static now, in the place on the dial where the voice had been.

"Anything interesting?" Ned Maddox asked, lying on the floor and looking at the ceiling.

Jin Lo shook her head, her hands trembling. "Not yet."

CHAPTER 7

The Magician

Benjamin was light-headed and distracted at breakfast. Janie's parents were annoyingly jolly, but at least they didn't call him Figment. And the scrambled eggs were good: salty and hot, not too wet or too dry—he had to give Mr. Scott that. But he felt far away, not quite in touch with the real world. He kept thinking about the After-room. Was his father really remaining close by choice? Or was he trapped in that place? Would Benjamin ever be able to go there safely, or would it always suffocate him?

The Scotts talked on around him.

"The twins' uncle is doing a magic show at the party," Janie said.

"Oh, *no*," her father groaned. "Like, pick a card—any card?"

Benjamin agreed with Mr. Scott, for once. When you had flown as a bird and become invisible, it was hard to get excited about someone waving a wand over a hat.

"He's supposed to be good," Janie said. "*Promise* you won't embarrass me?"

"He's the uncle on which side?" her father asked.

"You mean is he black or white?" Janie said, narrowing her eyes at him.

"I just want to imagine him in my mind!" her father said.

"He's their father's brother, I think," Janie said. "A Doyle."

"Okay, so a pasty white beanpole," her father said.

"Dad!"

"I might stay home," Benjamin ventured.

"I knew this was coming," Mrs. Scott said.

"You *can't*!" Janie told him.

Benjamin looked back at her, in a silent struggle. "I don't want to go," he said.

"But the twins have been so nice to us."

"It's true," Mrs. Scott said. "They have."

"Look, it's an afternoon magic party," Mr. Scott said. "How bad could it be?"

He was being sarcastic, but they were all three staring at Benjamin, worrying about him. Benjamin hated it. "Fine!" he said. "I'll go."

At the Doyles' house, the twins' mother took Benjamin's coat at the door. She was pretty and brown-skinned and looked like the twins, except that they were both taller than she was. She wore her hair pulled back and a lavender dress. "I'm so glad you could come," she said.

There were other university people at the party, and a buffet table in the dining room, and the Scotts disappeared into conversation. The twins took Benjamin and Janie upstairs to see their bedrooms, which were identical, with striped wallpaper and neat single beds and tennis trophies lined up on matching shelves on the walls.

Janie sat on Valentina's bed. "What kind of magic does your uncle do?" she asked.

"Close-up stuff," Valentina said. "Card tricks."

"He makes things disappear," Nat said.

"He's cutting me in half today," Valentina said. "He had a girlfriend who was his assistant, but she broke up with him for drinking too much."

"How does it work?" Benjamin asked.

"I can't tell you!" she said, smiling.

Nat said, "I'll bet you five bucks you can't figure out *any* of his tricks. They're really good."

"Is that his only job, being a magician?" Janie asked.

The twins glanced at each other.

"Actually, I think he makes more money playing poker," Nat said.

"Kids!" a voice called. "The show's starting!"

Downstairs, a corner of the parlor had been made into a makeshift stage, and the party guests gathered around it. The twins' uncle was tall, thin, and redheaded: a pasty white bean-pole, just as Mr. Scott had said, in a black tailcoat. He had pale green eyes and wore a silk top hat, which he swept off in greeting.

"Ladies and gentlemen!" he said, in a portentous voice. "I am Doyle the Magnificent!"

Benjamin groaned inwardly.

"Before we begin," the magician intoned, "I ask you to put

your hand in your pocket and identify some object there. Trouser pocket, jacket pocket—makes no difference, only please notice something you have carried here. It might be a slip of paper. It might be a key, a money clip, a pair of eyeglasses. Simply make note of the object and its contours, and leave it where it is." He stared at them all intently, with those unsettling green eyes.

Benjamin didn't want to play this game, but still he reached into his pocket and felt the small gold charm there. It was shaped like a human skull. He felt the smooth forehead, the indentations for the eyeholes, the grid of teeth. A sailboat called the *Payday* had once rescued him in the vast Pacific, with his father and Jin Lo aboard, and the skipper's wife had given him the charm to keep. "It's supposed to remind you that you're going to die someday," she'd said. "And I don't need to be reminded of that."

"Now, please turn your attention to this deck of cards," the magician said, and the show began.

Doyle the Magnificent was good. He produced cards out of nowhere. Benjamin was close to the front of the room, and he couldn't keep track of the hand movements. He was still trying to figure out the last trick when the magician asked a young man in a Michigan sweater to choose a card—any card—and show it to the audience. The student, who had pink ears that stuck out like jug handles, took a card from the deck and held it up. But then it turned out not to be a card. It was a piece of paper.

The magician plucked it from his fingers. "What's this?" he said. "Shall we read it?"

The young man's ears turned bright red, and he reached for the paper. "No!"

But the magician was tall and long-armed. He leaned back out of reach and squinted at the handwriting. *"Georgia,"* he read. "And a telephone number. Now, who might be the lovely Georgia who has given her number to this nice young man?"

Benjamin looked around and saw a girl in a red cardigan, just behind him in the crowded parlor, blushing furiously.

"There she is!" the magician cried. "You can tell because she's turned the color of her sweater!"

Georgia looked like she wanted to vanish.

"Oh, he's a very worthy young man, my dear!" Doyle said. "Getting an excellent education! You were right to give him your number. Let's give these two lovebirds a hand."

The audience applauded, laughing.

"Now, Georgia," the magician said, producing a small black tube. "You might want some lipstick to set off that fetching blush."

Georgia gasped, and pushed her way to the front, past Benjamin. "That's mine!" she said, grabbing the lipstick back.

At that moment, everyone realized what was going on. Benjamin reached into his pocket, and the little gold skull wasn't there. It had been there five minutes ago—he had felt it with his hand. Around him, people were finding their own pockets empty, and a murmur went up from the crowd.

The magician held up his hands for silence. "Don't fret, my friends," he said. "Your possessions are quite safe with me."

Benjamin checked his back pockets. All eyes had been on the magician the whole time. He had stayed on the makeshift stage. How had he stolen so many objects? Did he have an accomplice? Benjamin knew only one pickpocket good enough to go through all those pockets without getting caught, but Pip was in London.

"Next, a lucky coin!" the magician said, peering at the date on it. "A 1929 half dollar. Not such a lucky year. Who would keep a memento of the year the stock market crashed?" He gazed around the room, and his eyes settled on a man who looked about thirty, in a sweater and tie, whose lips were pressed firmly together, as if he was determined not to tell the magician anything.

"Ah," Doyle said. "I see. It was minted the year your dear wife was born."

The man's closed expression dissolved. His face was naked with astonishment. "How did you—" he began, but the magician made the coin disappear, showed his empty hand, and then made it appear again. He stepped into the audience to hand it back, and the owner checked the coin to make sure it was his.

"Yes?" the magician asked.

"Yes," the man with the coin said, amazed.

"And now," Doyle said, clapping his hands together, "I will saw my lovely assistant in half!"

A long box on wheels had been parked against the parlor wall, and Doyle rolled it out and demonstrated how it opened: nothing inside. Valentina came forward in a red sequined dress and black tights, slipped off her shoes, and climbed in.

Doyle produced a metal saw, made it wobble in the air, passed it through the middle of the box and separated the two halves. Two feet in black stockings wiggled at the end of one half. Valentina's head stuck out of the other. She had a forced, uncomfortable smile on her face, but the audience seemed impressed.

Benjamin looked for Janie across the parlor, to gauge her response to the show, but she was watching the magician reassemble his niece. Valentina climbed out of the box, held up an arm in triumph as the audience applauded, and curtsied.

"I would like to thank each of you for your patience," Doyle was saying. "And for being part of my humble show. I couldn't do any of this without you. We create the magic together!"

There was more scattered applause, mixed with murmurs about the stolen objects. But the magician was just preparing for his finale. He moved toward an old man with a white beard. "You sir, I would like to thank for the gift of your time," he said. "The most valuable gift. The one we can never replace." He held up a silver pocket watch by its chain and let it swing.

The man reached for the pocket watch with awe. "It was my father's," he said.

"It was five minutes slow, so I wound it."

The old man flipped open the silver cover to check.

Doyle turned to the twins' mother. "My dearest sister-in-law!" he said. "I can see you aren't pleased with my little tricks. But your guests will be made whole, just like Valentina was, don't you worry." He produced a small brass key from between his fingers. "And you may have the key to your liquor cabinet back. I know you were keeping it from me, in particular."

There was a ripple of laughter across the room. The twins' mother looked furious. She took the key from him and put it in her pocket.

Next, Doyle produced a fountain pen that Benjamin recognized. It was Janie's father's pen: silver, with vertical ridges on the cap. Benjamin watched as the magician found Mr. Scott in the crowd. "Your pen, sir," Doyle said. "And say, when are you going to use it to write again, instead of teaching those ungrateful kids?"

Janie's father took the pen stiffly, surrounded by his university colleagues. "Teaching is very—gratifying," he said.

"Mmm-hmm," the magician said.

Mr. Scott slipped the pen into his shirt pocket, his mouth pressed tight.

"And *you*, my dear girl," Doyle said, turning to Janie so abruptly that Benjamin saw her jump. "So full of secrets. I almost didn't take your little red notebook, as I knew it had

been taken from you before." He held up the notebook that Janie carried everywhere, and she snatched it out of his hand.

"Don't worry, I didn't read it!" he said, all mock innocence. The audience laughed.

Janie looked over to Benjamin, appalled.

Next, the magician held up a car key and studied it in the light. "A key for a German car—a Mercedes-Benz, I believe. Am I right?" He returned the key to a plump, shiny man in a blue suit. "They make good American cars right here in Michigan, you know," he said.

Approving laughter from the audience, and disapproving glances at the Mercedes driver, who took his key and made his way out of the room.

"*Auf wiedersehen!*" the magician called after him.

Then he produced a driver's license, held it up between two fingers, and read the name. "Nathaniel Lincoln Doyle," he said. "A brand-new license. I should probably keep this, for the safety of the pedestrians of Ann Arbor."

Nat grabbed the license from him, irritated. The audience laughed again. They were delighted with Doyle's jokes, and delighted to see their things. As each item was returned, the owners began to drift back toward the buffet in the dining room, talking and guessing at how he'd done it. The room thinned out.

By the time the magician turned his green eyes on Benjamin, the parlor was empty. Doyle seemed exhausted. His orange hair was damp, slicked back from his face. He held out a freckled hand and Benjamin felt the gold death's head drop into his palm. He was seized by the uncomfortable conviction that this magician could do *actual magic*. He could do things Benjamin had never seen before. The little skull was the same charm, unchanged: the smooth forehead, the eye sockets, the teeth.

"How do you do it?" Benjamin asked.

Doyle gave him a weary smile. There were beads of sweat at his temples. "A magician never tells his secrets!"

"It's not a trick," Benjamin said.

"*All* magic is a trick."

"You know what I mean," Benjamin said. "I need to talk to you."

Janie appeared with Benjamin's coat over her arm. "Let's go," she whispered.

"I *have* to talk to him," Benjamin said.

He turned back to the magician, but Doyle had vanished in the moment when Benjamin looked away. They checked the other rooms. Doyle wasn't at the buffet in the dining room, or in the front hall.

They found the twins in the kitchen, sharing a piece of cake. "Sorry, that was kind of weird," Nat said, with a grimace.

"You were great, Valentina," Janie said, her voice shaky and polite.

With a few quick strokes on a piece of paper, Benjamin drew the box and the way the assistant would fold up inside one end of it. "I don't know how you move the false feet," he said.

"I don't," Valentina said. "He does."

"How?" Benjamin asked.

"I don't know."

Benjamin frowned at his drawing, then said, "Can I have his address?"

"He won't tell you his secrets," Nat said.

"I just want to know where he lives," Benjamin said.

The twins looked at each other. Something passed between the two of them, without words. Then Nat wrote down an address over Benjamin's drawing.

"It's kind of a dump," he said.

CHAPTER 8

Keep Mum

The runners were scheduled to bring supplies, so Ned made a hiding place for Jin Lo in the brush beyond his hut. Until now, his offense had only been one of inaction. He should have reported the girl to his superiors as soon as she arrived, and he hadn't. But now he was actively hiding her, and that was a very different thing.

He'd been out here too long—that was the problem. During the war, he'd had a team: a translator, a Chinese weather expert, and a few Chinese guerrilla fighters. When the war ended, the others had danced on the beach, skinny from their limited food supplies, so happy to be going home. But Ned's parents were dead and he had no home to go to. He spoke Mandarin and Cantonese, and when naval intelligence asked him to go back to China, he did.

There were always warnings, in the service, about beautiful spies. About keeping your mouth shut when you went on leave. *Loose lips sink ships. Keep mum, she's not so dumb.* But this Chinese girl wasn't a spy. She was something else. He just wasn't sure what that something was.

He said nothing to the runners, while he helped them carry boxes of food and cans of kerosene up the beach. Jin Lo was utterly silent in the brush, as he'd known she would be. He hoped she was all right out there. It was a strange feeling, to worry again about someone else.

One of the runners handed Ned a sealed envelope. Then he helped them push off in their little boat. When they were gone, he tore open the envelope and found a message in code. He folded the piece of paper away in his shirt pocket and walked up to the hut.

Jin Lo emerged from the brush. Her steps were silent as she crossed the uneven, overgrown ground. She studied his face.

"Anything interesting?" she asked.

"Maybe chocolate," he said. "We can sort through the boxes and see."

She looked impatient. "About the men we are looking for?"

He shook his head. He had found himself unable to report her to his superiors. And unable to tell her what he was looking for. But if he didn't report her, then what was his purpose out here? And if he trusted her, then why not take her into his confidence? He felt pulled in two directions at once, caught motionless in the middle.

CHAPTER 9

The Deal

After the Doyles' party, Janie walked home with her parents and Benjamin. She had her fingers wrapped around the red notebook in her jacket pocket. Her parents were talking about the magician.

"He shouldn't be rooting around in people's pockets," her father said, still annoyed about his fountain pen and the dig at his stalled writing career.

"You have to admit he was good," her mother said. The broken earring the magician had taken from her pocket had been of no significance, so she'd only been amused.

"The first rule of show business is 'Leave the audience alone!'" her father said.

"No, it isn't," her mother said. "You're just envious. If you could write a screenplay that could pick people's pockets, you would."

"I want to pick the *studio's* pockets," her father said. "The audience—I just want to pick their *hearts*."

"Oh, is that all?" her mother asked, laughing. "How very unintrusive of you."

Her parents didn't seem to wonder how the magician had known about her father's interrupted career. They thought that *everyone* knew that, because it was the central fact of their lives, and on their minds all the time.

Janie hung back on the front porch when they got home. Her parents went inside.

"Benjamin?" she began, uncertain. "What did the magician tell you?"

"That he was just doing tricks."

"But you don't believe it."

"No," he said. "It's telekinesis, I'm sure of it! He took what was in people's pockets. Vili can do it a little, he can turn the pages of books—but not like *that*. I want to see if there's anything in the Pharmacopoeia about it." He reached for the screen door, to go inside.

"Benjamin!" she said, to stop him. There was a humming feeling inside her chest: an odd, anxious buzzing. "My notebook wasn't in my pocket."

Benjamin turned back, looking confused.

"My dress doesn't have any pockets," she said. "So I thought about the notebook, when he said to think of something. But the notebook was in my jacket pocket, under a pile of coats on a bed, on the other side of the house."

"You're sure?" Benjamin said.

She nodded. "The jacket was still there, under all the coats, when I went to get it. So he knew exactly what I was thinking. And then he got the notebook from the *other room*. How did he *do* that?"

Benjamin frowned down at the planks of the porch. "Maybe the twins helped him. They've seen your notebook."

She shook her head. "I don't think it was them. Nat was annoyed about the license. And Valentina was changing clothes, and then she was in the box. I think he can move things *and* he can read minds."

Benjamin nodded. "The two skills could be linked," he said. "They're both a kind of mental . . . extension. But there must be an explanation. We can do things that seem incredible, too."

The anxious feeling in Janie's chest grew stronger. "No, we can *make* things that are incredible," she said. "It's different. He's not using any potions, or elixirs. He can read the minds of a whole room at once, without any help."

Benjamin's mouth tightened. "That's even more reason to go see him. He might be able to help me talk to my father." He turned back to the door.

"He scares me, Benjamin," she said. "I don't think we should go there."

"We *have* to know what he can do," he said.

After school the next day, they stood in front of the address the Doyle twins had given them: a bar called The Mermaid, with peeling paint on the sign. The mermaid herself looked

kind of sickly, with a pale green tail and long faded hair. Janie was terrified. But she'd followed Benjamin to Nova Zembla, and he'd followed her to an island in Malaya. This was only Ann Arbor. Not the nicest part, but still: Ann Arbor! She kept telling herself that.

They went around to the side of the building, following the twins' instructions, and saw a weathered staircase leading up to the second floor. The wooden steps groaned beneath their weight as they climbed. Before Benjamin could knock, the door swung open.

Doyle the Magnificent squinted at them against the day-light. His hair blazed orange in the sun, and his pale eyes were rimmed with red. His dress shirt was unbuttoned at the throat. "I thought we'd finished our conversation," he said.

"We didn't even start it," Benjamin said.

"I have a birthday party to get to."

"Then let us in," Benjamin said. "We're not going away."

Doyle sighed and stepped back from the door.

The apartment had a stale, sour smell. The carpet was gray, and there were dishes in a small sink. Doyle slipped one limber arm under his suspenders. His shirt was bright white and beautifully ironed, out of place in the drab apartment. Janie guessed he took care of his shirts because they were part of his act.

"It's just one of those things that professionals do better," Doyle said. "Like—making croissants."

"Sorry?" Janie said.

"Ironing shirts," he said. "I never learned how to do it. A laundry in Germantown does a first-rate job. Just the right amount of starch." He turned to Benjamin. "Listen, kid, since you came all this way, I'll give you some advice. Death is not to be trifled with."

Janie struggled to control her thoughts, to keep them from Doyle.

"I was gonna tell you that when I gave your skull back," Doyle said. "I was tired last night, and I didn't want to start something. But here we are."

"What do you mean—trifled with?" Benjamin asked.

Doyle rolled his eyes. "Don't play around with me," he said. "I know you're looking for your dad."

Janie touched Benjamin's arm. She wanted to leave, and get out of the apartment where this man could read their thoughts.

"It's a bad idea, to go visiting dead guys," Doyle said. "You have to let him go."

"I can't," Benjamin said. "I need you to help me."

"Oh, no!" Doyle said, holding up his long, thin fingers. "You dabble in black magic if you want, traipse around on the dark side, but leave me out of it."

"How do you know so much?" Benjamin said. "Is it just from reading our minds?"

"*Just* from reading your minds?" the magician said. "You think that's a contemptible little party trick?"

"Well, we're right in the room with you," Benjamin said. "How hard could it be?"

The magician grabbed Benjamin's jacket and pulled him

close. "You show up at my door uninvited, and you ignore my good advice, and you're *rude*. I don't like it."

Benjamin wrinkled his nose. "You smell like whiskey."

"Two drinks!" Doyle said, but he pushed Benjamin away. "I've only had two drinks!"

"It's ten in the morning," Benjamin said, shaking his clothes straight.

Doyle looked sulky. "It's not easy knowing what everyone's thinking all the time," he said. "You might find yourself wanting a cocktail at breakfast, too."

Janie remembered boiling an herb called the Smell of Truth in London, to see if it would work as a truth serum. She had blurted out, under its influence, that she had a crush on Benjamin, and he had admitted to a crush on the beautiful and rich Sarah Pennington. It had been agony. She could see how knowing what other people were thinking could be painful.

"Can't you turn it off?" she asked.

Doyle shook his head. "Loud music masks it, a little."

"Does it run in families?" Janie asked. "Is that how the twins are so good at doubles? They know what the other is thinking?"

Doyle puffed out his cheeks. "No, the twins are just excellent tennis players," he said. "And *twins*. That's its own special weirdness."

"Maybe they have a version of it."

Doyle shrugged. "I never asked. And I wouldn't wish it on them. They're nice kids, who have enough to deal with."

"What about the telekinesis?" Benjamin asked.

"What about it?"

"How do you do it?"

"I just do."

"Look, you're the only person we know who can do real magic," Benjamin said. "I want to know more about it."

The magician considered them both wearily for a long moment.

Then he held up his hand and an orange flew into it, making a *thwap* as it hit his palm. Janie looked to see where it had come from, and saw two more oranges in a metal bowl on the table. The magician held up his hand again and the oranges flew across the room: *Thwap, thwap.* Then he began to juggle the three.

"It first started happening when I was a kid," he said. "I didn't understand it. I played baseball, and I always knew what the pitcher was going to pitch. In the field, balls would veer toward me a little." He angled his shoulders to demonstrate. "I could catch anything. I could have been a pro—except I couldn't hit the damn ball. Never figured out how to do that."

He walked away from the oranges and left them juggling themselves, circling in graceful parabolas past each other in the air. Janie stared at them. The buzzing feeling was back, but now it seemed like—recognition. And longing.

"Can you teach us to do that?" she whispered. The oranges went around and around.

"You can do it or you can't," he said. "And then it takes practice."

"So does baseball," Benjamin said.

"Look, you don't get to decide what interests you," Doyle

said. "You'll discover that, in life. I was more interested in girls than in baseball. So when I got a little older, and wanted to know if girls liked me, I started to concentrate on their thoughts. It was like tuning a radio, getting the signal. I had access to their minds! But after a while, I couldn't turn the radio *off*. And that was no fun, believe me."

They were all silent for a long moment, confronting the magician's burden. He lost interest in the circulating oranges and let them drop—*thud, thud, thud,* they hit the floor. One rolled toward Janie's feet. She wanted to pick it up and inspect it, but she thought she should say something.

"I'm sorry," she said.

"But I already *know* you're sorry," he said. "So what do you want, exactly? You might as well tell me, and stop trying to confuse me with a lot of scattered thoughts about orange juice on the carpet and the Smell of Truth, whatever that is. And yes, you have to know how to juggle in the usual way first."

Janie flushed, and tried harder to hide her thoughts.

"Don't bother, sweetheart," Doyle said. "You have an especially readable mind."

"I need to talk to my father," Benjamin said. "And I need to do it without getting sick."

"Well, he's dead," the magician said. "People die. Get used to it. That's what makes life so precious, right? *Tempus fugit.* Now, I have a gig to get to." He opened the door to shoo them out.

"I can help you," Benjamin said. "To screen out people's minds."

The magician eyed him. "You're just a kid."

"I've done harder things," Benjamin said. "You know I have, because you've read my mind."

Janie saw a glimmer of interest on Doyle's face. He closed the door. "How would you do it?"

"I'd make a filter," Benjamin said. "Just a damper, on the part of your brain that receives the signals. I designed a mind-connection powder once, and if I reverse the principles I used for that, it might work."

Doyle sat down on a sagging couch, his eyes glued to Benjamin's. "You're improvising so I won't kick you out," he said. "You think it would be hard, to make this filter, and you're hoping I'll believe you can do it. But you're also thinking that it's *possible*, and might even be kind of fun. A challenge. You haven't been interested in anything lately, except your dead dad. And you feel sorry for me, old two-drinks-for-breakfast Doyle."

Janie looked at the two of them with wonder. She wished she had just a little bit of Doyle's power to get inside Benjamin's head.

"I'll only do it if you'll help me," Benjamin said.

"Yeah, I got that part, too," the magician said. He leaned back on the couch. "You have no idea how exhausting it is. It would change my life, to have a filter. People are critical and nasty, you know? I'm too tall, I'm too skinny, my hair is too orange, my nose is too big, my jacket's out of fashion. So many niggling thoughts. And Janie, I know you're thinking that all those things are *true*."

"Sorry!" she said.

Doyle studied Benjamin. "You stopped breathing when you contacted your father."

"Yes," he said.

Doyle considered. "What you're really doing is accessing his mind, right? Which is a lot like what I do. I used to have a physical response to what other people were thinking. I would hyperventilate in the halls at school. It was awful."

"So what did you do?" Benjamin asked.

"There are ways to control the mental connection to other people. Your problem is that you have no control over your sympathetic nervous system when you contact your father. Your body gets flooded with adrenaline, and your breathing gets shallow, so you aren't getting enough air. You get dizzy, you feel sick."

"He stopped breathing *completely*," Janie said.

"If it is a similar process to what I'm doing," the magician said, "then I can show you how to control your breathing and your heartbeat while you do it." He narrowed his pale eyes at Benjamin. "But you can't chase your mother. She's too far gone. You can't follow her without dying. You understand me?"

Benjamin nodded.

"All right," the magician said. "So I'll teach you. But first you make me a filter."

Benjamin held out his hand. "Deal," he said.

CHAPTER 10

Malingering

In the morning, Benjamin told Mrs. Scott he had a cold. She sat down on the edge of his bed and rested the back of her hand against his forehead. "You seem all right," she said.

"I feel terrible," he croaked.

She frowned. "Okay. You can stay home, with or without a cold. But just for today."

After she went downstairs, Janie, dressed for school, appeared in the doorway of Benjamin's bedroom. "You could have told me," she said in a fierce whisper. "I would have stayed home, too!"

"We can't *both* have a cold," he said.

"Why not? I could've gotten it from you."

"Your parents wouldn't buy it. They'd think we were staying home for—other reasons."

"But I want to help!"

"Okay," he said. "I need a triple-necked boiling flask from the chemistry lab. You can bring it home at lunch."

"You mean *steal* it?"

"Just borrow."

She frowned. "You won't go to the After-room while I'm gone."

"Of course not," he said. "Not until I learn how to do it right."

She looked doubtful. "Okay."

While the Scotts ate breakfast downstairs, dishes clanking like cymbals, Benjamin lay in bed and practiced breathing deeply and slowly, paying attention to the shape and size of each intake of air. He had to control his sympathetic nervous system, the magician had said. Because it was overly sympathetic. He inhaled and his lungs expanded, exhaled and his chest sank back again.

When he finally heard Janie and her parents leave the house, he swung himself out of bed. The Scotts had an office at the university, but you never knew when they might pop home to check on him, or to get lunch. He might not have much time.

He'd made a false bottom in one of his drawers with a piece of thin plywood from the school wood shop, and from beneath it he took out his father's leather-bound book, the Pharmacopoeia, with the embossed Azoth of the Philosophers on the front: a circle inside a star made of seven pointed triangles, with an upside down triangle inside the circle. The Pharmacopoeia had been passed down in his family for generations. Its pages were full of alchemical symbols and diagrams, with handwritten notations in the margins about problems or side effects. His father had written in a few notes himself.

Next he took out a cardboard box full of jars and packets. A few were things he'd brought from Malaya in his suitcase: his father's last belongings. But some were new, ordered from a mail-order apothecary in Philadelphia. He'd met the postman on the street before the Scotts could see the box and ask questions.

He carried the book and the box downstairs to the kitchen, where he paged through the Pharmacopoeia's entries on telepathy and clairvoyance. He'd spent two years with the Pharmacopoeia as his only textbook, and his Latin had gotten much stronger. He didn't have to laboriously translate the pages anymore. He could just read and think.

On one page there was a drawing of the insulae, one in each hemisphere of the brain, deep in the cerebral cortex. Below the picture was written: *Perception. Empathy. Music. Digestion. Disgust (especially smells). Awareness of other minds.*

If there was a part of the brain that allowed you to read minds, then the insula was the best candidate. It was interesting that it also processed disgust, and regulated digestion. Benjamin's father had once said that thinking about other people's thoughts—imagining their experience—might have begun as an awareness of the state of other people's stomachs. It would have been useful knowledge, in early humans, as a way to avoid poisoning: If that person feels awful, I will not eat what he eats. If cavemen spent a lot of time thinking about other people's digestion, that must have led to their thinking about other people's state of mind.

So maybe the magician had an overactive insula—or two, one in each hemisphere of his brain. But how did his insulae become so powerful and refined that he could read exact thoughts—the thoughts of an entire room full of people? Had he been born with the ability, or had it arisen on the baseball field, as he watched the pitcher and wondered about his plans? Were there other telepaths like him? Could Benjamin learn to do it, with practice? Uncontrolled, it was making the magician's life miserable. But if he could turn it on and off, it would be a useful tool.

There were no specific instructions in the Pharmacopoeia for what Benjamin wanted, so he would have to improvise. He closed the book and began to work. He should really wait for Janie and the boiling flask, but he was impatient. *He* was the vessel, his father had said so—he didn't need Janie. He had made the powder by himself. He hauled out the Scotts' deepest stockpot, filled the bottom of it with water, and arranged his materials on the counter.

He thought about the insula's connection to the stomach, and reached for a packet of *Mandragora officinarum*, ground into powder. He poured some of it into the stockpot.

Then he thought about what might dull pain. It would help if the magician didn't mind so much what people thought. Benjamin poured in some oil of clove. He was working intuitively, measuring things out, setting the stockpot to boil.

It felt good to be working. This was what he was supposed to do. It wasn't just losing his father that had made him plunge into despair—it was losing his sense of purpose. He felt cautiously excited. Almost happy.

Then something went wrong. A white foam started to spill out of the stockpot. Benjamin turned off the heat but the foam kept billowing out. He clamped the lid on and still it was spilling everywhere. The pot made gurgling noises and jumped on the stove. He heard the front door open and close. Light footsteps, just one pair.

"Oh, no!" Janie said.

She grabbed a potholder and helped him hold down the lid, standing on her toes and bending forward to keep foam from getting all over her clothes.

"I'm sorry!" Benjamin said. "I don't know what happened!"

They carried the pot to the sink, leaving a river of foam behind them, and finally the pot stopped oozing. Benjamin wanted to save all those precious ingredients, but they were already sliding down the drain. The white froth was in the sink, on the floor, on the tile counter, inside all the gas burners. His shoes and trousers were soaked. He looked around at the mess. He should have waited for the boiling flask.

Janie wiped her hands on a dishcloth, went to the telephone in the hall, and dialed.

"Hello," she said, in a very brisk, grown-up voice. "This is Marjorie Scott—Janie Scott's mother? I'm afraid she's come down with the same cold Benjamin has. Yes, it's a shame. I'm going to keep her home from school this afternoon. Thank you. I hope so, too." She hung up.

Then she took a bundle of blue sweater out of her knapsack and unwrapped the delicate glass bulb, clear and round with three long necks, and handed it over.

"Thank you," Benjamin said.

"Mr. Walters almost caught me taking it."

Benjamin looked up from the flask in his hands. "*Did* he catch you?"

"No," she said. "I faked a coughing fit. He's terrified of getting kids' germs. He'd heard you were sick, and he just backed right out of the room."

Benjamin smiled. "That was a good idea," he said.

Janie brightened and then blushed: Concern and pleasure and pride and embarrassment raced across her face, one after the other. Benjamin's own face felt strange, and he realized that the muscles around his mouth weren't used to smiling.

He set the flask on the counter. "I think the interaction with the steel pot was the problem. Glass will be better."

Janie took a mop and bucket from the broom closet, all seriousness now, and pulled on a pair of rubber gloves. "I'll do the counter," she said. "You do the floor. But from now on we work together, okay? I help make the mess, or I don't clean it up."

He nodded.

As they cleaned the kitchen, he explained what he'd been trying to do, and they began again from scratch. This time they came up with a chalky-looking liquid that didn't boil over, and they decanted it into an empty wine bottle. Benjamin put the Pharmacopoeia away in its drawer, and Janie wrapped the clean boiling flask in a sweater in her knapsack. They scrubbed the kitchen until it sparkled. Janie made grilled cheese sandwiches to explain the obvious cleanup and cover the lingering smell.

"What is this, home ec?" Mr. Scott asked, when her parents came back.

"I called in sick after lunch," Janie said.

Mrs. Scott put her hand on Janie's forehead. "Why didn't you call me?"

"You were teaching. I didn't want to bother you."

"Do you feel better?"

"Much."

Mr. Scott was suspicious. "So what did you two do all afternoon?"

"Worked on some chemistry problems," Benjamin said.

Mr. Scott raised an eyebrow. "Not biology problems, I hope?"

"You're both going to school tomorrow," Mrs. Scott said. "You look healthy as horses."

"Do I smell clove?" Mr. Scott asked, sniffing the air.

"That's my shampoo," Janie said. She leaned on the kitchen counter, and Benjamin saw her wipe away a stray patch of white foam with her elbow. "How are your students?"

"Full of excuses," her father said, meaningfully.

"Did you have your talk about suspense?" Janie asked.

Mrs. Scott made a wry face. "I'm not sure it sank in. They

get an idea for a plot turn or a big event, and they just put it in right away, at the spot where they thought of it. I wish they had more patience."

Benjamin was not feeling very patient himself. He wished he could take the filter to Doyle tonight. But he felt Mr. Scott's eyes on him.

"What *should* they do?" Janie asked.

"Well, lay the groundwork, lead the audience, let them anticipate what's going to happen," her mother said. "Incipience is everything."

"What's incipience?" Janie asked.

Benjamin thought she was laying it on a bit thick, this engaging-daughter, how-was-your-day business. Her father already smelled a rat. But Janie was avoiding Benjamin's eye.

"It's when something's about to happen but hasn't happened yet," her mother said. "Like—the couple in the movie have met but haven't kissed yet. Or you know someone's hiding behind a door but he hasn't jumped out yet. It's kind of agony, but it's exquisite, too."

Benjamin thought of the bottle of white liquid, out on his bed where he had left it. Had he left his door open? What if they went upstairs ahead of him and saw it?

"But you can't put off the big event forever," Janie said. "The characters can't just sit around eating grilled cheese sandwiches and waiting."

"No," her mother said. "But a little grilled cheese is okay, while you anticipate something else."

Benjamin coughed lamely. "I'm going upstairs," he said.

"Need to be healthy tomorrow, you know?" He felt Mr. Scott's eyes follow him as he left the room. He needed to work on his acting if he was going to be doing this work again. He could never have fooled the chemistry teacher with a coughing fit, like Janie had.

He took the stairs two at a time and stashed the wine bottle in his knapsack. Downstairs, they were still talking about suspense. Mr. Scott mistrusted Benjamin for all the wrong reasons, but Benjamin would still have to be careful, under those vigilant eyes.

CHAPTER 11

Fishing

J in Lo sat in the shade outside the little hut, looking at the silver ocean. She was stronger every day, and the water didn't seem so endless and desolate now. Ned Maddox had taken a mask and snorkel and something called a pole spear, propelled by heavy rubber bands, and he was swimming among the reefs, trying to spear a fish for dinner.

He had shown her on the chart exactly where they were, on a tiny island surrounded by reefs and shoals. The shallow and dangerous water kept the island safe and ignored. And yet Jin Lo had floated right over the reef in the night, when the surf was low, and come to rest on his beach. She could have landed on any number of deserted rocks, but she had landed *here*, on a morning when Ned Maddox was in his banyan tree looking for the missing American. He had pulled her out of the water alive, and he had a radio, and was willing to let her use it. The chances were too small to calculate.

Ned Maddox was an orphan like she was, and had lived a hidden life for years. Jin Lo watched him wake up each morning on the floor of his hut and he never had hazy moments of face-rubbing and confusion. He was asleep, and then his eyes opened, and he was fully conscious and alert. When she was little, her father used to tease her for stretching and rubbing her eyes in the morning before school. "Monkey preening," he called it. But that was before she had learned that you had to be always on your guard. At some point, Ned Maddox had learned it, too. They both knew that danger could come at any moment, and you had a better chance if you could sleep anywhere, and wake up as quickly as possible.

She watched him hunt in the water, his snorkel investigating the reef. His feet kicked slowly. The bare skin of his back was tan and freckled.

His discarded shirt was beside her in the sand, inside-out, the cotton worn thin. She reached out to touch it, just to feel the soft fabric, but it crinkled slightly. That wasn't what she expected, and she pulled the shirt closer and turned it over.

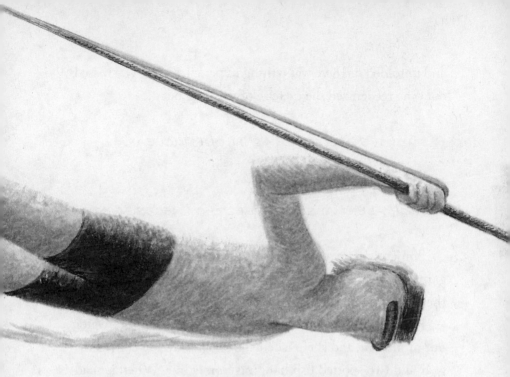

There was a buttoned pocket. A piece of paper inside. She looked up and saw his snorkel catch the sunlight, and then his feet kicked up into the air as he dived.

Ned Maddox had saved her life. Did she, therefore, owe him the respect of not looking through his pockets? She had never felt as strongly about ethics as the apothecary had. If an action might help your cause, and your cause was right, then other considerations were not so important. And anyway, this man, Ned Maddox, was spying on her country. China might be headed down a perilous road, but it was still her country. Could it be wrong to spy on a spy?

She decided it would not hurt him for her to see what was in his pocket. She undid the button, took out the slip of paper, and unfolded it. There was writing in pencil, some of it crossed out. She recognized the exercise of working out a code:

FUGITIVE HAS STOLEN 8-IN. DIA NUCLEAR
   ARTILLERY SHELL
TARGET BELIEVED CHINA
HIGH ALERT ABSOLUTE SECRECY NECESSARY

Something on the beach caught her eye: Ned Maddox gathering his fins. She folded the paper and stuffed it back in the pocket. How had he gotten out of the water so fast?

He walked up the beach, smiling and shaking the water out of his hair, and she pushed the shirt away. He carried his gear and two spotted fish hanging from a line. When he had first shaved his beard, his face had been two-toned, his chin pale, but now the color was evening out. He held up the fish, triumphant. They were both speared right through the head, and Jin Lo felt sad when she saw them. She thought they had probably enjoyed their lives, poking in and out of the reef. But then her stomach growled. Life was compromise.

Ned Maddox came into the shade where she sat, plucked a large leaf, and set his catch down on it. The fish were grouper, fat and shiny, with spots the size of large coins, as beautifully decorated as porcelain pots. He took a knife from the scabbard on his leg and neatly slit the fattest one up the belly, holding it gently in his hand. There were drops of salt water on his sun-bleached eyelashes. The freckles on his face stretched when he smiled.

"We've got dinner," he said. "Better than canned soup!"

He stripped out the bloody insides, keeping them on the large leaf.

"I was thinking about why I landed here," she said. "Of all the islands."

He nodded. "I was thinking about that, too," he said, starting on the second fish. "I'm not a big believer in predestination. Horoscopes, that stuff. Some people say they can tell the future from fish guts." He looked at the bloody pile of intestines and shook his head. "I don't believe that. But I can't shake this feeling that you were *sent* here for some reason. And I don't mean by the Commies, as a spy."

"My old teacher said that the universe is always doing its work," she said. "And we are only part of it."

He pulled out the guts of the second fish and laid them aside. "I'd like to believe that."

"He used to read tea leaves," she said. She could see her old teacher now, staring into the dregs of his cup when he was struggling with a problem. Jin Lo had never been sure whether it really worked, or was just a way for him to meditate on an answer.

"So what's the work the universe is doing now?" Ned Maddox asked.

She thought of the broken code in his pocket. *Nuclear artillery shell. Target believed China.* "I think it will become clear."

"I hope so," he said.

He took the guts down to the beach to wash them into the water, where they would be eaten by something else. Then they carried everything back inside, and Ned Maddox pan-fried the fish on his little stove. It was crisp and light and delicious. Jin Lo thought she had never eaten something so recently alive, and there was an odd sorrow in it.

For dessert, Ned Maddox produced a silver can from his box of supplies. "No labels," he said. "It's dessert roulette. I never know what I'm getting. But I have a good feeling about this one." He wiped his pocketknife on his shorts, opened the can and peered inside. "Peaches!" he said. "We're in luck."

He poured the peaches into two bowls, drizzled evaporated milk over them, then slid one bowl across the table to her.

As Jin Lo watched, the milk spread in the shape of an explosion: a narrow stem between two glossy orange peaches, with a billowing cloud at the top, against the curved rim of the bowl. A chill passed through her body.

"They're really good, I promise," Ned Maddox said.

Jin Lo had been so careful with her secrets for so long, but now she felt compelled to speak. Not because she had looked in his pocket and owed him something. Not because of the message in the peaches. She just knew it was the right thing to do.

"I want to tell you something," she said.

CHAPTER 12

The Filter

Janie didn't sleep well, after she and Benjamin made the filter. It was untested, and they were giving it to someone they didn't know. She had a dream in which the magician drank the chalky liquid and turned into a white rabbit staring reproachfully at her with red eyes. In another dream, he turned into a small green toad. Then he became a stag, which reared and ran off into a dark forest that hadn't existed a moment before. She woke up exhausted.

After school, they went to see Doyle. Janie dragged her feet, following Benjamin up the creaking stairs beside the bar to the magician's apartment.

Again, Doyle opened the door before they knocked. He was dressed for another magic show, in white tie and black tailcoat, and his orange hair was combed slickly back. He looked from one to the other of them, green eyes gleaming.

"You have the filter!" he said.

"Maybe you shouldn't try it right before a show," Janie said.

"It's just a birthday party," he said. "I don't need to know what those brats are thinking. I'd rather *not* know. Does it work?"

"You're the only mind-reader we have to test it on," Benjamin said.

The magician rubbed his hands together eagerly. "Then shall we try?"

"We don't know if it's safe," Janie said. "There could be side effects, or consequences you don't expect. It might make you dizzy, or make you talk funny."

"That would all be worth it," he said.

"Even if the kids couldn't understand you?"

"I'll do a silent show," he said. "Visual tricks! Stuff with balloons!"

"If it works," Benjamin said firmly, "you'll teach me the rest of what I need to know to contact my father safely."

"Of course, of course!" the magician said.

Benjamin produced the wine bottle from his knapsack and handed it over. "I'd start with a tablespoon, no more."

The magician studied the label like a wine expert. "1948!" he said. "A very good year. It's a little white for a burgundy, though." He uncorked the bottle and Janie watched with apprehension as he took a quick swig. She hoped it wouldn't kill him. Or turn him into a rabbit.

He made a face. "Nasty stuff."

"It's not supposed to taste good," Benjamin said.

"Okay," he said, turning to Janie. "Think of something."

"Like what?"

"I can't tell you," he said. "It has to be something I don't know!"

So she thought about her grandmother's earrings, which she and Benjamin had melted down in London so they could make an invisibility bath.

The magician squinted. "Earrings," he said. "From an old woman. Something about water."

"Right," Janie said, disappointed.

"No, it's good!" the magician said. "It's all hazy, getting hazier. Your brain is usually like a movie screen. It's working." He took another swig from the bottle.

"Careful!" Benjamin said. "Don't take too much."

"Think!" Doyle commanded, pointing at Janie.

So she thought about Jin Lo, whom they'd last seen heading after Danby and the uranium, and how strong and smart and self-contained she was, having been orphaned when she was very young.

The magician frowned. "A girl," he said. "Something about a girl." Then his face broke into a smile. "That's all! And barely that! It works!" He put his hands on his knees, looking straight into Janie's eyes. "Now think something cruel about me."

"No," she said.

"Come on! I need to test this."

So Janie thought about what the twins had said—that

Doyle's assistant-girlfriend had ditched him for drinking too much. She added that his apartment smelled bad, and that he gave her the creeps a little.

The magician beamed. "You're doing it? You're thinking something rotten about me?"

Janie nodded.

"Nothing!" he cried. He turned to Benjamin and crushed him in a hug, lifting him off the floor. Then he set him down and danced around the room, doing a strange, long-legged jig. "Nothing! My own thoughts! Such freedom! I don't know what you're thinking and *I—don't—care!*"

"Do you feel all right?" Janie asked.

"I feel *wonderful*! You can't imagine! The silence!"

"Just don't take too much at once," Benjamin said. "And let this first dose wear off, so we can learn how long it lasts."

"I don't want it *ever* to wear off!"

"You *have* to," Benjamin said. "We're testing it. This is the test."

"Fine!" Doyle said.

He was still dancing around, lifting one knee high, then the other. It was impossible not to be pleased for him, in his goofy celebration, and Janie felt herself smiling. He grabbed her hand and twirled her around, then around again.

"I'm so happy!" he cried.

"You won't be able to cheat at poker anymore," Benjamin said.

"Who says I cheat?" He spun Janie one more time, and the room whirled past.

"Of course you do," Benjamin said.

Doyle let Janie go. She caught the wall and steadied herself. The room kept spinning. "Not enough to get caught," he said. "Just enough to win."

"Well, you won't even be able to do that," Benjamin said.

Doyle lifted his chin. "I don't need poker anyway."

"Can you live on birthday parties?" Benjamin asked.

"If I did enough of them."

"*Are* there enough?" Janie asked.

Doyle frowned. "No."

"So what are you going to do?" Benjamin asked.

"There are lots of ways to make money," Doyle said. His eyebrows shot up. "Hey, I want to do something for you!"

"I know," Benjamin said. "You're going to teach me how to contact my father."

"And I'd like to learn telekinesis," Janie put in.

"No, no—*more* than that!" Doyle said. "I could get you a lot of money. Some associates of mine in Detroit would be *very* interested in your ability to contact dead people."

Janie felt her smile vanish.

Benjamin's expression hardened. "What associates?" he asked.

"Oh, people I play poker with. People with money! Moola, moola!"

"Have you *told* them about us?" Janie asked.

"Of course not!" the magician said. "Just keep it in mind, if you're ever in need. These people are *connected*, if you know what I mean."

Benjamin's body had gone rigid. "You can't tell them about us."

"You can't tell *anyone*," Janie said.

"It was only a suggestion!" Doyle said. But something was different about him now—Janie had the ominous feeling that something was very wrong.

"If you breathe a word of this to anyone, we'll never make you the filter again!" Benjamin said.

Doyle shrugged. "A chemist I know will analyze it and make it for me. He's very good with drugs."

"No!" Benjamin said, and he lunged for the filter.

The magician, who was almost a foot taller, held the bottle over his head by the neck, just as he'd held the girl's phone number out of reach at the party. It was a practiced move. "Let's not overreact, now," he said.

"That's my formula and it's a secret!" Benjamin said.

A nasty edge crept into the magician's voice. "Not anymore."

Janie's chest tightened with anguish. Why had they trusted Doyle? Her father had told her the story of the scorpion who stings the frog who helps him cross the river. When the dying frog asks *why*, the scorpion says, "It is my nature." Was this Doyle's nature? Or had they made him this way with the filter? He'd been so happy and generous a moment before.

Still holding the wine bottle out of reach, the magician pushed them toward the door. "Out," he said. "Good-bye. Go. Don't bother to keep in touch."

He gave them each a last shove. Janie stumbled out onto the rickety landing after Benjamin.

"Wait!" Benjamin said. "I did my part! You have to teach me what to do in the After-room!"

"I don't have to teach you anything, you little wretch," the magician said, and he slammed the door.

CHAPTER 13

The Cricket and the Flame

Ned Maddox sat in his banyan tree, eyes on the horizon, thinking about what Jin Lo had told him. She claimed that she and her friends could contain a nuclear explosion. It sounded ludicrous, but Ned had heard rumors about what had happened to the Soviet hydrogen bomb on Nova Zembla. At first it seemed that the Russians had messed up, done their calculations wrong. Everyone enjoyed thinking that, because it made them feel safer. But then a Russian sailor defected, and turned himself in to the U.S. Navy, and he said that something much stranger had happened to the bomb. It had *started* to explode, but then shrank back in on itself, and afterward there'd been no radiation on the frozen ground. Not a pip from the Geiger counter.

That demanded an explanation, and this girl who'd washed up on Ned's island had one. She and her friends had been on Nova Zembla, and had contained the explosion with a sort of net, a very strong polymer that contracted in the presence of radiation. Then they'd mopped up the remaining radiation with something called the Quintessence. Ned still didn't really understand that part. Jin Lo said that the Quintessence was just a nickname for this particular oil. The word meant the fifth element and the essence of all life, but the oil was an extract that came from a flowering tree.

She had also shown him, in small ways, that she had strange powers. She had paralyzed a cricket on his table, then set it free. She had taken a little salt in her hand and lit a blue flame from it, watching it dance, then closed her hand to put it out. Ned had been duly impressed. But something else had happened. It had to do with the serious, absorbed look on her face, while she brought out her tricks. It made him feel like that cricket: entirely at her command. So maybe she could stop an atomic explosion with some kind of magical net. Who was he to say that she couldn't?

If it were true, then the U.S. Navy would be very, very interested in talking to her. They would want her methods for themselves. They certainly wouldn't want them falling into the hands of the Chinese Communists, or the Soviets. If the American nuclear arsenal was useless, then America's power in the world was over. Done. *Kaput.* And Ned believed in his country. He thought that the land of the free was not a bad place for power to reside.

But he couldn't deliver Jin Lo to be interrogated by people who wouldn't understand her. He shouldn't have left the piece of paper in his pocket, of course, but he'd discovered that he didn't mind that she'd looked. It meant she'd been curious about him. She had asked him what a nuclear artillery shell was.

"It's a nuclear bomb that can be fired from a big gun," he said. "Like any artillery shell."

Jin Lo's face grew pale. "This exists?"

"Sure," he said.

"That's terrible."

"They can do a lot of damage," he admitted.

"And what does '8-in. dia' mean?"

"It means the missing nuclear shell has an eight-inch diameter," he said, making a circle with his hands, his fingers not touching. "There are different sizes of shell, depending on the size of the gun—just like regular artillery."

"This one is small?"

He nodded. "It's new, just a prototype."

"Tell me about the commander," she said.

"His name is Thomas Hayes. He's a respected naval officer, decorated in the war. His son joined up after him, and was killed in the Communist shelling of Quemoy. The son was just a kid. And now he's dead. I think Hayes wishes we'd gone after China, but we didn't, so he wants to do it himself."

"He wants revenge," Jin Lo had said.

"It's a crazy way to get it."

"People are not rational when their families are killed," she'd said.

Now Ned scanned the horizon through his binoculars, from the banyan tree. The sea was glassy and blue, mirrored silver where the sun blazed off it. He saw nothing out there, no fugitive Americans, no boats. *Target believed China*, the message had said, but China was an awfully big target.

"Where are you, Commander?" he muttered. "Where are you planning to go?"

CHAPTER 14

Followed

Days went by, and Janie and Benjamin went through the motions of school and dinner and homework. Benjamin spent even more time alone in his room, reading the Pharmacopoeia. When they made the filter, Janie had thought he might be emerging from his misery, but the magician's betrayal had knocked him back down the hole.

She wished that Count Vili had left an address, a way for them to contact him. He had been their protector, and he should have been in touch. The apothecary was dead, and Jin Lo was on the other side of the world. So wasn't it Vili's duty to stay in contact?

She was picturing the apothecary's kind, bespectacled face, and missing him with a keen ache in her chest, when another image came into her head. It was like a fleeting dream that might melt away and vanish, and she tried to hold it in her mind while she figured out what it was. It was a book, a leather-bound book, but not the Pharmacopoeia. It was smaller, and worn, but not by seven hundred years of use. It had a snap clasp to hold it closed. She went upstairs, and walked like a sleepwalker into her parents' bedroom.

On the bureau was her mother's leather address book. It closed with a snap, just like the image in her head. The cover was worn from having been carried around by her mother since college.

She let the daydream go, and picked the book up. It was heavier than it looked. Was this snooping? She would be furious if her parents read her diary, but this wasn't a diary. She unsnapped the cover and looked at the paper tabs running down the right side of it: ABC, DEF. She picked up the tab that said TUV, knowing her mother wouldn't trust herself to remember Vili's many aristocratic surnames. And there he was, *Count Vilmos Hadik de Galántha*, in her mother's neat cursive. With an address in Luxembourg.

Janie's heart pounded. He had left an address with her parents. But why hadn't he told her he'd done that? Why not just leave the address with her?

Then she remembered the state she and Benjamin had been in when they returned from Malaya. She had been kidnapped and locked in a mine. Benjamin had been drugged and imprisoned and lost at sea. They had watched Benjamin's father die, and they had come home grief-stricken and guilty, barely able to look at each other. Maybe Vili had found her parents easier to communicate with, or maybe he'd tried to earn her parents' trust by being a responsible adult among adults—not a near stranger (and possible creep) in contact with their daughter.

But his reasons didn't matter now. She could write to him!

She went to her bedroom to look for letter paper, and found Benjamin crouched in front of her bureau, digging through her bottom drawer.

"What are you doing?" she asked, although she knew. He was looking for the powder.

He spun to face her, clutching a handful of blue sweater. "I just need to take it one more time."

"It isn't safe," she said. "And you should ask me, not search my room!"

"But you'd say no."

"Of course I would!"

"I've been practicing controlling my breathing," he said. "Just like the magician said."

"You almost died," she said. "He didn't teach you enough." She held up her mother's little book. "I found Vili's address. I'm going to write to him and tell him what's going on. We need him."

Benjamin looked at the book. "Your parents had his address? All this time?"

She nodded.

"Why didn't Vili give it to *us*?"

"We were a mess," she said. "I don't blame him." She didn't tell him about the strange dream image that had come into her mind, of the address book. She wanted to think more about that first. "Let's write a letter."

"A telegram will be faster," Benjamin said.

So they sat down at her desk with a blank piece of notebook

paper. What could they say in a communication that could not be private, when they had established no code to use with Vili? And how would they explain about the After-room? Or about Doyle? Janie's pen hovered.

"You write 'stop' at the end of a sentence," Benjamin offered. "And you pay by the word."

So she wrote:

B in touch with father STOP. Some danger involved STOP.

"Better not to say 'danger,'" Benjamin said. Janie crossed it out and started again.

B in touch with father STOP. Request your advice STOP.

But that wasn't the whole story. Doyle had threatened to tell people about them, people who sounded suspicious and criminal.

B communicating with father STOP. Request your advice STOP. Some trouble here STOP. Unsure of exact nature STOP.

That was pretty vague, but mostly true. Janie thought Vili would recognize it as a call for help. They walked to the

Western Union office to send the telegram, pooling their cash to pay for it.

"That's it?" the clerk asked, reading the message. He was small, with round glasses.

"That's it," Janie said.

"No signature?"

"No thanks," Benjamin said. Vili would know who had sent the telegram—he didn't know anyone else in Ann Arbor.

The clerk pursed his lips, then shrugged. "It's your money," he said.

The next morning at school, the Doyle twins found them at Janie's locker. Nat looked uncomfortable, and Valentina was fiddling with her bag strap.

"Can we ask you a question?" Nat asked.

Janie nodded, nervous about what the question might be.

"When you saw our uncle, did he seem—all right?" Nat said.

"Why?" Benjamin asked.

Valentina said, "He showed up last night with a broken nose and a black eye. He asked our mother to sew up his eyebrow."

"He wouldn't go to the hospital," Nat said.

"He's been losing at cards," Valentina said.

Janie winced. Of course Doyle was losing at cards, if he was using the filter. He had won before because he knew what cards everyone else had. But why was he still playing? Benjamin had warned him not to.

"He's also gotten so *mean*," Valentina said. "He says terrible things. He told our dad he was getting fat. It's like he doesn't care about anyone else."

"We just wondered if you noticed anything strange when you went to see him," Nat said.

There was a silence as Janie considered how to answer. She felt Benjamin doing the same thing beside her. She decided to address the immediate problem. "Can you get him to stop playing poker?"

The twins shook their heads in unison.

"He wants to win back his losses," Valentina said.

"But he can't," Janie said desperately. "He *won't*, not now."

Benjamin coughed, and the twins looked puzzled. "How do you know?" Nat asked.

Janie fumbled for an explanation. "Because—he's panicking," she said. "He'll just get in deeper."

"I still don't understand how he could lose," Nat said. "You've seen what he can do, how he *knows* stuff."

Janie looked down at her shoes. A bell rang.

Valentina said, "I'm sorry. We shouldn't be dragging you into this."

Janie went to class feeling guilty and confused. All day, the words in her notebook went in and out of focus. To distract herself, she tried to move the pencil on her desk without touching it, but it didn't budge.

After school, she met Benjamin on a bench near the tennis courts.

"We created a monster," she said.

"It's not our fault that he's playing cards when he has no advantage," Benjamin said. "I warned him."

"We should have thought about the side effects," she said.

"What side effects?"

"The lack of empathy," she said. "Not caring about anyone else's feelings."

"That's not a side effect," Benjamin said. "That's the *main* effect. It's what he asked for, to be free from other people's thoughts."

"He asked not to know them, telepathically," she said. "But the filter is too strong. It makes him not even *imagine* other people's thoughts. He doesn't care what anyone else thinks or feels."

"What's the difference?" Benjamin said.

"There is one," she said. "We saw it happen, remember? He was so happy, dancing around, and then he changed in front of us and threw us out."

"Because we didn't want to sell the powder to his friends," Benjamin said.

"I think it was more than that," Janie said. "And they don't seem to be his friends anymore. Friends don't break your nose."

They sat in unhappy silence. They'd taken a sad, telepathic magician, and created a sociopath with gambling debts.

"Maybe he'll run out of the filter soon," Janie said.

Benjamin sounded glum. "He'll just have his chemist friend make more."

"We could try to find him, and explain why he has to stop playing poker."

"He won't listen."

Janie looked off across the street and saw a man in a blue sedan, parked beneath the trees, looking back at her. He wore dark glasses and didn't drop his gaze. "Don't turn around now," she said, "but there's a man watching us."

"Where?"

She lifted her chin in the man's direction.

Benjamin stretched his legs out in front of him and settled his arms on the back of the bench, just happening to glance off toward the car. Then he looked up at the sky as if to check the weather, or look at a bird. "How long's he been there?" he asked.

"I don't know."

"You're sure he's watching us?"

"Pretty sure."

"Maybe he's just having a rest in the shade."

"I don't think so."

"Should we start walking home, and see what he does?"

They stood, gathering their things, and tried to walk away normally, but Janie thought they wouldn't fool anyone. The blue sedan pulled away from the curb. Janie had been followed by federal marshals in Los Angeles, and in New Hampshire she'd been dragged into a car and kidnapped while she was walking down the street. She did not want to repeat either experience.

"He's following us," she said. Her heart began to race.

"I know," Benjamin said.

"Should we go somewhere else, instead of home?"

"Where?"

"I don't know!"

They kept walking, down a residential street in the direction of her parents' house.

"Let's stop," Benjamin said. He took her hand, which was shaking, and they stood on the sidewalk facing each other.

"I'm scared," she said.

"We're just having a romantic moment here, right?" he said. "And he's going to have to cruise on by, or else say something. And then we'll know more."

"I don't want to be dragged into that car," she said.

"If he gets out, we'll run."

The car came alongside them and paused for a moment. Janie's hair blew across her face, and Benjamin brushed it away. When his fingertips touched her cheek, she jumped. He leaned toward her and her face grew hot. She didn't want to kiss Benjamin as *cover*, after so long, but she didn't know how to explain that. She could feel the man in the dark glasses staring at them.

Then the car kept driving, slowly. Janie turned her head out of reach of the kiss, and the taillights rounded a corner and disappeared from sight.

She slipped her hand out of Benjamin's grasp, without looking at him. "Let's go home," she said.

CHAPTER 15

The Commander

Thomas Francis Hayes was born and raised on a cattle ranch in Oklahoma, far from the sea, and his first love was a border collie named Jazz. Jazz was a working cattle dog who considered the family his primary herd, and he was happiest when Tommy and his parents were all in one room, around the dinner table, and he could be sure he'd done his job. Then he dropped to the floor, folded his paws, and watched them, satisfied. When the family spread out around the house, he would try to urge them back together.

If the family was his herd, then Tommy was his particular responsibility. They ran together, worked together, played together, hunted together. Jazz slept at the foot of his bed, and Tommy slipped Jazz scraps from his plate.

Jazz died when Tommy was fifteen, and it was the first great tragedy of his life. He wrapped an old orange blanket around the strangely motionless body—Jazz had never been still, running even in his dreams—and lowered him into a hole dug in the field behind the house. His father gave a speech about what a fine dog Jazz had been, loyal and smart and brave, and Tommy wept.

When it was time to shovel the dirt over the blanket, Tommy was shocked that such a thing could happen, that dirt could fall on the still body and the world could go on without Jazz in it. Every morning he woke, expecting the sandpapery tongue on his face that urged him to get up and greet the joyous day, and then he was plunged into despair when the truth came rushing back.

He joined the navy when he finished high school, and was sent to officer training in California. He joined the Pacific fleet, rose through the ranks, and met a girl on the beach in Waikiki. Cassie was wearing a white two-piece swimsuit and had an orchid tucked behind her ear. She was a mix of things, like many people in the islands—Hawaiian, Japanese, *haole*— with black hair and hazel eyes that tilted up at the corners like a cat's. He had not known that such girls existed in real life. He felt like the hero of a film, with her: a film with sappy, romantic songs and waves crashing in the background.

They married, took a house in Honolulu, and had a son named William who was as beautiful as his mother, a relentlessly cheerful baby, fat hands always reaching for the world. As a boy, William wanted to know how ships worked, and he wanted to be in the navy like his father. But the year he turned seven, the Japanese bombed Pearl Harbor, and their life became a different kind of film.

Hayes's war was hard and long. So many sailors and pilots

were lost beneath the waves. Japanese planes hid behind the clouds, ready to dive and crash into the U.S. ships, to give up their lives to kill. It affected your mind, that awareness that death could come screaming down at any moment. On land, there seemed only to be starvation and mud and misery.

Hayes was a captain by 1945, and was standing on a captured airstrip in the Solomon Islands when he heard about the attack on Hiroshima. Death again, screaming down, obliterating a city in a flash of light and a billowing cloud of radiation. Japan intended to fight to the last man and woman—civilians and housewives were armed with knives and guns against the invasion. But now the emperor had surrendered, because of the new bomb. So it was a good thing, this terrifying new weapon. Hayes was fairly sure of it. War had given him armor in place of skin: a carapace like a crab's. That soft, vulnerable boy who had buried his face in the dog's fur and wept was gone.

His son was eleven then, and Hayes hoped that the boy could grow up in a world not torn by war. William spent the next years surfing before school, coming home with salt in his hair and his board under his arm, and tinkering with engines. In college, he signed up for reserve officer training, and he was likeable, with an easy authority, destined to be a fine officer. He never talked too long, or swaggered; he remembered people's names.

But then came the civil war in China, and William wound up on Quemoy. Chairman Mao was starving his own people, in the name of revolution. Chiang Kai-shek had withdrawn to Taiwan, and his reinforcing of two tiny islands so close to the mainland was like poking a great beast with a sharp stick. The shells came raining down on the islands. On that godforsaken rock that no one cared about except Chiang and Mao, the mechanics couldn't figure out the trouble with a Jeep, and someone said that William was good with engines. He was standing beneath the hood when a 130mm Chinese shell struck.

One moment Ensign William Hayes was in the world; the next he was gone. A young radio officer who had been William's friend brought the news to Hayes, and broke down crying.

Cassie left after their son's death—there was too much sadness between them. After that, the only good moments of the day were those few seconds when he woke from sleep, thinking that his son was still in the world. Then the truth crashed down like a wave, pinning him to the bed, leaving him drenched and breathless. He slept less, but craved sleep more—not for its own sake, but for those few bright seconds on waking, when his son was alive.

The chief medical officer said that sleeplessness would start to affect his brain, and prescribed pills, but the pills made Hayes's mornings groggy and confused, and erased the moment when his son seemed still alive. So he threw them away. He would conquer this on his own, as he had conquered everything else.

But without his son, what was the point? He went round and round about that question. When the Joint Chiefs of

Staff in Washington recommended a nuclear attack on China in September, Hayes thought he had his answer. A spectacular revenge.

But Americans were tired of war, and they didn't want a new one over two islands no one had ever heard of. So President Eisenhower rejected the idea, and Hayes was enraged. Not just because of William. What about the people Mao had enslaved? His own people who were starving? Korea under Mao's thumb?

He began to think, night and day, about the new 8-inch nuclear shell, a thing of beauty, in its smooth titanium casing. The light casing reduced the weight, and so did the delicate new mechanism. He lay awake contemplating the simple genius of its design. He had not slept for weeks.

One morning while it was still dark, he went to the chief artillery officer and told him he had orders to transport one of the new shells to another ship. Hayes seemed to be outside his own body, watching the conversation without much worry about which way it would go. He had a great deal of trust built up among the officers, and he would squander it all. The artillery officer was puzzled at first, but Hayes spoke of sealed orders and high-level instructions. They loaded the shell into a padded aluminum box, and then into a wooden crate. Two young seamen loaded the crate into a boat for transport.

"Shall we come with you, sir?" one of the seamen asked.

"Yes, please," Hayes said, because he feared he might fall asleep. And it would be useful to have young, strong arms to help him. These two seamen did not seem especially bright or curious. And they were William's age—the age William would have been—which made him firm in his resolve. Hayes had cash in a lockbox, and he brought it all, plus warm clothes, and a large empty canvas duffel bag. He also took a case of chocolate bars, on the chance that they might come in handy.

When he set out in the boat with the two young men, he transferred the shell into the duffel bag and tested its weight. He could lift it, with the long shoulder strap, though he wouldn't be able to carry it far. At dawn, they came in sight of a Taiwanese fishing boat.

"Bring us alongside," he said, as if he had planned this meeting all along. They hailed the fishing boat, and Hayes asked to see the captain in private.

The captain, in his tiny cabin, was nervous—he probably had an illegal smuggling operation going. Hayes offered the man cash to take him and his luggage aboard, and keep his presence secret. He explained that this was part of a sensitive secret plan to help Chiang Kai-shek. They agreed on a price, and Hayes sent the two seamen back to the battleship, with more talk of secrecy. The young men were so fresh-faced and earnest in wishing him well that he felt a stab of conscience, but only a small one. He thought of William, and of the starving millions. He knew that what he was doing was right.

Late that morning, they came in sight of another fishing boat, and Hayes repeated his conversation with the new captain, and transferred his luggage across. He asked to be taken to the Grand Canal, the great man-made waterway that went north to Beijing, and he picked out the tallest fisherman among the crew and asked to buy his clothes. A price, again, was reached. A wide-brimmed fisherman's hat covered his foreign face.

In the canal, Hayes surveyed the large boats and small boats, the freighters and junks and scows. After a time, he chose a flat, steady-looking canal barge. It housed a small family circus: acrobats who played in the canal towns. The daughters, who looked no more than five or six, did an act in which they walked on their hands. Hayes offered the suspicious barge captain cash and eight chocolate bars, and suddenly they had room for a *gweilo* passenger—why not? Everything had a price.

A storeroom was converted into a cabin. Hayes, in his broad hat and the fisherman's clothes, stashed his duffel bag beneath his cot, along with the rest of the chocolate. It made him happy to think of the satiny titanium shell hidden there: his precious cargo, his gift for Chairman Mao.

CHAPTER 16

Syncope

Janie was rattled, as she and Benjamin let themselves into the house. The U.S. marshals who had followed her in Los Angeles seemed like they belonged to another lifetime, to a fading dream. It had been terrifying, but the result was that she had moved to London with her parents, and met Benjamin and his father there, and her life had begun. So she wouldn't wish away those two marshals in their car now, no matter how awful it had been at the time.

She tried to think that maybe *this* car, too, was just a messenger from the next stage of her life. But it didn't feel that way. Janie didn't want to have any more adventures in which people might die. She knew she should tell her parents about the sedan, and the man in the dark glasses, but then she would have to explain about the magician, the powder, the After-room—everything.

Her mother was in the front parlor, reading student assignments as usual, and Benjamin went straight upstairs.

Janie dropped her knapsack by her mother's chair and flung herself across the couch.

"Everything all right?" her mother asked.

"Can we go away somewhere, for the summer?" Janie asked.

Her mother was still reading. "Mmm—maybe."

"I wish we could go right now."

That got her a direct look. "Why?"

"Just, you know, to be out of school. Same as you."

Her mother tossed the stapled paper on the ottoman and stretched in her chair like a cat, yawning. "I don't know what we can afford. Where do you want to go?"

"Maybe back to London to see Pip?"

Her mother laughed. "Not on what we're getting paid."

"We wouldn't have to stay anywhere fancy," Janie said.

"We'd still have to get four people across the Atlantic."

"How about Los Angeles?"

Her mother shook her head. "The Studebaker would never make it. And train tickets, sleeping cars—we're just not making enough money."

"I wish you could get a writing job."

"Yes, you've said that," her mother said. "You think we don't want that, too?"

"Sorry," Janie said. She didn't want to make her parents feel deficient.

Her mother had a little carved wooden Japanese figurine of a mouse that she used as a paperweight, and Janie concentrated all her thoughts on pulling it toward her from

the side table. The little mouse
sat crouched over the seed in its
paws. Nothing happened. Janie
got up from the couch.

At the top of the stairs, she
knocked on Benjamin's bedroom door. He didn't answer.

She knocked again.
"Benjamin?"

No answer.

She said, "Benjamin, are you okay?"

Nothing.

She pushed open the door, and saw him lying motionless
on the floor with his eyes closed. Then, as in a nightmare, she
saw the glass of water on the nightstand. And the jar of powder she'd hidden so carefully.

"Benjamin!" she cried, pulling him up to sitting. He
slumped over in the other direction, and she struggled to keep
him upright. Was he breathing? She felt for a pulse in his
neck. It was there, but barely.

She heard her mother's feet on the stairs, and rolled the jar
under the bed. Then she slapped Benjamin's face. "Wake up!"
she said. "Wake *up!*"

"What happened?" her mother cried, behind her.

"Breathe!" she begged him. "Just please *breathe!*"

"You say he fainted," the doctor said, at the hospital. They'd
given Benjamin something to open his airways and then

something to make him sleep, and now he lay unconscious in the hospital bed. The doctor was short and balding and full of concern, with fuzzy gray hair at his temples.

"Yes," Janie said. "And then he wasn't breathing."

"Does he have a history of syncope?"

"Of what?" she said.

"Of fainting."

"It happened once before."

"*When?*" her mother said.

"The other day," she said, sheepish.

"And you didn't *tell* me?"

"He was fine, and he didn't want to worry you."

"Janie!" her mother said.

"We'll keep him here for observation, do some tests," the doctor said.

If they drew blood, would they detect the powder? Would they know what it was? "Can't we just take him home?" Janie asked.

"I'm afraid not," the doctor said. "We'll take good care of him."

"Then I'll stay here," she said.

"You need to eat dinner," her mother said. "And do your homework."

"*Homework?*" Janie said. "Are you serious?"

Her mother sighed. "All right. I have to go pick up your father. But then I'm coming back and you're eating dinner, even if it's in the hospital cafeteria."

"Fine."

When her mother and the doctor left, Janie took Benjamin's heavy, sedated hand. She wasn't just angry with him for stealing the powder back. She was angry that he'd put her in a position where she had to be the gatekeeper, and *then* he'd stolen it. They were supposed to be friends—more than friends. She didn't want to be hiding the jar and nagging him about the importance of staying alive, while he kept running toward the After-room.

She thought about writing to Vili again, but what more could she say, safely? A nurse came in, a trim black woman in a starched white uniform. The nurse took Benjamin's wrist and looked at her watch to count his pulse.

"Do you think he'll sleep for a while?" Janie asked.

"If he knows what's good for him," the nurse said.

Then she left, and Janie sat watching Benjamin for signs of consciousness. A few minutes later, she heard voices in the hall, the nurse telling someone that visiting hours were over.

"It'sh very important," a man's voice said. The voice was familiar to Janie, but also mushy and strange. She listened, trying to puzzle it out. *Doyle*.

"You can't go in there," the nurse said.

But Doyle pushed his way past her. He had purple bruises under both eyes. His nose was crooked, his jaw swollen. "I need more of thad shtuff," he said to Janie.

"Sir," the nurse said, putting herself between him and the hospital bed. "I have to ask you to leave."

"I jusht need a minute," he said.

"You look *awful*," Janie said.

"You think I don't know thad?"

"Do you *know* this man?" the nurse asked.

Janie nodded, staring at Doyle's battered face. "It's okay," she said.

"It's not okay," the nurse said.

"You should have stopped playing poker," Janie told Doyle.

"I know!" he said. "I was shtupid. But the shtuff is wearing off, and I can't go back to the way I wazh."

"I'm going to get an orderly," the nurse said, and she disappeared down the hall.

"I thought your chemist could make it," Janie said.

"He said it wazh imposhible. I told him it couldn't be. *Kidzh* made it!"

"Do you know that someone's following us?" Janie asked.

Doyle's bruised eyebrows came together in a frown. "Who?"

"A guy in dark glasses, in a blue sedan." Janie felt tears stinging her eyes, and she willed them back. She wouldn't cry in front of Doyle. "I wish we'd never met you! Benjamin almost died because you wouldn't help him!"

Doyle seemed to notice Benjamin in the hospital bed for the first time. He stared. "Whad happened?"

"He tried to talk to his father," she said.

"I told him to knock thad off."

"You also promised you'd teach him how to do it safely!"

The nurse came back with two burly men in white scrubs, who seized Doyle by the arms. Janie wondered what the nurse had heard. She hoped it hadn't been too much.

"Oush!" Doyle said. "Careful! My ribzh!" He dragged his feet as the two orderlies carried him out the door. "Zhanie, you have to help me!" he cried.

Janie turned away. Doyle should have stopped playing poker. He should have taught Benjamin what he promised. But everything went back to the filter. They shouldn't have given it to Doyle without thinking harder about what it might do. It had been wildly irresponsible, just handing it over. The apothecary would never have approved.

"He's gone," she said to Benjamin, who gave no sign of hearing.

She sat at his bedside. The room was silent. She wished she had brought her homework after all—anything to keep her mind from spinning around the wrongness of what they'd done, and the question of what they should do now. She felt that buzzing, anxious feeling again, rising in her chest.

A paper drinking straw was on the little table by Benjamin's bed, with a glass of water. Janie focused on the straw, pulling it toward her hand. She thought it shifted slightly, angling toward her, or maybe it was just a trick of the light.

She blinked and tried again. At first nothing, and then the straw slid off the table and shot into her hand. The anxious feeling in her chest turned into triumphant, liquid joy, suffusing her whole body.

The nurse came back into the room. "He's gone," she said. "You want to tell me who that was?"

"He's—a magician," Janie said. "He's our friends' uncle."

The nurse frowned. "That man is *trouble*. You all right?"

Janie nodded, clutching the straw in her hand. "Thank you," she said. "I'm fine."

CHAPTER 17

Conscience

Jin Lo sat listening to Ned Maddox's radio, trying to decipher patterns in the cloud of signals, making notes on a piece of paper, looking for meaning. The U.S. Navy was searching the tiny islands in the China Sea for the rogue commander, Thomas Hayes, but she thought that was wrong. He wouldn't be in the islands. The commander was a military man, and he knew that orders came from the top. So she thought he would go after Chairman Mao. To get to Mao he had to go to Beijing. To get to Beijing by water, which was a naval officer's natural element, he had to go up the Grand Canal.

She presented this theory to Ned Maddox.

"That's crazy," he said.

"He is crazy," she said. "From grief."

"And you know this because—you're psychic? Is that another one of your tricks?"

"No," she said.

"So I'm supposed to risk my career for a guess."

"You would be helping your navy if we found him," she said.

"I'd also be abandoning my post."

"So tell them you're leaving," she said.

"Because a strange girl washed up on the beach and told me to?"

"Tell them you think he is in the canal."

"That's not how it works," he said. "I'm stationed here for a reason. I have orders."

"Your orders are to help your navy," she said. "To look for enemies."

"Right," he said.

"So?"

"So there's a protocol," he said. "There's a chain of command."

"But they are looking in the wrong place," she said.

"You don't know that."

"I do."

"I would need evidence to explain why I wanted to go."

She tilted her head. "So you will let a nuclear explosion occur in China. And *that* will be your evidence."

"I'm not letting anything happen!"

"You are," she said. "By not acting."

"Stop pretending to be my conscience!"

"I am your conscience," she said.

"You're not," he said. "I have my own, thank you very much!"

Jin Lo sighed. She knew Ned Maddox had not asked for her to show up and start making demands. But no one ever asked for the task they had been given. "You remember I told you my teacher said that the universe is always doing its work," she said.

"Yeah," he said. "You said that."

"*This* is what the universe is doing, Ned Maddox. *We* are what it is doing. Come with me and see. Or I will go alone."

"You don't have a boat," he said.

"You hide one in the mangrove swamp."

He frowned. "How do you know that?"

"I am not stupid."

"And if I say you can't take it?"

She looked him in the eye, to make sure he knew she was serious. "I will," she said. "You cannot do your work and watch me all the time."

CHAPTER 18

A Vanishing Act

Janie's parents made her go home from the hospital to sleep, over her protests. At the house, she checked the mail, in case anything had come from Vili.

"Did anyone telephone?" she asked.

"Why?" her father said. "You expecting a call from your agent?"

"Just asking," she said, sullen. Sometimes her parents forgot that she was not a child. She'd been in boarding school, and had a job washing dishes in an Italian restaurant. She'd been to Nova Zembla—although that had been chemically erased from their memories.

In the morning, the hospital called to say that Benjamin was being discharged. The doctors couldn't find anything wrong with him, but they wanted him to stay home and rest.

"I'll stay home, too," Janie said.

"No, you'll go to school," her father said.

"I won't miss anything important."

"School is your job," her father said. "We'll work at home and keep an eye on him."

So her parents dropped Janie on the sidewalk outside the school, on their way to pick him up at the hospital. She had retrieved the jar of powder from under his bed and put it in her knapsack for safekeeping, but that didn't make her feel any better.

The blue sedan didn't seem to be hanging around the school, at least. It was still early, and the Doyle twins were practicing on the tennis courts. Janie watched them wistfully. A game of tennis on a spring morning seemed so simple and straightforward. You couldn't worry while you played tennis. Nothing mattered but getting to the ball. She walked around the chain-link fence to the court.

"Who's winning?" she asked.

"We're just hitting the ball," Valentina said.

"*She's* winning," Nat said.

He picked up balls with a quick flick of his racquet against his toe. They both looked happy from playing, but then Janie thought she could see the worry come back into their faces, like a storm cloud gathering.

"Our uncle was supposed to come to dinner last night," Valentina said. "But he didn't show up."

"Maybe he didn't feel like it, with two black eyes," Janie said.

Nat looked confused. "Did we tell you he had two black eyes?"

"Have you seen him?" Valentina asked, eager.

Janie winced inwardly. Why couldn't she keep her mouth shut? "He came to the hospital last night, to see Benjamin."

"Benjamin was in the *hospital*?" Nat said.

Janie nodded. "This weird thing happened where he stopped breathing."

"Like asthma?" Valentina asked.

"Sort of," Janie said. "Do you know who your uncle plays poker with?"

Nat flicked up another ball. "His name's Joey Rocco," he said. "They used to call him Joey the Haberdasher. He ran liquor in Detroit, back when it was illegal. He went to prison and he's retired now, but our dad says he's still a crook."

"Wait, is Benjamin okay?" Valentina asked.

"I think so," Janie said.

The first bell rang, and the twins picked up their bags to go change.

Joey the Haberdasher. A nickname like that seemed an ominous sign. What would her mother and father do if someone came to the house for Benjamin? Her parents had many admirable qualities, but they were not equipped to deal with gangsters.

Janie couldn't concentrate on anything in school. In chemistry, she sat at her desk with her chin in her hand and stared at a row of glass beakers, trying to slide one of them across the stone lab counter. Mr. Walters was droning on and on.

"Miss Scott?" he said.

Janie sat up straight.

"Would you care to explain how that last reaction works?"

She looked at the blackboard. The notes looked like incoherent scribbles. A beaker fell to the floor with a crash.

"Who did that?" Mr. Walters snapped.

Looks shot around the room, but no one had been anywhere near the lab counters.

"Janie, you can clean it up, for not paying attention," Mr. Walters said.

She nodded and stood, her face hot, and got the broom and dustpan from the corner of the room. It took her the rest of the class to chase down all the glinting pieces. She let her hair fall over her face to hide the small smile of triumph she could feel on her face.

When school finally let out, she avoided the twins, who might have more questions, and hurried in the direction of home, but the blue sedan cruised up beside her. It was a Chevrolet and said *Bel Air* in fancy letters on the side. The driver rolled the passenger window down and leaned over the seat. She caught his dark glasses out of the corner of her eye.

"Afternoon, miss," he said.

She sped up her stride, gripping her knapsack strap, wondering if she could swing the bag as a weapon if he got out of the car. It was heavy with books.

"Just stop a minute, miss," he said.

She shook her head *no* and kept walking.

"Where's your boyfriend?" he asked.

Her hands were sweating.

"I said, miss, where's the boy?"

"What boy?" she asked.

"The apothecary's kid."

She glanced sideways. The dark glasses had blue lenses. What had Doyle told these people? "He left town," she said.

The man had to pull around two parked cars, but then he sidled back into the curb. "Left *town*?"

She nodded. "He got really sick, so they sent him to a better hospital. On a plane."

"What kind of sick?"

"They don't know. The doctor had never seen anything like it."

He frowned. "Was it from taking that powder?"

Janie's heart plunged into her stomach. "What powder?"

"The one he maybe left behind?"

She renewed her sweaty grip on her knapsack, trying not to think about the glass jar nestled inside it. "He didn't leave anything behind," she said. "I'd know."

"Would you, now?" the man asked.

"Of course."

"No suspicious jars or packages? Glass bottles?"

"No," she said. "I'm not supposed to talk to strangers."

He had to pull around two more parked cars. Then he cruised back over. He stretched his hand out the window, holding a business card between two fingers. He had very white shirt cuffs and black enameled cufflinks. "My number," he said. "If you run across anything."

Janie took the card, which said only *EN-4800*. No name. "Okay."

"What hospital did they send him to?" he asked.

"I think it was in Minnesota," she said. There was a good hospital there, but she couldn't remember the name.

"The Mayo Clinic?" he asked.

She nodded. "That one."

The man lowered his dark glasses and looked at her over them. The look in his eyes made her shudder. "You telling me the truth, my girl?" he asked.

"Yes," she said.

"I hope so," he said.

The car pulled away. Janie watched, holding her breath, until it had rolled around the corner. Then she ran all the way home. What if Benjamin had gone out for a walk and had been spotted? She ran up the stairs to the front porch and threw open the door.

The front hall and the parlor were empty, and she felt panic rising. Had Joey the Haberdasher been here already? Was the man in the car just distracting her? Had they taken Benjamin and her parents away?

In her mind, she saw Doyle's bruised eyes, his broken nose and swollen jaw.

"Benjamin!" she called, out of breath.

"We're back here!" her father's voice said.

She ran to the kitchen and found the three of them sitting at the table as if nothing had happened. Benjamin was eating a bowl of soup, and his face had color in it. Her parents looked positively giddy.

"Janie, you'll never guess!" her mother said. "We have a *job*!"

CHAPTER 19

Deus Ex Machina

The cable had come before lunchtime. Janie's parents had been asked to rewrite a script for a movie that was shooting in Italy. They were to go to Rome at once to meet the director, and it meant leaving on a morning flight.

"They'll pay everyone's way," her mother said. "Yours and Benjamin's too. Janie, it's *Italy*! Cinecittà! And a writing job!"

"I didn't think we'd ever get one again," her father said.

"But it means you have to miss the last two weeks of school," her mother said. "Do you mind too much?"

"Of course she doesn't mind," her father said. "Who minds missing school to go to *Rome*?"

Janie sat down at the table, her legs collapsing under her with relief that Benjamin and her parents were fine. But she was confused about whether to be happy. Rome? That should be good news. Her parents had a job. They would be leaving town at exactly the right moment. But it all seemed too good to be true. Was it a trap? "Can I see the telegram?" she asked.

Her mother slid it across the table. "You can make up the schoolwork," she said. "It's such an opportunity! We can stay all summer. You wanted to go away, remember?"

"Benjamin wants to go," her father said. "Right, Figment?"

Benjamin was watching her. "If Janie does."

Janie ignored them and read the message:

DAVIS AND MARJORIE SCOTT:

FILM NEEDS REWRITE ON SET. PLEASE
REPORT TO CINECITTÀ, ROME, EARLIEST
POSSIBLE. FLAT ARRANGED FOR FAMILY
OF 4. FLY TOMORROW. SPEAKING TO AGENT
ABOUT YOUR FEE. PLEASE REPLY ASAP.

There was that Italian word they'd been saying: *chee-nay-chee-TAH.* "Cinecittà is a movie studio?" she asked.

"Where Fellini works," her father said. "He's a genius!"

"They're doing a film in English, and they want us to rewrite it," her mother said. "We talked to our agent, and it's legitimate. He called us long distance."

"The poor guy thought we'd never get another job," her father said.

"He didn't know what our fee should be, so he just made up a number. And they said okay!"

"Or whatever the Italian is," her father said. *"Okay-dokay."*

"Va bene," Janie said, automatically.

"See, you can translate for us! It's perfect!"

"I don't know that much," she said. "I can say *Dai, dai, dai, ragazza!* That's what they shouted at me when I was too slow washing dishes in the restaurant. And I can order food."

"So we won't starve!" her father said.

Her mother peered into her face. "Oh, Janie. Please don't kick up a fuss like when we went to London. You were such a pill."

"What?" her father said. "How can you be a pill about *Rome?*"

Janie's mind was racing. This was too elaborate to be a trap. Joey Rocco might have an Italian name, but he wouldn't send them all the way to Rome to trap them, when he was right here in Michigan. So why did she have so much trouble believing that her parents could get a writing job? They'd done it before. They were funny and talented. She'd seen them spin out stories, adding twists and surprises, and talking about character. That was what they did best, what they were supposed to do. "I want to go," she said. "I really do. I'm just surprised, that's all. I mean, not *surprised.* It's great. You deserve it."

Her parents sat back in their chairs, grinning with relief. "You scared us!" her father said.

"We have so much packing to do!" her mother said. "A transatlantic flight! It's so glamorous. I'm going to find the suitcases." They both went up the stairs, and their voices receded.

Janie studied Benjamin. He really did look healthier. "How are you feeling?"

"Much better, thanks," he said.

"Doyle showed up at the hospital, wanting more filter."

Benjamin scowled. "I hope you told him to get lost."

"The nurse did," Janie said. "She had orderlies carry him out. His face is all smashed up. The twins think he owes money to a retired mobster named Joey Rocco. I'm sure that's who sent the guy to follow us. That guy asked where you were today, and I told him you were sick and had gone to Minnesota."

"And he believed you?"

"He seemed to. There's a big hospital there, he knew the name. He wanted to know if you'd left any powder behind, and I said no."

"So is Rocco behind your parents' job?" Benjamin asked.

"That's what I thought at first," Janie said. "But why would he send us to Rome?"

"It makes no sense."

"So maybe it's just a job. A real job."

"It's convenient timing, right?" Benjamin said. "Kind of a coincidence?"

"Well, except that they're trying to get work all the time. So maybe now is just when it happened."

Benjamin frowned. "I hope so. I don't trust coincidences."

"Do you have any of those mushrooms that help with languages?"

"Two small ones," he said. "They won't do much."

Just then she remembered the straw in the hospital room, and the beaker on the lab shelf.

"Benjamin, look!" she whispered. She held up her hand

and concentrated on the telegram on the table. It was harder to do it with Benjamin watching—it made her self-conscious. But after a moment, the piece of paper trembled as if there were a breeze in the room, then slid across the table into her hand. She pinched it with her thumb and forefinger, feeling a wild exultation.

His eyes widened. "How did you do that?"

"I've been practicing," she said. "To distract myself, when I get upset. Try it!" She put the telegram down.

Benjamin stared at the piece of paper, and held up his hand to summon it, but nothing happened.

"I couldn't do it at first, either," she said.

Benjamin glared harder at the telegram.

"Janie!" her father called from upstairs. "Benjamin! Come pack!"

They spent the evening getting ready to close up the house, her parents gleeful and frantic. Janie tried to make sure Benjamin didn't stand near any windows, and couldn't be seen from the street. They ate a picnic dinner of all the perishable food in the house: the rest of the soup, cheese with apples, an open box of crackers, a loaf of bread.

Janie slept badly that night, drifting in and out of dreams in which the blue sedan kept appearing around every corner. Then her father was shaking her awake, singing, "Oh, what a beautiful morn-ing! Oh, what a beautiful day!"

Janie groaned and pulled the covers over her head.

"Up!" he said. "*Arrivederci*, baby!"

"Mmph," she said. "That means good-bye."

Then it all came back: Joey the Haberdasher. The Bel Air. The telegram. Rome. She struggled out of bed. She found the jar of powder and considered throwing it into the fireplace, or pouring it down the drain, but instead she stashed it in her suitcase with her hairbrush and toothpaste. You never knew.

The sun hadn't risen when they climbed into the taxi. Benjamin wore a wool cap pulled down low over his eyebrows and his collar up. The taxi took them to the airport, where Janie was seized by nervousness as they presented their passports. She couldn't believe that the ticket agent would really think this English boy was her cousin, Benjamin Scott. But the agent smiled and sent them right through, saying, *"Buon viaggio."*

On the plane, Janie looked at every one of the other passengers as she found her seat. When she was sure the man with the dark glasses wasn't on board, she bunched her jacket up against the window and went back to sleep.

CHAPTER 20

At Sea

Ned Maddox's boat, hidden in the mangrove swamp, was deliberately ragged and patched-together, to blend in among the working boats in Chinese waters, but it was also fast and seaworthy, with a small berth in the bow where two people could comfortably sleep. It was the perfect boat in which to move unnoticed, and Jin Lo wondered again at the fact that she had washed up on Ned Maddox's beach, of all the possible beaches.

They loaded the lockers with provisions and fuel cans and blankets and warm clothes. Jin Lo coiled her hair up under a hat, to look more like a boy. Ned Maddox backed the boat out of its hiding place, turning it toward the sea when the inlet became wide enough. He would have to stay hidden much of the time—as a foreigner, he would draw attention.

"What if we're stopped?" he asked. "What's our story?"

"I am bringing my American husband to meet my family in Beijing," she said.

An uncomfortable look crossed Ned Maddox's face. He

pushed the throttle forward, and the boat started to lift and plane, heading north toward Hangzhou and the mouth of the Grand Canal. The sun was setting over China, all orange haze. Fish raced beneath them, going about their business, knowing nothing of the stolen bomb that could poison their waters for years to come.

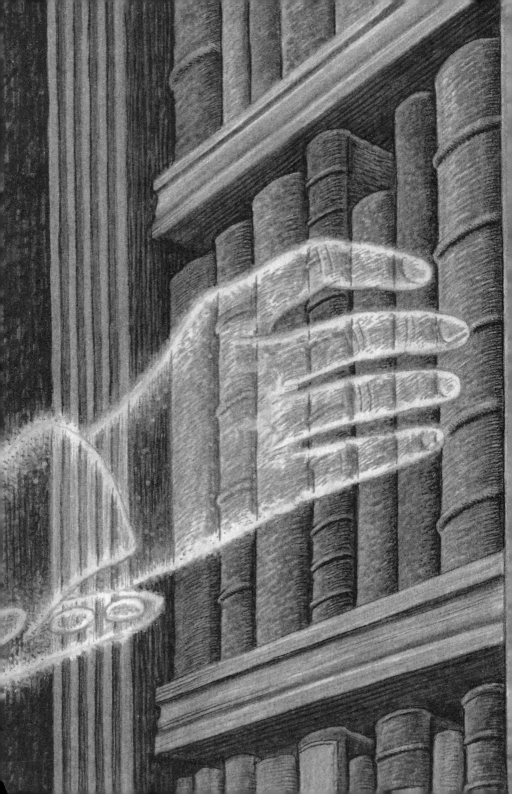

PART TWO

CHAPTER 21

Cinecittà

When the Scotts and Benjamin changed planes in New York, Janie again surveyed the passengers for the man in the dark glasses, or for anyone who might be watching them with sinister intent. But no one was, as far as she could tell. The other passengers were all absorbed in their own travels. She told herself to stop worrying and to be proud of her parents for getting a job at exactly the right time.

Her father, meanwhile, was acting like a starry-eyed kid. "Italian cinema is the best thing happening in film right now," he said. "You have to see *I Vitelloni*."

"What's it about?" Janie asked.

"Youth," he said. "Young men. Boredom."

"Sounds great," Benjamin said, in a voice that said it didn't.

"Don't be smart," her father said. "It's also about finding a moral compass. You might find it useful."

Janie said, "You're usually so cynical about show business."

"A film like that is *art*!" he said. "And you'll find I'm much less cynical when I have a job."

They arrived at Ciampino Airport rumpled and tired, and her parents went looking for their bags. As they walked through the terminal, Benjamin passed Janie the two small dried mushrooms that made languages easier to learn.

"You keep one," she whispered.

"They'll do you more good," he said. "One's not really enough."

Her mother turned. "Don't dawdle," she called.

Janie popped the mushrooms into her mouth and chewed.

A taxi carried them the short distance to the studio. The streets were dusty and scrawled with graffiti. Many of the walls of buildings were crumbling at the corners. Strange smells came through the open windows of the cab, not all of them good.

Her father tried to talk to the driver, and the mushrooms made the mangled, enthusiastic sentences intolerable to Janie. *"Vamos a hacer un film, qui!"* he said.

"Dad, that's mostly Spanish," she said.

"He understands me."

"Yes," the driver said. "I understands!" But really, he wanted to practice his English, so they were spared her father's Italian.

The studio had a high wall with a gate in it, and inside, a receptionist gave them directions. The buildings were all painted the same brown and reminded Janie of huge cardboard boxes, lined up in rows. The only buildings that looked real were fake: a city street set with storefronts and apartments, held up by scaffolding behind.

An actor walked by in a dark suit, his face an unnatural orange, with tissues tucked into his stiff white collar to protect it from his makeup. He gave Janie a brilliant smile. *"Ciao,"* he said, in a deep, warm voice.

Benjamin, who'd seemed asleep on his feet, came fully awake, and looked from the actor to Janie.

"Um, *ciao*," she said, taken aback.

"Hey, that's my daughter, chum!" her father said.

The actor reached out and shook her father's hand. *"Complimenti,"* he said. "Good job." He gave Janie's mother a wolfish grin, too, then turned back to look at Janie again as he passed.

Her face felt hot. Benjamin watched the actor go.

"Welcome to Italy," her mother said wryly.

A short, silver-haired man in a green suit came rushing out of the nearest cardboard-box building. *"Buon giorno!"* he cried. *"I signori Scott! Benvenuto!"* He kissed her mother on both cheeks and pumped her father's hand.

Then he turned to Janie and clasped her hand in both of his. She was surprised to feel him slip her a piece of paper, unseen. *"Come stai, carina?"* he asked. "I am Tonino Clementi. Call me Tony. Your parents are saving my film. Let me show you where you live! Did you keep your taxi?"

"Our bags are in it," her father said.

"Wonderful!" he said. "Come!"

He rushed off toward the studio gate, and her parents followed.

Janie unfolded the piece of paper. It was a handwritten note:

Welcome to Rome! Hope all suits. Tomorrow you must see the Trevi Fountain. Around ten?

x Vili

Janie suddenly felt as though everything was a film set, not just the street with the scaffolding. At the edge, the world might end, and she would fall off. She showed the note to Benjamin.

He read it and looked up at her. "Vili's *here*?"

Her parents had turned to call them onward, so she folded the paper quickly into her pocket. Outside the gate, Tony crowded them into the waiting cab.

As they drove, Tony told them about the neighborhood. "There is a ruin of the old aqueduct over here," he said, waving. "That brought the water. The ancient Romans knew how to do everything. Running water, a bath every day, poetry, philosophy, the most beautiful houses. Then Europe forgot these things for three hundred years, and lived in holes. In filth. It is absurd."

The cab stopped at a nearby building, and Tony showed them into a flat on the second floor. The apartment was simple and the plaster walls were scarred where chairs had scraped against them, but it was clean. Between the living room and the kitchen was a small table with four chairs. They put down their suitcases and looked around.

"It's not a palace, okay, you know?" Tony said. "It's, what you say, *comodo*."

"It's perfect," Janie's mother said.

Tony beamed. There was a basket of oranges on the table. "A little gift from me," he said. "They are dark red inside, in the Roman way. For your breakfast. And look, there is a *balcone!*"

Glass-paneled doors opened out onto the balcony, and yellow light poured through. They stepped outside.

"You like it?" Tony asked.

They said that they did, very much. Janie still felt that everything was staged and unreal. And maybe it was.

"The script is *una porcata*, I'm telling you," Tony said. "It needs everything new. New *dialogo*, new scenes, a new girl, new heart." He struck the left side of his chest with his right fist.

"We're good at heart," her father said.

"You start tomorrow," Tony said. "There is a very good trattoria on the corner, for your dinner. Tell Angelo I am sending you. I leave you to unpack. *Ciao! A domani!*" He gave Janie a wink, and she looked away, embarrassed.

Her parents went to open cupboards. Janie and Benjamin stayed out on the balcony.

In a low voice, Benjamin said, "So—do you think Vili set all this up?"

"We did write to him," she said. "And say there was trouble."

"Does he know movie people?" Benjamin asked.

"He knows *everyone*."

Her mother called out, "Did you guys pick your rooms already?"

"Could Vili invent a whole movie so fast?" Benjamin whispered.

"I don't know," Janie said. "It seems real, right?"

"I don't know what a real movie seems like," Benjamin said. "What will happen when they find out Vili's behind it?"

Her parents were still inspecting the flat, their happy voices ringing out with discoveries, and Janie was filled with resolve.

"We're not going to tell them," she said. "So they won't."

CHAPTER 22

Roman Holiday

Janie woke at four a.m., her body hopelessly confused about what time it was. She had been dreaming about playing badminton in Penny Meadows's backyard in Los Angeles with Penny and her mother. That had really happened, once upon a time. Janie must have been eight or nine, and after a few games she had realized that Penny's mother was missing the birdie on purpose, cheating to let the girls win. Mrs. Meadows was kind and generous and made delicious brownies, but Janie had been furious with her. She didn't know the word "condescension" yet, but she knew the feeling of not being taken seriously because she was a child.

She had stormed home that day and asked her parents if they let her win at games on purpose. Amused, they said no. They said the world was a tough place, and it was important to learn that you didn't always win. You needed both luck and skill to do it, and you had to know how to lose gracefully.

In her exhausted state, in the strange room in Rome, the

badminton incident loomed in her mind. As fervently as her parents wanted to make a living as writers again, and as unfair as their treatment in Hollywood had been, she knew they wanted to get a job on their own merits. They would be crushed if Vili had made the whole thing happen.

Tony had asked them to come to breakfast at the commissary, so all four of them walked to the studio and checked in with the receptionist at the gate. The commissary had white tablecloths and silver water pitchers, and men in suits having breakfast meetings. The waiters were deferential to Tony and brought coffee for everyone and a plate of cone-shaped pastries. Janie sniffed the coffee and her father raised his eyebrows at her.

Tony described the movie her parents were going to rewrite, with a lot of enthusiastic hand gestures. It was about a Swedish princess, frustrated with her constrained life—she can't do this, she can't do that—until her English cousin shows up and they have an adventure in Rome.

"That's *Roman Holiday*," Janie said.

"No, no!" Tony said. "This script was from before." Then he saw someone he knew, waved in greeting, and left the table to say hello.

"It's the exact same movie," Janie said to her parents. In *Roman Holiday*, Audrey Hepburn played a visiting princess who sneaks out of her country's embassy in Rome. Gregory Peck played the handsome American reporter who shows her around the city.

"Well, Shakespeare used existing stories, too," her father said.

"Old stories," she said. "Audrey Hepburn got an Oscar for *Roman Holiday* last year."

"That's why they need us to fix this one!"

"Will you two go scout locations for us?" her mother asked. "We need places for the characters to go exploring."

"You mean besides all the places they went in *Roman Holiday*?" Janie asked.

Benjamin kicked her under the table.

"Ow," she said.

"Of course we'll scout," Benjamin said. "Should we start with the Trevi Fountain?"

Tony, returning, overheard. "The Fontana di Trevi!" he said, his face betraying nothing but pride in his city. "You must go there. You throw a coin in, to make sure you'll come back to Rome. I will arrange a car for you."

The chauffeur-driven car, black and shiny, left them in the center of the city, and they stood in front of the Trevi Fountain, with the roar of water all around them. The fountain was an enormous sculpture, with wild-looking horses ridden by muscular men, and a god standing over them all—maybe Neptune? Or Triton? At the base were giant rocks that the water poured over. Janie thought it would be a good place to have a conversation you didn't want to be overheard, because the roar of the water drowned out everything. Then she wondered if she was capable of a simple, appreciative response to anything anymore—just, *It's magnificent. What a nice place.* No imagining how it might aid a secret life.

"Do you think that's Neptune?" Benjamin asked.

"Oceanus, actually," a voice said.

Janie turned to see Count Vili beside her, round and sleek as a seal, wearing a white linen suit and a green silk scarf. "Vili!" she cried, and the noise of the water swallowed it up. She wanted to throw her arms around him, but that seemed inappropriate at a clandestine meeting. He leaned over to kiss both her cheeks in his European way.

"Oceanus was one of the Titans," he said. "The god of the great river that surrounds the world. This was originally the mouth of an aqueduct, bringing water to the city. And are you settled? Is everything acceptable?"

"Yes, sir," Benjamin said, shaking his hand.

"Thank you for getting my parents a job," Janie said, a little stiffly.

Vili waved a hand in dismissal. "It was easier than going to Michigan myself, at this time," he said. "And I have been thinking they should be writing again. Some people are born teachers, but perhaps not your parents."

"Is it a real film?" Benjamin asked.

"Of course it is!" Vili said, looking insulted.

"We thought you might've invented the whole thing," Janie said.

"That would take a little longer," he said. "No, I assure you, it's perfectly real. Though perhaps I gave it a little nudge.

Now, shall we walk to the Spanish Steps and you can tell me how you are? Your telegram was a bit—vague."

They walked through the narrow cobblestone streets, around corners and up hills. The count had always been nimble for his size, and he set a brisk pace, swinging his blackthorn walking stick. They told him about Benjamin's discovery of the After-room, and how he'd stopped breathing when he took the powder to go there, and about the magician who could read minds but didn't want to. Benjamin told him about the deal they'd made with Doyle, and the way the magician had changed after taking the filter, how he'd refused to teach them what he'd promised, and no longer cared about other people's thoughts or feelings. Janie described how Doyle had been beaten up for poker debts to a retired gangster called Joey Rocco, and how a man had started following them in a car, asking about the powder.

"When the telegram came about a job in Rome," Benjamin said, "we thought it might be a trap."

"Of course, you would," Vili said thoughtfully.

"I'm so glad it was you," Janie said. Telling the story had made her feel grateful for their escape, and less concerned about her parents' egos.

"Your magician is brave to play poker with that man," Vili observed.

"Doyle used to know what cards everyone had," Janie said. "So he could always win."

"Which is cheating," Vili said. "So I imagine his friend has built up some resentment, over time. If I'd known about your Rocco, I might not have brought you to *Italy*, of all places. But this is the only place I have film connections."

"Do you think Rocco has family here?" Janie asked.

"The American crime syndicates are not closely linked to the Sicilian and Neapolitan families, I believe. They formed among immigrants on their own. But we might as well be watchful."

"Have you ever heard of anything like the After-room?" Janie asked.

"Never," Vili said. "I'm very interested."

They arrived at the base of the vast travertine staircase of the Piazza di Spagna. The Spanish Steps stretched up toward a church at the top with two square towers. Young people stretched out on the sun-warmed marble, enjoying the bright afternoon. Tourists idled around the fountain at the bottom.

"I have an appointment to keep," Vili said. "But you might look in at that house there. It's where the poet John Keats died."

Janie had read the "Ode on a Grecian Urn" in school— *Beauty is truth, truth beauty*—and some of the poet's letters, which she had liked. "Okay," she said, looking at the house at the base of the steps.

"It's a museum now," Vili said. "I must be off."

"Wait!" Janie said. "Is it a secret that you're here?"

"I'll drop your parents a note, to say that I happen to be in town."

"You won't let them know that you nudged the movie a little?"

Vili smiled. "Now, why would I tell them such a thing?"

"Because beauty is truth, and truth beauty?"

"Oh, not always," Vili said. "The old urn was wrong about that."

Then he was gone, and Janie and Benjamin went into the Keats house. They climbed to the upper level, where they bought a ticket from an English girl not much older than they were. Letters and manuscripts were in glass cases, along with portraits of Shelley and Byron.

In the poet's little bedroom, a window looked out at the fountain below. Keats had been dying of tuberculosis here, coughing up blood and struggling to breathe, and Janie thought she could feel, in this room, how he had wanted to live, but also wanted to be out of pain. It was as if some part of him was still here.

She studied a portrait of Fanny Brawne, the girl Keats hadn't lived long enough to marry, and read the "Ode to a Nightingale" in an open book:

> Darkling I listen; and, for many a time
> I have been half in love with easeful Death,
> Call'd him soft names in many a musèd rhyme,
> To take into the air my quiet breath;
> Now more than ever seems it rich to die,
> To cease upon the midnight with no pain,

While thou art pouring forth thy soul abroad
In such an ecstasy!

She thought about Benjamin and the After-room, and wondered if he was half in love with easeful death.

"Look at this," Benjamin said.

He was standing by a biography framed on the wall. It was a chronology of Keats's life, beginning with his birth on Halloween in 1795. She skimmed the first few lines. Keats had lost his father when he was only nine, and his mother to tuberculosis when he was fifteen. Janie couldn't help thinking that Benjamin had lost his parents like that. Then it said that John Keats had become an apothecary's apprentice at sixteen, in 1811.

She turned to Benjamin. "Did you know that?"

Benjamin shook his head. She saw the movement reflected in the glass, and thought someone was standing behind them, over Benjamin's shoulder. She looked, but the room was empty. She turned back to the biography on the wall.

"Do you feel something here?" she whispered.

"What do you mean?" Benjamin asked.

"Like maybe he hasn't left?"

"That's the effect they're going for," Benjamin said, looking around at the books, the letters, the keepsake locks of hair, the room with its early nineteenth-century furniture. A white plaster death mask made from Keats's face was mounted in a glass case on one wall. His eyes were closed, his face smooth, and it made her shudder.

"There's something *here*," she whispered. She thought she saw movement again and whirled. Again, nothing was there.

The English girl from the ticket desk popped her head in. "You two have any questions?"

"Yes," Janie said. "Has anyone ever said this place is haunted?"

"Loads of people," the girl said, laughing. "It's wonderful, isn't it? It feels like he's still here."

They went down the narrow staircase out of the house, then started to climb the weather-pocked travertine of the enormous Spanish Steps. The gloom and sadness of the house dispersed, but its windows still stared down at them. Janie was watching the windows for a sign of what she had seen, but someone thrust a flower at her—a little boy selling roses—and she almost stumbled. When she looked back at the building, it looked empty.

At the top of the steps, they were crossing the street when a truck came around a corner, very fast. Janie reached for Benjamin's sleeve to pull him back, but the fabric slipped out of her fingers. She heard the driver's indignant shout, the roaring complaint of the engine. The truck hit a puddle and splashed mud.

"Benjamin!" she cried into the noise.

The truck barreled away down the narrow street. Benjamin was standing very still. The truck had missed him by an inch.

"That truck could've killed you!" she said.

He shook his head as if to wake himself. "I didn't see it coming."

They both looked down at his mud-splattered clothes. The poem was still in Janie's head: *Now more than ever seems it rich to die.* She caught both of Benjamin's shoulders. "Listen to me," she said. "Dying is not an option. Do you understand that?"

He nodded, but his eyes were vacant and dazed.

CHAPTER 23

Termini Station

Doyle had drunk the last drops of the filter, and he was on his own. Which meant he was *not* on his own. Other people's minds came back with a vengeance, crowding his thoughts. He drank whiskey and went to bed with a pillow over his head, but nothing helped. The apartment walls were thin, and the neighbors' dreams invaded his sleep.

He also began to feel *remorse*, a sensation that had vanished with the filter but now came back, the Furies tearing at his chest with their long, sharp fingernails. He felt awful for criticizing his sister-in-law, for calling his brother fat, for driving his girlfriend away. For throwing the kids out of his apartment. He should've been nicer to the kids, if only out of self-interest! He might have cadged another bottle of the stuff.

He wondered if Benjamin was all right. Doyle remembered being sixteen and doing stupid, dangerous things. Walking on train tracks, jumping off bridges into murky water. Clinging to the back of a moving car and sliding through the icy streets in winter. Had he stopped doing any of that because it wasn't safe? No. So would Benjamin stop chasing his dead parents? No.

He hadn't meant to tell Joey Rocco about what the kid could do. He'd never been good at keeping his mouth shut. When he started losing at poker and owed Joey money, he got desperate, frantic. He'd been improvising, trying to find some way to offset his debt, and he just blurted it out.

He figured Joey wouldn't believe him, but the old gangster was interested. Turned out Joey had always been suspicious about Doyle's luck, and had him watched for signs of cheating, but found nothing. So he was ready to believe that there were ways of knowing things that didn't have an easy explanation. It could be very useful, in his line of work, to talk to the dead. When Doyle told him Benjamin could talk to his dead father, Joey believed it right away.

Joey the Haberdasher, ex-convict, was supposed to be retired, but someone like him could never actually retire. So he sent one of his goons to follow the kids home from school, which exasperated Doyle. You couldn't be tailing kids in cars! It just spooked them. The whole Scott household vanished. *Poof*: They were gone.

Doyle went to their house in Ann Arbor and jimmied the lock. There were signs that they'd packed up quickly and left. He rubbed a pencil over the pad of paper in the kitchen, and saw the indentations of the last thing written: an address in Rome.

So now Doyle was standing outside the Termini railway station in the Eternal City, under the long cantilevered roof, waiting for some cousin of Joey Rocco's to collect him. He had wanted to say no, to refuse to chase the kids across an ocean, but his nose was still tender, his eyes still bruised, and he was worried that Joey might send someone to break his kneecaps. Doyle liked his kneecaps. They were knobby and freckled and sprouted ginger hair, but he was attached to them.

He hunched his shoulders against the drizzle of other people's thoughts. Nothing was as vapid as people's thoughts on their way to a train. They wanted a pack of gum, a drink, another look at that girl in the tight skirt. They wanted a calzone, a coffee, a seat facing forward, a newspaper. On and on. It didn't matter that Doyle didn't speak Italian, except a few vivid curse words. Everyone's *wanting* came through bright and clear: amber liquid in a clear glass, an empty train seat, that smooth curve of skirt. It all flashed through Doyle's mind as it flashed through the minds of the people walking past.

Until he found a giant standing in front of him.

Doyle, who was six feet four himself, followed the brown suit from the lapels up to the face. The man's craggy nose had been broken more than twice, and his hair was thick as a wire brush. He held out a business card between fingers like Polish sausages.

Doyle took the card, which read only *Salvatore Rocco*, then looked back up at the giant who'd delivered it—a bodyguard? He wasn't sure. Because there was something remarkable about the giant. Doyle struggled to recognize it at first, but then he understood: No thoughts came off this guy at all. His mind was a perfect blank. He picked up Doyle's suitcase and turned away.

Doyle had to run a little to catch up, because the giant had such long legs. But the mental clamor around them dimmed. It was as if the giant's silent mind cast a cool, calm shadow, like the shade from an umbrella. The other voices couldn't get in, as long as the giant was close. Doyle took extra steps to stay in that quiet orbit, basking in the stillness and peace.

CHAPTER 24

A Disappearance

Vili sent Janie's parents a handwritten note, as he'd promised to do, and invited them to dinner at the trattoria down the street from their apartment. There were shiny knots of hot garlic bread in baskets on the table, and the place had a rich, warm smell of tomato sauce. Vili ordered for everyone in fluent Italian, and the owner, Angelo, seemed to approve of all his choices, and to find them interesting, a challenge.

Benjamin had needed to change out of the clothes the truck had splattered with mud, so he was going to catch up, to join them in a few minutes. That made Janie nervous, but she told herself he would be fine. She tried not to look at the empty chair they had left for him, or to picture the truck barreling down the street.

Her father leaned across the table to Vili. "So how did you know we were here?" he asked.

"I read about it in the film news," Vili said.

Her father brightened. "Seriously?"

"Of course," he said.

"And you just happened to be in Rome?" her mother asked.

"I like to be here whenever I can," Vili said. "I keep a little flat near the Piazza Navona. And I know your director, Tony, a little bit."

Janie waited for her parents to object to this coincidence, but they didn't. They were too pleased to have been in the film news.

People—European aristocrats, no less—were reading about them! Janie wondered which magazines had stories about movies that hadn't been made yet, mentioning writers who weren't famous. Could Vili produce a printed story if they asked to see it?

"That's what I love about Italy," her father said. "It's small enough that everyone knows everyone, within a certain world. It's *charmant*."

"That's French," Janie said.

"I know it's French!" he said. "I'm using a French word to express an Italian quality. Stendhal did it too, I think you'll find."

Janie was about to say that French was Stendhal's native language, so he expressed *everything* in it. Instead she told herself to stop correcting her father. It didn't matter what words he used.

Angelo brought a steaming bowl of ravioli to the table, and everyone oohed and aahed.

"Did you throw a coin into the Trevi Fountain?" Janie's mother asked while Vili dished the ravioli out.

"No, we forgot," Janie said.

"Then you have to go back," her father said.

"We saw the house where Keats was living when he died. It's a museum now."

"How romantic!" her mother said. "Is it pretty?"

Janie nodded. "Vili, did you know Keats was an apothecary's apprentice, at sixteen?"

"Ah, yes, of course," Vili said. "I'd forgotten."

"No kidding!" her father said.

"Like Benjamin," her mother said.

Janie thought about their strange experience in the house. What had she seen? An imagined shadow, a strange reflection. She wondered where Benjamin was. How long could it take him to change?

"We're meeting the cast tomorrow," her father said.

"Mr. Clementi—I mean Tony—has a girl he wants for the princess," her mother said. "And there's some British actor for the boy, because he's under contract and they need to use him. No one seems crazy about him."

"Maybe Pip could be in it," Janie said.

"Writers don't get to make those decisions," her mother said.

"If you had a strong opinion," Vili said, "I imagine you could voice it."

"Yeah, we could voice our way right back to Michigan," her father said. "Just in time for summer school."

"You might find filmmaking different in Italy," Vili said. "Things are more adaptable here."

"Well, I don't want to chance it," he said.

"I wonder where Benjamin is," Janie said. "Maybe I'll run back and see."

"Not alone in the dark," her father said.

Janie rolled her eyes—the apartment was a block away—but her father missed it, because Angelo arrived with a plate of tiny fried fish, each no bigger than a string you'd tie around your finger as a reminder of something important.

"*Qué manera!*" her father cried.

Janie bit her tongue to keep from telling him that was Spanish.

"I'll walk her back," Vili said, pushing away from the table. "No one can say I'm not getting enough food."

Janie's parents, warmed by the meal and the excitement of their new job, didn't object. Janie wondered if, on some deeply buried level, they knew that Vili was their benefactor, and were grateful to him. He held open the restaurant door for her.

The night was cool, after the warm, bright restaurant, and the air felt good on Janie's face as they walked back to the flat. "There was something I wanted to tell you, about the Keats house," she said.

"Yes?" Vili said.

"Well, he seemed to still sort of be there."

"Who?"

"Keats. Just faintly. I thought I saw him in a reflection. But maybe I was imagining it."

"Perhaps not," Vili said. "Perhaps your experiments with this After-room have made you more—aware of another dimension."

"I'm afraid sometimes that Benjamin would rather be there than here," she said. "He almost got hit by a truck today."

"Ah," Vili said. "That would be a problem."

"And it's so strange that Keats was an apothecary's apprentice. I thought maybe that was why you'd sent us there."

"I wish I'd been so clever," Vili said.

They were inside the building, climbing the stairs. Janie opened the flat with her key, and it was dark inside. "Benjamin?" she called.

Silence.

She fumbled for a light switch in the unfamiliar apartment, and it revealed empty furniture. She ran to Benjamin's room and flipped the light on there. His muddy clothes were hanging over a chair. She turned back to Vili in despair.

"There's a note," Vili said. He took a slip of paper from the table in the main room, and Janie read it.

Going to look at the ruins of the aqueduct, as a location. Not hungry. See you soon.
—B.

But something else caught her eye. There had been three oranges left in Tony's welcome basket on the table. Now the basket was empty, and there were three bright oranges on the floor.

CHAPTER 25

Visitors

When the Scotts went off to dinner, Benjamin started to take off his muddy clothes. His near miss by the truck had rattled him, although Janie's frantic response had rattled him more. The truck *hadn't* hit him, after all.

He sat on the bed thinking about the strange presence at the poet's house. What was the relation of that haunted feeling, the otherworldly sense that someone was there, to the After-room, where he knew his father was? Were dead people hanging around everywhere, and he'd just never noticed it before? He was able to communicate with his father because they'd both taken the mind-connection powder, before his father died. But Janie had felt the poet's presence first, and she hadn't taken the powder since last year. Keats had never taken any, unless he'd developed something like it in his time as an apothecary.

The powder. The night was warm, and Janie had gone to dinner without her jacket. She'd taken it off when she thought Benjamin was going with them, or she wouldn't have left it behind. He was pretty sure she'd left the jar in the pocket—*here*, in the apartment. The thought made him nearly dizzy with longing.

But he wasn't going to go to the After-room on his own. He had promised. He had to get to dinner. First he had to find a clean pair of trousers, and pull on his socks. Then his shoes. One had slid under the bed. The laces were knotted. Everything was so difficult. He knew that Janie's parents would require conversation of him. There would be questions and jokes—her father's terrible jokes.

There was a knock at the door.

He assumed it was Janie, coming back to check on him, and he opened the door.

In the hall stood Doyle the Magnificent, ginger-haired and seedy, in a tan raincoat. Beneath his eyes were fading bruises, green and yellow, sliding down his face, so that he looked like a moldy cheese.

"*Buona sera!*" Doyle said. He was standing with the tallest man Benjamin had ever seen.

"What are you doing here?" Benjamin asked.

"Making amends. I'm sorry I was such a jerk. Come on, let's go see your pops."

Benjamin glanced up at the giant.

"Don't worry about Gianni," Doyle said. "He never speaks, and he doesn't understand English. He barely thinks, or at least I can't hear it. It's amazing—if I stand very close to him, he actually *dims* other people's thoughts."

"Why is he here?"

"He's our driver," Doyle said. "Wait'll you see the car! C'mon, let's go."

"Why would I *ever* trust you again?" Benjamin asked.

The magician tilted his head to one side. "People make mistakes, Benjamin. To forgive is divine, and it's also *adult*. Don't be a child."

"I'm expected at dinner."

"What, to talk about the fake movie and listen to bad jokes?"

"How do you know about the movie?"

Doyle threw his head back in impatience. "Do we have to go through this again? The filter's gone. So what's in *your* head is in *my* head."

"The Scotts will worry about me."

"You'll leave a note. Do you have a curfew?"

It wouldn't have occurred to the Scotts to give Benjamin a curfew, because he never went out. "Not exactly."

"Then get the powder and let's go, before I have Gianni throw you over his shoulder. It will be much more dignified for you to walk down the stairs."

Benjamin looked at the two men. The giant could certainly overpower him, if he wanted to. So was he being kidnapped? Somehow, he didn't think so. And either way, going with them seemed like a way to move forward. Doyle could help him talk to his father. If Benjamin didn't go, he would be stuck in this exhausting holding pattern, doing pointless things. Scouting locations for a movie that only existed to give Janie's parents something to do.

"Just a minute," he said.

He went to Janie's room, where her blue jacket was hanging on the doorknob. He reached into the pocket and touched the smooth glass jar. He felt a sting of conscience. But the powder didn't belong to her. *He* had made it. He slipped it into his own jacket pocket and felt a rush of power.

"Now leave a note," Doyle said. "Find some excuse. You're out for a walk."

Benjamin scribbled a note.

"Let me see," Doyle said, and he read the note over. "The aqueduct!" he said. "Very clever."

Benjamin went to leave the note on the table, and saw three oranges in a basket. He looked at Doyle, standing at the door next to Gianni, who dimmed other people's minds. But *dimmed* wasn't *shut off*. So could Benjamin scramble the transmission of his own thoughts?

He concentrated on the memory of the Trevi Fountain, to block whatever might get through to Doyle. The great muscular water god, the rampant horses, the triton charioteer blowing a shell as a horn. The rushing roar of water that drowned out everything. He tipped the basket and spilled out three oranges on the floor. The rush of water. The leaping stone horses. The crowds throwing coins over their shoulders.

"Come on!" Doyle said. "Before they come home!"

Benjamin followed him down the stairs.

"Been to the Trevi Fountain, have you?" Doyle asked.

"Yes," Benjamin said.

"Spectacular, no?"

"Sure is," Benjamin said. *Horses. Tritons. A rush of water.*

"Did you throw a coin in?"

"We forgot," Benjamin said. *Coins*, rusted turquoise on the bottom of the pool.

A dark red Alfa Romeo, polished to gleaming, was parked outside the building. It was the most beautiful car Benjamin had ever seen, but getting into a stranger's car suddenly seemed a very bad idea. He hesitated. Doyle opened the door and Benjamin took a deep breath and told himself he was moving forward. He climbed in. Doyle got in after him. The giant folded himself improbably into the driver's seat, and the car pulled away from the curb.

CHAPTER 26

The Herbalist

Jin Lo steered the boat into the harbor at Xiangshan, in search of a telegraph office and supplies. She had written to Vili in code, with an old cipher devised by the apothecary, and she needed to send her message to Luxembourg. And their food and fuel were running low.

With Ned Maddox hidden in the boat's cabin, she walked into town. She nodded to people she passed, so they wouldn't wonder who the unfriendly stranger was, but she also tried to seem as uninteresting as possible, unworthy of their attention. The telegraph office was closed, so she asked directions to an herbalist's shop, and was sent to a small house in a crowded lane. When she knocked there was no answer, so she pushed open the door.

The first room in the house was a bare kitchen with a concrete floor and a pot simmering on the stove. Jin Lo passed through a hanging curtain into a second room lined with rickety shelves holding rows of bottles and jars. An old woman in a loose shift sat in a chair, sizing her up.

"Good afternoon," Jin Lo said.

The old woman nodded.

Jin Lo walked along the shelves, feeling oddly calmed by the familiar rows of glass bottles and porcelain jars. She chose carefully, scooping dried leaves and powders from the bottles into small paper packets, under the herbalist's watchful eye.

"You have a good supply, grandmother," she said.

"The best," the woman said.

"May I visit your garden?"

The old woman's look turned to one of suspicion. "Everything is here."

Jin Lo made an acknowledging movement of her head. "There are certain things that would be better fresh," she said. "More effective."

"Dried is just as good," the woman said.

Jin Lo had a chocolate bar from Ned Maddox's navy provisions, and she took it from her bag and set it on the little table where the woman sat. "It would be a great honor to see your garden," she said.

The chocolate in its bright white wrapper disappeared so quickly into the folds of the shift that it was almost like a magic trick. "Come with me," the old woman said.

They went to the garden, laid out in neat rows in a little plot behind the house. Jin Lo walked on the boards that ran through it and understood that this was no ordinary herbalist. Her old teacher had given her a passphrase to identify others in China, however scattered, who were doing the same ancient work. Jin Lo spoke the words idly, as a passing comment on a patch of rhubarb, the roots of which were effective at suppressing fever: "The *da-huang* will soon come into flower."

But the old woman didn't take it as an idle comment. Her face lit up, and after a moment of searching her memory, she answered as Jin Lo had known she would, with the pass-phrase's correct response: "Then the fruit will take wing."

Jin Lo smiled at her. "My name is Jin Lo," she said.

The woman took her hand and held it, then led her back inside to show her the contents of a cabinet hidden in the wall. Jin Lo had never seen such treasures. Everything she might have dreamed of finding was there.

"Tell me, grandmother," she said, when she had gathered everything she wanted. "Why is the telegraph office closed?"

"They were passing information to Chiang," the herbalist said. "Mao's army came and destroyed the machine."

"I see," Jin Lo said. "Tell me another thing. Can one buy fuel without papers or a ration ticket?"

The woman considered. "You can pay?"

"I can."

The old woman wrote a name and address on a slip of paper. "He will sell a little fuel, but you must go as soon as you have it. He is not strong in his convictions, and might give you away."

Jin Lo took the address and thanked the old woman. She returned to the boat, burdened with packages.

"Was it successful?" Ned Maddox asked.

"Halfway. The telegraph machine was destroyed."

"So now what—Bat-Signal?"

She was interested. "What is Bat-Signal?"

"Something from a comic book. A spotlight in the sky."

She shook her head. "That won't work."

"It was a joke," he said.

She frowned. "Jokes are not useful."

"Does everything have to be useful?"

She stared at Ned Maddox. It was a question that barely deserved an answer. Of course everything should be useful.

He said, "I'd argue that jokes *are* useful, because they make you laugh, and that makes everything else easier."

"It did not make me laugh," she said.

"I've gotten used to making jokes for myself," he said. "I'll try to do better."

Jin Lo shrugged. "If you wish," she said, and she set about sorting her new store of supplies.

CHAPTER 27

Honor

When Benjamin, Doyle, and the giant arrived in the room at the Hotel Majestic, a man sat waiting. He wore a light gray tailored suit and his hair was swept back. He seemed unnaturally still, in one of two deep leather chairs. Benjamin thought the man looked like a snake, coiled and waiting to strike, and he turned to Doyle. "What's going on?"

"Relax," Doyle said. "Just listen to what he has to say."

"Please sit," the man said.

He had an Italian accent and a smooth, resonant voice. The voice seemed snake-like, too: slithery and cold-blooded.

Benjamin sat in the second chair, his legs trembling. If this man was the snake, Benjamin was the mouse. Doyle and the giant remained standing, and Benjamin had the uncomfortable sensation of being guarded, his escape cut off.

"My name is Salvatore Rocco," the coiled man said. "You may have heard of my cousin Giuseppe, in the city of Detroit."

"Joey the Haberdasher," Benjamin said, trying to sound brave.

Rocco smiled a thin smile. "My cousin was an apprentice tailor once, in his youth. It is difficult to escape one's past. Doyle tells me you have a remarkable talent."

Benjamin shook his head.

"Ah, you are modest, too," Rocco said. "Doyle tells me that he promised you something, and did not fulfill his promise. In my life, in my work, honor is everything. When a man gives you his word, he gives you a piece of his soul. I have brought Doyle here to recover this piece of his soul."

Benjamin swallowed. "That's not the reason I'm here. You don't care about his soul."

Rocco paused, then said, "My mother died last year. Sometimes, when I am alone in a room, I smell her perfume. I believe she is trying to speak to me. She has something to say. I would like to speak to her once more, and I believe you can help me. But first, Doyle will teach you what he promised."

"Where, here?" Benjamin said.

Rocco opened his hands and looked around at the elegant room. "There is something wrong? You will talk to your father, and then I will talk to my mother."

Benjamin considered. Janie would say he shouldn't go to the After-room alone—or surrounded by strangers—but the jar of powder was so heavy in his pocket. He had come so far. And Doyle knew how to help him. "All right," he said. "But I want just Doyle in the room."

Rocco tilted his head. "Why?"

"It's too distracting, to have other people around."

Rocco nodded. "Very well," he said, and he stood. "My own suite is upstairs." Accompanied by the giant, he left and closed the door.

Benjamin could feel his heart beating in his chest as Doyle filled a glass with water. Benjamin tapped a few grains of powder into the glass, swirling them around until they dissolved. Then he and Doyle sat down in the two chairs, facing each other.

"You remember what I told you about the breathing," Doyle said.

"Yes," Benjamin said.

"That's how you stay tethered to your body. It's easy to get caught up and forget where you belong."

"Okay," Benjamin said. "You're sure you know how to do this? I mean, with dead people?"

Doyle shrugged. "In my experience, living people give you more trouble. And we're *not* going after your mother, right? Just talking to your dad who's close by. Nice and safe."

"Right," Benjamin said.

"Okay," Doyle said. "First think about where the breath

starts, with your diaphragm, how it fills up your lungs, all that stuff. Sounds kind of goofy, I know."

Feeling self-conscious, Benjamin took a breath, noticing it expanding his lungs from his stomach to his collarbone. Janie had figured out how to do telekinesis. He ought to be able to figure out *breathing*. He thought about all the little air molecules bouncing around inside him. Then he exhaled, feeling the muscles in his chest relax to empty the air out. He inhaled again, imagining the oxygen-rich air coming in, passing through his alveoli into his red blood cells. He exhaled: the used air full of carbon dioxide flowing out.

"The hard part," the magician said, "is to have a conversation while you're keeping that tether—while you're thinking about breathing. You have to do both things at once. Like rubbing your belly and patting your head. Try talking to me, while you pay attention to that slow, steady breathing."

Benjamin concentrated, keeping his focus on the inhalation, the exhalation. With effort, he said, "What should we talk about?" His voice sounded artificial and forced.

"What you want to say to your father," Doyle said.

Benjamin felt a hitch in his breath. "I just want to see him."

"But what do you want to say, specifically?"

A long moment passed, during which Benjamin realized he wasn't breathing at all. It was none of Doyle's business. But finally he squeezed out: "That I'm sorry."

"Sorry for what? Are you breathing?"

"No."

"Sorry for what?"

Benjamin took a noisy, shallow breath through his nose. He wanted very much not to cry. "For what I did."

"And what did you do?"

"I was trying to save us." He felt the tears coming. "I made a smoke screen. But I did it wrong, and it poisoned him—*I* poisoned him."

The magician let out a long, low whistle. "Is that true?"

"Yes," Benjamin said, miserable.

Doyle shook his head. "You must've had that in a concrete vault, in that skull of yours. I had no idea."

"Janie knows." Benjamin's throat felt so swollen that he could hardly get the words out. "It's why—I can hardly talk to her."

"Janie doesn't think you're responsible for it," the magician said.

"She should."

"But she doesn't. I'd know if she did."

"But she should! I *am* responsible!"

"She knows it wasn't your fault."

"But it *was*."

"Are you breathing?"

Benjamin shook his head again. The room was blurred and his jaw was trembling.

"So let's try this again," Doyle said. "And work on the heartbeat, too. You have to slow it down. Keep it from racing, the way it's doing now."

Benjamin turned his attention to his heart and found that it was pounding against his rib cage, trying to escape. He imagined it slowing. His muscles were tingling with adrenaline, and he imagined it draining out of them.

After a minute, he whispered, "It's working."

"Good," the magician said. "Now—keep your heart slow and add the breathing."

With effort, Benjamin did. The slow, full inhale. The emptying exhale.

"Okay," the magician said. "Why do you want to see your father?"

Benjamin breathed in. Heart slow. "I want him to say that he forgives me," he said. He breathed out. "I want to know that he does."

"Good," the magician said. "Are you breathing?"

"Yes," Benjamin said.

"All right," the magician said. "Drink up."

CHAPTER 28

In the After-Room

Benjamin was in the dark, but the dark was different. Clearer, somehow. He had the same sense of a room without corners, but now it wasn't so hazy. He saw the particles shimmering in the distance, but he would not be drawn toward them. His mother was too far away, he understood that now. Outside the boundary of the room, closer than the glinting particles, he could see figures. Human figures, but shadowy and gray. And drifting. There had been no figures before, and these were drawing closer.

He started to feel the adrenaline rush again, the pounding heart.

Breathe in. Back in the hotel room, his lungs filled. *Breathe out.* They emptied. His body was anchored in the leather chair, in the world of the living.

The drifting figures swayed, and grew more distinct. Some wore modern clothes. Others wore robes, one a tunic, one a high-waisted gown. One young man wore a frock coat with a high collar like the portrait of Keats in the museum, and

Benjamin peered at him to see if it was the same face, but he couldn't tell. Another wore a white shirt that bloomed with black blood.

Breathe in. His lungs filled. *Breathe out.* They emptied.

There was the hazy figure of a small child out there. And a woman with a baby. There were so many of them, looming closer. He shouldn't be visible to them, because he was only here in his mind. So why were they gathering close?

"Because you're alive," his father said, startling him.

Breathe in. Breathe out. "Dad?"

"They want to be close to you," his father said. The voice was much clearer than it had been before. It still seemed to be the result of great effort, but it resounded inside Benjamin's head. "They know you have a body, they can sense it. They aren't ready to let go of their lives."

"My mother isn't with them," Benjamin said, scanning the gray faces.

"No," his father said. "She was much too practical to hold on to human form, your mother. But she's nearby. I'll be with her soon."

Benjamin was puzzled by the emotion in his father's voice, and then realized it was joy. Anticipatory joy. He wondered if he had heard his father express anything like it before. "You want to go to her," he said.

"I do," his father said.

Benjamin felt oddly resentful and jealous. His father wanted to leave him, and go be with his mother. The two of them had a happiness that had nothing to do with Benjamin; he had hardly been there for any of their lives together.

Benjamin had told Doyle that he wanted to ask for his father's forgiveness, but now he didn't know how to do that. He couldn't find the words.

"You have to help Jin Lo," his father said.

"I do?" Benjamin said. That was a surprise. They hadn't heard from her in so long. And she never seemed to need anyone. "Can you communicate with her?"

"In brief flashes," his father said. "She took your powder once."

"Does she have the uranium?"

"No. She's on the trail of something else."

"What? Where? Is Danby there?" Just the thought of Danby filled him with a perilous rage that threatened to undo his careful concentration. *Breathe in, breathe out.*

"I don't think so," his father said.

"So what do I do?" Benjamin said. "How will you tell me?" The room began to flicker. "Help me stay here! I'm slipping!"

"You have to turn outward, Benjamin," his father's voice said. "You need to live in the world."

The gray figure in the frock coat still waited, like a cat outside a fishbowl. His face was clearer now, the face of the plaster death mask in the poet's house. As Benjamin lost his hold on his father's mind, the ghost loomed forward, reaching for Benjamin, arms outstretched, with a look of fixed determination. Benjamin recoiled from the misty gray hands, but couldn't escape. He felt a cold shudder pass through him. It was there in his bones, and then gone.

Then darkness. The smell of furniture polish. The smooth leather chair beneath him, and the faint sounds of traffic outside.

CHAPTER 29

Oranges

Janie, staring around at the empty apartment, reached for her pocket to make sure she had the powder, but she wasn't wearing her jacket. Where had she left it? She raced to her bedroom and found it hanging on the doorknob. She felt the pockets, her heart sinking.

No jar. How could she have been so careless?

"I take it he's not really at the aqueduct," Vili said.

"He's with Doyle," she said. "And they have the powder!"

They hurried back to the restaurant, where Vili paid the bill and excused himself. He had work to do, he told her parents.

Janie, trying to hide her agitation, told them that Benjamin had gone to look at the old aqueduct.

"At night?" her mother said.

"It's not that late," Janie said.

"But it's a ruin," her mother said. "It sounds dangerous."

Janie tried to sound nonchalant. "It might be a good location. Romantic, you know?"

"You're not going looking for him," her father said.

"No," she said. "He'll be back soon."

Her parents chatted happily on the walk home, and went to bed, exhausted. Janie took a chair out to the balcony to sit and watch the street below. Vili had promised to start looking for Doyle and Benjamin, but where would he start?

She tried closing her eyes and summoning memories, in case the faint traces of powder in her body might let her see through Benjamin's eyes, but it didn't work. It just made her sad about the vibrant, stubborn, imaginative boy she had known, before the brightness was washed out of him by grief. It wasn't recklessness that had nearly gotten him killed by a truck, it was apathy. He didn't seem to care about anything in this world anymore.

But at least he'd left a message. The oranges on the floor gave her reason for hope. It reminded her of the old Benjamin's coded letters: inventive and intimate and confidential, a communication just for her. He'd known she would think of the magician when she saw the fallen oranges. She clung to that thought as she watched the empty street for his return.

The next thing she knew, it was morning, and someone was shaking her arm.

"Mmmph," she said in protest. The sun on the balcony was painfully bright, and her neck was stiff from sleeping in a chair.

"Were you out here all *night*?" her mother asked.

"I guess so," she said, rubbing grit from the corners of her eyes.

"Oh, Janie. What were you thinking? And Benjamin's gone out already."

Janie sat up straight, remembering that Benjamin had

been taken by Doyle. But she had to pretend she thought he'd gone to see the old aqueduct. "He's not here?"

"He came home, didn't he?" her mother asked, alarmed.

Janie ran to his bedroom, which was exactly as it had been. The same wrinkles in the blanket from the night before. She could hear water running on the other side of the wall—her father in the shower. She grabbed her jacket, to get out while she could. Two parents were more of an obstacle than one. The important thing was to keep them calm. And to find out what Vili had discovered.

"Wait!" her mother said. "Should we talk to the police?"

"No!" she said.

"But what—"

"I know where Benjamin is," Janie lied. "Can I have money for a cab?"

"Oh, Janie, we have to go to work," her mother said. "We don't have time for a crisis!" But she was reaching for her purse.

"There's no crisis," Janie said, very firm. "Go to work. It's all fine." She took the cash her mother offered, stuffed it deep in her pocket, and ran down the stairs.

"Be careful!" her mother called after her.

"I will!" she said, without looking back.

At the address Vili had given her, near the Piazza Navona, the count answered his door unshaven, his hair uncombed, in carpet slippers. He was usually so neat and sleek and smooth.

"Benjamin didn't come home," she said breathlessly. "What did you find out?"

Vili stepped back to let her in. His apartment wasn't grand, but the ceilings were high, with ornate moldings, painted white. There was a kitchen with a deep marble sink, and a little sitting area with a gold rug. A floor lamp next to the sofa cast a warm glow.

"I found a boy who'd seen a strange car parked outside your building," he said. "It was an Alfa Romeo, red and shiny. It made an impression. I offered him money if he tracked it down."

"How would he do that?"

Vili shrugged. "Roman street children are resourceful. And others will have noticed a particularly beautiful car."

"So we just wait?"

Vili nodded.

"Did you sleep last night?" she asked.

He shook his head and rubbed his stubbled chin.

"There must be something we can do!" she said. "I don't think I can stand this."

But she didn't have to stand it for long, because the doorbell rang. A small, ragged boy with wide eyes and bony cheeks stood outside. He had close-cropped hair and missing teeth. He acted dramatically winded from running: hands on his knees, panting.

"This is Primo," Vili said. "My scout and spy."

Primo, suddenly recovered, held out an open palm, and Vili dropped some coins into it. The boy studied the coins, then gestured for them to follow, but first Vili had to put on his shoes: leather boots with laces to tighten and tie.

Janie exchanged a look of impatience with Primo: Grown-ups were so slow! Finally the boots were on and laced, and she handed Vili his blackthorn walking stick.

The boy scampered off down the street as if released from a slingshot.

Janie and Vili followed, down narrow Roman streets, over uneven cobblestones. They walked up a curving avenue to find Primo posed next to a shiny, dark red car, hands on his hips. Vili looked up at the windows above them, and Janie followed his eyes. Benjamin could be in any of them.

Primo, waiting for praise, looked disappointed. Weren't they pleased? He'd only been contracted to find the *car*, not the people in it.

A doorman stood on the sidewalk, and Janie saw that the brass plaque next to him read HOTEL MAJESTIC. He seemed reluctant to answer Vili's questions at first. But then a banknote changed hands, and the doorman's attitude changed. He opened the door, but closed it before the street boy could follow them.

Janie and Vili entered a lobby with a plush red carpet, then walked up the stairs, circling a steel elevator cage. Down a long white hall-way, Vili knocked at a door with the gilt number 208 on the white paneling.

Janie thought maybe
no one was in. Then the door
opened, and Doyle stood before
them. The bruises beneath his eyes had
faded and drooped. He put a finger to his lips
and stepped back from the door.

"He's fine, you see?" he whispered. "Sleeping like a baby."

There were two huge leather chairs in front of a window.
Benjamin was curled up in one of them, covered with a blanket. His eyes were closed and his hair stuck out in all directions. The blanket rose and fell with his steady, peaceful breathing as he slept.

CHAPTER 30

Ashore

Jin Lo tied up the boat in Hangzhou Bay, thinking there must be a working telegraph here. The port was huge and busy, and the city stretched out beyond, full of people going about their business, making a living, or trying to. Walking on dry land felt strange and good. The ground was hard and solid beneath her feet, and her head swayed with the remembered motion of the waves.

She stopped to buy some vegetables at an open stand and saw, out of the corner of her eye, a tall man with light hair. When she turned, he disappeared around the corner of an old building.

The plump woman at the vegetable stand smiled at Jin Lo. "A friend of yours?" she asked.

Jin Lo was annoyed at herself. Part of being uninteresting to strangers was not being interested *in* strangers. To be curious was to make people curious about you, which was exactly what she wanted to avoid. "No," she said.

"I saw him this morning in the market," the vegetable woman said. "He's very handsome. And very tall. A foreigner."

Jin Lo said nothing, but put her greens and eggplants into her bag.

"You don't like handsome men?" the woman asked, teasing her. "You don't like love?"

"I am only passing through," Jin Lo said.

"Ah, then it's fate that you should meet!" the woman said.

"Where is the telegraph office, please?" Jin Lo asked, her voice stiff.

The woman pointed down the street and grinned, with missing teeth. "Good luck, my girl!"

Jin Lo left, feeling irritated. The woman would remember her now. Jin Lo had a story. She was not just a forgettable stranger buying vegetables, but a coy girl destined to fall in love with a handsome foreigner.

But the man had seemed so familiar—it had caught her off-guard.

She walked in the direction the woman had pointed, moving neither too fast nor too slow, and found the telegraph office.

Inside, the clerk frowned at the message she handed him, which was clearly not in English. If the Party had destroyed telegraph machines for sending secret messages, then this clerk would not send it if he thought it was in code.

"It is Romanian," she lied.

"Ah," he said. "Romanian." He searched her face for signs of foreignness.

She dropped her eyes to the counter. This was twice that she was becoming memorable. The Romanian girl who looked

Chinese. The Chinese girl who spoke Romanian. "I am only delivering this message," she said. "A family message, to a cousin."

He waited for her to tell him more. But she said nothing, and finally he gave up, and began to tap out the signal. "There was an Englishman here this morning," he said, to fill the silence.

"Oh?" she said, remembering the tall man rounding the corner.

"Sending a message to Korea," the clerk said.

"In English?" she asked.

"In Latin," he said, with a shy pride. "Romanian and Latin, both in one day!"

Jin Lo held very still. She did not want to disturb the air around her. She knew, now, why the man in the street had looked familiar. He was skinnier now than he had been, almost gaunt. "Did the Englishman have white hair in front?"

"Yes!" the clerk said. "You know him?"

"I saw him in the street," she said.

"Maybe something frightened him!" He laughed.

Jin Lo didn't answer. She was trying to think.

"It made his hair white!" the clerk explained, pointing to his forehead.

Jin Lo nodded, to show that she'd understood the joke in the first place. Jokes were useful, Ned Maddox said. She tried to smile.

Finally the clerk finished sending her message, and she thanked him and slipped out the door.

She walked back to the docks, trying not to look hurried. She had been searching for Danby for so long, and now he was *here*, and she wasn't ready. The American commander with the stolen shell was a more urgent problem than the uranium: Hayes had a functioning weapon, and was prepared to use it. But the commander could be anywhere, and Danby was right *here*! She could feel people watching her. She was walking too fast. She tried to slow down, but couldn't.

What were the chances that she and Danby would send a telegram in the same office, on the same day? Were they better or worse than the chances that she would wash up on Ned Maddox's beach? *The universe is doing its work,* she thought. But did the universe really want her to run into Danby, unprepared?

The answer, apparently, was yes, because a moment later he stepped out of a building and stood in front of her. He wore a faded shirt, open at the collar, and worn khaki pants belted tight over his bony hips. His hair had grown out on top into its old curls, but there was still the white forelock, startling on a man who could not be more than thirty-five.

The Soviets had sent him to Siberia, and it had turned his hair white.

"Hullo," Danby said. "I thought it was you. You have the most distinctive step. A long, efficient step, the spine very straight and strong, the chin neither raised nor ducked."

"Where is the uranium?" Jin Lo asked.

"With my friends, on their boat," he said. "Shall we walk there together?"

He took her arm as if they were only going for a stroll, but his grip was like a steel clamp. Would Ned Maddox see what was happening as they approached the harbor? He was supposed to be staying out of sight. She was amazed that Danby, a foreigner in possession of dangerous contraband, would walk about so freely. But he had always been reckless.

"Who are your friends?" she asked.

"Now, that's a funny story," he said. "They're pirates."

She waited to see if this was a joke. He was still propelling her inexorably toward the docks. "Pirates?" she said.

"Maybe you've heard of their leader, Huang P'ei-mei," he said. "She's quite a woman."

Jin Lo had heard of Huang P'ei-mei, since her childhood. The pirate queen was a legend, with a vast network of boats. "I thought she was only a story."

"Oh, no," Danby said. "Quite solid flesh. I ran out of fuel and was starving when one of her boats came upon me."

"They took the uranium?"

"Cargo is cargo," he said. "I have persuaded her to transport it north and sell it, as I planned."

"So you are partners?"

"No one is partners with pirates!" he said. "She won't give me a penny. But you're going to help me change that."

Jin Lo tried to wrench her arm free, and stumbled as he dragged her forward.

"*Don't* draw attention," he hissed. "That's no good for either of us."

They were back at the docks: the smell of salt, and fish. The calls of men unloading boats.

"I'll tell you how this is going to go," he said evenly. "I will introduce you to the legendary Madame Huang. You'll compliment her, tell her you have heard of her exploits, and that will please her. You'll do a few of your magic tricks. She's very superstitious, and she'll want to keep you as a pet. Then we'll go north and sell the uranium. And you'll help me get my money."

It was funny, in a way. All Jin Lo had wanted was to find the uranium, and now that Danby was *here*, and taking her to it, she didn't want to go. She had to find the American commander and the missing shell.

"Stop struggling," he said. "This is a rare chance. You can tell your grandchildren that you met the famous pirate queen!" He was steering her away from Ned Maddox, along the tied-up boats. She could not be taken to the pirates, not now.

When they were close to the edge of the water, between a sampan and a small cruiser, she put her foot in front of Danby's to make him stumble forward. When he was off-balance, she heaved his whole weight onto her shoulder, using his grip on her arm, and then ducked and flipped him toward the harbor. His feet went sailing skyward and he splashed headfirst into the brown water, between the two boats.

Jin Lo turned and ran. Danby rose to the surface and she heard him splutter, shouting unintelligibly. When she reached Ned Maddox's boat, she leaped aboard and untied the lines. Ned Maddox came up from below and started the engine, without asking questions. He acted quickly. She did value him for that. They backed away from the dock, narrowly missing a scow with a little boy in it.

As Ned Maddox steered out of the harbor, Jin Lo saw Danby, wet through, struggling onto the pier, hauling his thin body out of the water.

They picked up speed. "Who *was* that?" Ned Maddox asked.

"The Englishman I was looking for."

Ned Maddox looked back. "But then—why are we leaving?"

"We don't have time. We will find him later."

"But he's here!"

"This is not the moment."

She looked back and saw Danby, sodden with seawater, watching them go. She could not take on a band of pirates now. But how would she ever find the uranium again? She wished the apothecary were here to help her think it out.

But then a thought broke through her confusion: *Danby will follow you.*

And she felt much calmer. Of course. Danby would not give up. He would come to her.

CHAPTER 31

An Aubade

Janie sat in one enormous club chair in the hotel room and watched Benjamin sleep in the other. He looked much younger, with his eyes closed and his hair sticking out from under the throw blanket. She wondered about the years after his mother died, when he had lived with only his father. Had Mr. Burrows read him books and tucked him into bed? Had he cooked dinner for the two of them, patched up Benjamin's skinned knees, and helped with homework? Or had he been too grieving and preoccupied?

She couldn't imagine losing either of her parents. But losing both—Janie thought Benjamin was handling it all pretty well, considering.

Benjamin stirred, in the big chair. He stretched, hands balled into fists, and his mouth gaped in a yawn. He blinked at Janie and pushed himself to sitting. She felt a flush of relief that he was safe, that something terrible hadn't happened. He rubbed at his eyes with his knuckles.

"Hullo," he said.

She smiled. "Hi."

"Have you been watching me sleep?" He tried to flatten his hair, but it didn't help.

"Not for long."

"How'd you get here?"

"Vili hired a street kid to find the car."

"It's a nice car."

"Very. And recognizable."

"Is Doyle still here?" he asked.

She nodded toward the door. "In the hall, talking to Vili."

"And Rocco?"

She frowned, confused. "Rocco? You mean Joey the Haberdasher?"

Benjamin shook his head. "His cousin. Never mind. Listen, I was *there*, Janie, with my father! We had a whole conversation! And there were other people there, too."

"Dead people?" she asked.

He nodded. "They were outside the After-room, looking in. They knew I was alive."

"What did they want?"

"They miss it here. I think I saw the poet, Keats, and he tried to, well—" Benjamin hesitated. "Come *through* me. Into this world."

"Did he?" she asked.

"I'm not sure. My father says we have to help Jin Lo."

"Help her find the uranium?"

Benjamin shook his head. "It's something else. He says

I have to turn outward." His face crumpled. "I miss him so much, Janie. No one I love can ever die again. I mean it. You can't die. Okay?"

Janie was startled, and wasn't sure how to answer. She was teasing out the logic of what he'd said, thinking of algebra. Did the transitive property apply in those sentences? *No one he loved* could ever die. And *she* couldn't die. So therefore—had he really meant it? "Okay," she said.

"Promise?"

"I promise," she said.

He was silent, staring at the floor, his hair wild in all directions. Then he looked up at her. "You didn't answer."

"I just promised."

"No, I mean the other thing." His face was twitching with emotion.

"I didn't know if you meant it," she said. "The whole equation, I mean. Did you?"

He nodded.

"Well, I love you, too, Benjamin Burrows," she said, feeling a smile take over her face. It seemed absurd that she had never said it before, and absurd that he didn't know it in his bones.

He smiled and the room seemed to brighten, as if the curtains had been thrown open to the morning light.

"Move over," she said. She climbed into the club chair beside him, and he put his arm around her shoulder. She tugged the blanket over their knees and rested her head against him. They were in some weird hotel room, with the awful Doyle outside in the hall, and still she never wanted to leave. She just wanted to stay here, with her hip tucked against Benjamin's hip, her leg pressed against his. But something nagged at her.

"So wait," she said. "Who's Rocco's cousin?"

"I gave him the powder."

She sat up, her heart lurching. "You did *what*?"

Then Doyle came into the room, with Vili behind him. The magician raised his eyebrows. "Some chaperones we are."

"You gave some *stranger* the powder?" Janie said.

"It's all right," Benjamin said. "Rocco just wants to talk to his mother. He keeps smelling her perfume. He thinks it's a message."

Doyle laughed. "Oh, boy. Dead people using smells to communicate. That's such a hack story."

"Don't they?" Benjamin asked.

"Sure," Doyle said. "But the message is usually 'Hey, I stink, you should bury me.'"

"So you think this Rocco was lying?" Janie asked.

"Of course he was lying!" Doyle said. "His buddy got offed. He wants to know who killed him."

"Why does he want to know?" Janie asked, although she was afraid she knew the answer. And this was not how Benjamin's father had intended him to carry on their work.

Doyle rolled his eyes. "So he can whack the guy, of course."

CHAPTER 32

The Capo

Salvatore Rocco, alone in his suite on the top floor of the hotel, looked at the jar of powder on the table. Fear was a strange emotion for him. In the war, he had lived in the mountains with the partisans, fighting the Germans. He was flush with youth and passion then, lean and flexible as a green branch. He had once scrambled up the side of a Panzer tank and dropped a grenade into the cockpit. He could still feel the hard, knobby surface of the grenade in his hand, and the expectation that any second it would explode. He could feel the impact in his knees as he jumped down to the ground, and hear the concussive blast behind him as he ran.

His friend Carlino had been with him in the mountains, and had fought and run by his side. They had been children together, like brothers. Carlino knew all of his secrets, had helped him in every step of his life. And now Carlino was gone, his body pulled cold and still from the river. Sal had searched for witnesses, for men who might talk, for anyone who knew who had killed Carlino, and found no one. When his cousin in Detroit told him there might be a way to ask Carlino himself, it had felt like a gift, a sign.

He picked up the jar and shook it. It was not a true powder but was granulated, like coarse salt. He and Carlino had both grown up in the church, altar boys in white robes, watching the swinging incense hang in the air, listening to the priest tell stories of hellfire. They had seen the dark paintings of demons and torment. And they had both broken many commandments. Sal hadn't counted lately. *Thou shalt not kill. Thou shalt not steal.* He had committed mortal sins. But there had always been a reason for what he had done. In the beginning, it was the Germans. The first thing Sal ever stole was potatoes from a barn when he and his fellow partisans were starving.

But the commandments were absolute. The stone tablets Moses brought down from the mountain had not said *Thou shalt not kill except when fighting Nazis, or in self-defense, or in some other situations, listed below. Thou shalt not steal unless thou art near death with hunger fighting in a just cause, or hath a family to support, or if perhaps an irresistible opportunity to get rich presenteth itself.*

One could confess, of course, but confessing was not in their line. So was it possible that Carlino was really in that place the priests had described, with the demons and the flames and the torment, the eternal suffering? The pitchforks? Would the powder take Sal there? The boy, Benjamin, claimed to have gone to an in-between place, a dark room where he could talk to his father. So was that limbo? Did Sal believe in limbo? Did he believe in hell? If he didn't, then why were his hands trembling?

There was a light knock at the door. Sal Rocco hadn't answered his own door in years. It wasn't safe for a man like him, with many enemies, to go blithely opening doors, but he had sent his bodyguard away, because he'd wanted to contemplate the powder and its possibilities alone. He sat in his chair, unsure what to do.

There was another light knock, and then a girl's voice called, "Mr. Rocco? Signore Rocco? Don Salvatore?"

He went to the door. Outside were Benjamin, who looked unhappy, and a girl. Her hair seemed not entirely under control, her eyes worried.

"I'm Janie, sir," she said. "That powder's not going to work, and I didn't want you to be angry about it when nothing happened. You won't see your friend, because he didn't take any of the powder before he died. That's how it works, you both have to take it. Benjamin is only connecting to his father's mind, he's not really—well, *going* anywhere."

The first thing Sal felt was a flood of relief, like a drug in his bloodstream. He stumbled back into the room, leaving the door open. *He didn't have to try it.* The girl took the jar of powder and slipped it into her pocket, but he didn't care. An iron weight lifted from his heart. Then the relief was followed by a flush of shame, because it proved that he really had been afraid. He was becoming a coward, in his middle age. Then both sensations were replaced with bitter regret, because now he would never know who had killed his friend. He sat down, lowering himself into a chair.

"I'm sorry, sir," Benjamin said, his eyes on the floor. "I should have realized it wouldn't work for you. Since my father died, I don't think clearly. It's very frustrating."

Sal nodded. "I understand."

"Thank you, sir," the boy said.

"But you gave me your word."

The boy looked up, with the fear and uncertainty Sal had seen so many times in the eyes of his underlings. "Sir?"

"You will go for me, and ask your father what happened to Carlino," Rocco said. He felt his old power flooding back. He was Salvatore Rocco. He could discover what had happened to Carlino, without having to go where Carlino was. He was not a *sgarrista*, running his own errands. Why had he ever thought he should be? People went to unpleasant places *for* him. It should have occurred to him to send the boy in the first place.

"Wait—he can't go," the girl said.

Sal Rocco looked at her, this impertinent child. "Why not?"

"Because he was just there," she said. "It doesn't work twice in a day, it just makes you dizzy and sick, and you don't make contact."

"Then he stays in this hotel until he can go," he said.

"But he can't!" she said. "My parents—"

Rocco drew himself up. "Your parents don't concern me. What happened to Carlino concerns me. I will not let the boy leave. I can send you both to the bottom of the river, if I wish."

"Wait," the boy said, his eyes bright with intelligence. "There might be another way."

CHAPTER 33

The Go-Between

Janie climbed the narrow stairs at the Keats House, wishing she had Benjamin beside her. He'd said it felt as if the poet had *come through him*, using Benjamin's presence in the After-room to pass back into the world—and not just in the fleeting way that they had sensed him hovering around his house. Benjamin thought the poet would know what had happened to Rocco's friend, or could find out. So now Janie was looking for a ghost, in the house where he had died over a hundred years ago.

The tall building was strangely quiet.

The girl selling tickets wasn't at her desk at the top of the stairs, so Janie stood there for a moment, listening to the silent rooms, and then stepped into the wood-paneled library.

As her eyes adjusted to the dimness, she saw a semi-transparent young man in a double-breasted frock coat, his hair curling over his high collar, browsing the shelves. He reached for a book, but his hand passed right through it, and he swore quietly. Janie drew in a breath. Benjamin had been right. This wasn't a vanishing reflection, or a vague feeling of haunting. The youngest and saddest of the Romantic poets was standing in front of her, in his nineteenth-century clothes. He'd been twenty-three when he died, and he looked even younger.

She cleared her throat. "Hello," she said.

The ghost turned, startled. "Hello!" His voice was high and thin. "Can you see me?"

"Yes," Janie said.

"That other girl couldn't. She heard my voice and ran away. Is she a housemaid?" He had an English accent, more formal-sounding than Benjamin's.

"No," Janie said. "She sells tickets."

"Tickets to what?"

"Your house. It's a museum—about you."

He smiled. "That's absurd," he said, though he seemed pleased. "Why can *you* see me?"

Janie hesitated. "I think because I took this powder," she began. "It—well, you were an apothecary once, right?"

"For a short time," the poet said.

"Were you—an ordinary apothecary?"

He gave her a hard look. "I have never been ordinary."

Janie wasn't sure that he had understood the question, but it would be time-consuming to explain, so she went on. "Well, my friend Benjamin isn't an ordinary apothecary either, and he made a powder that allows two people to see through each other's eyes."

"Oh!" the poet said. "What a beautiful thought! Did he do it to communicate with you?"

Janie blushed. "Yes."

"I imagined such a thing, with—a certain young person. When we were far apart."

"You never tried it?" she asked.

He shook his head. "Only in my mind."

She could feel him drifting, getting caught up in memories, so she went on. "So, because of the powder, Benjamin still has a connection with his father, who died recently. So Benjamin went to talk to him—"

"Ah, your friend is the one who was *there!*" the poet said. "On the other side! Who was living!"

Janie nodded. "Right."

"It was irresistible, his presence," he said. "Like a fire when you have been very cold, when you thought there was no more warmth in the world."

"He says—you came *through* him?"

"I suppose so," Keats said. "I just wanted to be close to this warm, living world. So I waited for the moment when I could feel that he was about to return, and I *pounced.*"

Janie felt uncomfortable. She was pretty sure that was not

supposed to happen. "So—I think the reason I can see you is because I took the powder, too."

"I see," Keats said. "Well, perhaps you can help me. I am looking for a book with information about—this young person. Whom I loved. But I cannot open the books." He passed his hand through the shelves to demonstrate.

"You're looking for Fanny Brawne," Janie said.

The poet looked shocked. "You *know* her?"

"Well, she's—dead, of course. She's been dead a long time."

His face blurred with grief. "Of course," he said. "Yes, of course. That would be so. But if I could discover *when* and *where* she died, then perhaps I could find her."

"Okay," Janie said.

"You'll help me?" His face was suffused with happiness. For a transparent and misty face that didn't always hold its shape, it was remarkably expressive.

"First I have a question," Janie said.

"Yes?" he said, impatient.

"It's about someone who was in that—other place. The in-between place."

"Oh, they're all terribly dull," he said, with a wave of his hand. "Utterly single-minded. They're obsessed only with getting back here."

"I need to know who killed one of them," she said.

The poet laughed. "Do you know how crowded it is there? I came here to *escape* those wretched bores!"

"Could you try?"

"No," he said, turning back to the shelves. "It's impossible."

Janie felt dismayed, and tried another tack. "There's an idea in your letters—" she began.

The poet drew himself up in indignation and stretched to an astonishing height, his head drifting up toward the ceiling. "A lady should never read a gentleman's letters!"

"But—they're published!" she said. "Lots of people have read them. They're famous."

He drifted back down to size, curious. "How did the publishers get them?"

"From your friends, I guess," she said. "And from Fanny's children."

"Her *children*?" His face wavered and pulsed with horror.

"She mourned you for a long time, before she married."

"*Married!*" he wailed.

"But—she was so young when you died. Wouldn't you have wanted her to have a life?"

He recovered himself. "Of course. Of course I would. I did. I do."

"So, you wrote in your letters about 'negative capability.'"

Keats looked eager again, and Janie wondered if his moods had shifted this quickly in life, or if it was just part of his ghostly driftiness. *Mercurial*, that was the word. "Of course!" he said. "Did you understand it?"

"I think so," she said.

"Well?"

She felt self-conscious. She had been excited by the idea of negative capability when she first read about it. She thought it was something like what the old gardener had told them, back in the Chelsea Physic Garden—the thing that had made her believe she might actually become a bird. But she had never expected to be quizzed on the concept by the poet himself. "It means—that you don't always need rational explanations," she said. "You can trust that mysterious things happen, and live with the strangeness of it, and allow for many different possibilities. So your mind isn't bound by rationality, I guess. You thought Shakespeare had it."

"Yes!" he said. "Exactly!"

"You have it, too," she said, encouraged. "That's why I think you can find this man who was killed. He died in Rome, not that long ago, and no one knows how."

Keats shook his head, blurring his features. "There are so many people out there. You have no idea."

"But I think this one is close by!" she said. "He might even know that we're talking about him now. He might be hovering, like you used to hover around this house. Just think about it for a minute, and see if you can find him. His name is Carlino. Please try. And then I'll find out where Fanny is for you."

The look on the poet's face when she said Fanny's name was touching. He had really loved her. "Oh—very well!" he said. "Let me think."

He closed his eyes. As Janie watched, his transparent body seemed to lose form, to drift apart into a nebulous cloud, as if he were no longer an individual being, with an individual's memory. He was merging, becoming part of something larger. And the room seemed to drop in temperature. Janie shivered.

It was hard to judge the time passing, but she thought he had been dissipated in that formless cloud of smoke for several minutes.

Then the high-collared frock coat materialized, together with the spilling curls and the handsome, expressive young face. "I have the answer!" he said.

"Yes?"

"But it's terribly sad."

"What is it?"

The poet folded his misty arms. "First you find what happened to Fanny! I must know that you know!"

"Fine!" Janie scanned the bookshelves and found a biography of John Keats. She pulled it down, and looked in the index under the Bs:

Brawne, Fanny, 124–6, 137–9, 165;
   marriage 362;
   death 368

She flipped back to page 368, the poet watching her expectantly. She felt a little nervous. Was she doing the right thing? Would Fanny want to see him? The poet had been Fanny's first love, who died tragically. If Benjamin died, and Janie lived fifty more years and married someone else, and they were all long dead, would she still want to see Benjamin? But it wasn't even a question. Of course she would.

"Well?" the poet asked.

Janie hugged the open book to her chest. She didn't trust him; he could just drift through walls and leave. "I have it. But you go first."

He sighed. "All right. Your Carlino wasn't murdered. He was delivering a package by the river, waiting for someone on the bank. A bird flew up out of the brush and startled him, and he stumbled and fell in. Near the Piazza del Popolo. He couldn't swim, and his clothes were heavy, and maybe he'd had a few drinks. And he drowned."

"He just *drowned*?" she said.

"It happens!"

"So no one did it, no one pushed him."

"An accident. Terribly sad. He's very sorry, apologizes to his friend, says something about a sack of stolen potatoes, as proof that the message is from him. Now—where is my Fanny?"

Janie read from the book. "She died in London, and was buried in Brompton Cemetery. She was sixty-five. Her married name was Fanny Lindon."

"Sixty-five!" Keats said. "And married! My lovely Fanny!"

"I'm so sorry," she said.

"But I must go to London at once!" And he passed through the bookcase and disappeared, off to find Fanny Brawne.

Janie slid the book back onto the shelf and ran past the empty ticket desk, down the stairs, and out into the Piazza di Spagna. She had to get back to the hotel to tell Rocco and Benjamin what she knew.

CHAPTER 34

A Squall

On a clear twilit evening, Jin Lo slept while Ned Maddox steered the boat north along the coast of China. She was dreaming of flying, searching for barrels that contained something she couldn't identify, when she heard him call her name.

She ran up on deck and Ned Maddox pointed to the horizon. A fishing boat, larger than theirs, was steering to intercept them, and powering along at a deliberate pace. All thoughts of sleep were gone.

"Pirates," she said.

With her supplies from the herbalist, she had prepared two bottles of liquid, and now she uncorked both, pouring them together into a bucket of water. A fine mist rose up, and quickly coalesced into a dense cloud. It started to grow.

"What is that?" Ned Maddox asked.

"A storm, to protect us."

The cloud rose above them, gathering strength, a column

of dark, roiling fog. "Does it *know* it's supposed to protect us?" he asked.

The pirates had drawn closer, and Jin Lo saw a stout woman on the deck, in simple black cotton clothes, with her hair pulled severely back. Beside her stood Danby, tall and thin, with his white forelock. Jin Lo's intuition had been right, he had followed her, but she wasn't ready for him yet.

The dark cloud picked up moisture and enveloped the boat, so they couldn't see their pursuers. Rain began to fall.

"Go faster," Jin Lo said, and Ned Maddox pushed the throttle forward.

As they ran, they carried the storm with them, pouring out of the bucket, seeding the clouds overhead and sucking up water from the sea. The pirates would have a long, snaking squall to fight their way through, and heavy winds. Lightning shot out of the cloud. Jin Lo squinted into the rain that pelted her face.

"How do you know that lightning won't hit *us*?" Ned Maddox shouted.

"We'll outrun it," she said.

"I can't see anything!" he shouted, rain in his eyes.

But the storm was exhilarating, and finally they broke through into the clear twilight. Jin Lo was oddly elated. Danby was still behind her, still within reach. The storm trailed in their wake, the pirates lost in it, but Ned Maddox raced on ahead.

CHAPTER 35

A Telegram

Janie ran all the way from the Keats house to the Hotel Majestic. The doorman wasn't outside. She ran past the front desk and up the stairs around the slow elevator cage. On the top floor, dizzy and breathless, she knocked on the door of Rocco's suite.

No one answered.

She knocked again, and called, "Benjamin?"

Nothing. She put her ear to the door and heard no voices and no movement.

She descended the carpeted stairs more slowly, thinking. At the reception desk, she asked if Mr. Rocco had gone out.

"You are a moment too late, miss," the clerk said. "He has left the hotel."

"What about the boy who was with him?" Janie asked.

The man shrugged.

"Did they leave a message for me? My name is Janie Scott."

The man rummaged among the papers on his desk, then shook his head.

Janie went outside. She looked up and down the curving

avenue. It didn't make any sense. She felt in her pocket for the jar of powder. At least she still had that. But why would Benjamin leave? Why wouldn't Rocco wait for the news about his friend?

She started walking down the hill, and ran into the boy Primo. *"Sai dov'è Benjamin?"* she asked.

Primo shook his head.

"Gli altri?" she said. "Vili? Doyle?"

He nodded and tugged at her sleeve, then led her on a bewildering path between buildings to Vili's flat. The count's face was shaven when he opened the door, but he looked careworn.

"Is Benjamin here?" she asked.

"No," Vili said, frowning. "He's not at the hotel?"

"No one's there. They've left."

"Oh dear," he said. He produced some coins from his pocket and gave them to Primo with instructions in rapid Italian. The boy scampered off down the street, and Vili stepped aside to let Janie into the flat.

Doyle was sitting on the couch in the sitting area, his long legs stretched out on the rug. "So?" he said. "What news of the dead guy?"

"He wasn't murdered," she said. "He fell into the river."

"Oops," Doyle said. "You really talked to the poet? To Keats?"

"Yes," she said. "But now no one's at the hotel. Why didn't you stay with Benjamin?"

"What, now I'm a babysitter?" Doyle said.

"You got him into this!"

"A telegram arrived from Jin Lo," Vili said. "It was forwarded from my house in Luxembourg. Primo brought it to me, and I came back here to translate it. I thought it was safe to leave the hotel. Rocco is a man of his word."

Janie was torn between concern for Benjamin and curiosity about the telegram. Jin Lo had been out of contact for so long. "What did she say?"

"She thinks an atomic weapon has been stolen from the Americans, to be used against China. She's trying to find it."

Janie felt as if alarm bells were going off all around her head. "Can we go to her?"

"Not in time."

"Maybe we could fly as birds." Of course that was impossible, but when she pictured Jin Lo without anyone to help her, it made her feel desperate.

"It's much too far," Vili said. "And far too dangerous."

"I'd like to fly as a *man* in an *airplane*, back to Michigan," Doyle said.

Janie turned on him, all her helpless frustration finding a target. "You can't leave. You know too much. You already sold out Benjamin once."

Doyle held up his hand. "I give you my solemn word that I will keep your secrets."

"That's worth *nothing*. And if an American bomb goes off in China, and Russia attacks the United States, you won't be safe at home."

"Then my number's up," Doyle said. "At least I'll be *home*."

"You could help us stop it," Janie said.

"An atomic bomb? You're out of your mind."

"You can do things we can't."

"Yes," Doyle said. "I can understand when I'm out of my depth. That's a specialty of mine."

"We'll make you a new filter," she said, because that was the one thing she knew Doyle wanted. "A better one."

Doyle scowled, but she felt his interest rising. "Look, I'm not a good team player," he said. "Cooperation puts me in a vile mood."

"That's the deal," she said. "Take it or leave it."

He eyed her, and she knew he was reading her mind. "You're not sure if Benjamin can make a better one," he said.

"No, but we'll try."

They stared each other down. Doyle's talents might be useful, but he really was a pain in the neck.

"All right," Doyle said. "But you have to stop thinking what a jerk I am."

"Well, stop being a jerk, and I'll stop thinking it!"

"Let's hear the telegram, and I'll explain why all your plans are stupid."

"That's not helpful," she said.

"I'm already having regrets about this," Doyle said. "Just tell me exactly what your China girl said."

So Count Vili spread out the pages on which he'd decoded Jin Lo's message. The essence was this: Jin Lo believed that a U.S. Navy commander had removed a nuclear artillery shell from his ship. His only son had been killed in the shelling of the islands. The commander, disappointed that there had been no U.S. retaliation against China, had taken the shell and disappeared. Jin Lo was trying to find him, and believed he was headed up the Grand Canal to Beijing.

"That hasn't been in the news," Janie said. "I mean the stolen shell. Has it?"

"I imagine the U.S. Navy is keeping it quiet," Vili said. "It would be a great embarrassment."

"Does Jin Lo have a plan?"

"She seems to be in pursuit. And to have an ally in the navy."

"And if she finds the commander?"

"I don't know. She doesn't say."

They sat in silence. Janie toed the expensive-looking rug. China was so far away. When they had gone after the hydrogen bomb in Nova Zembla, it had taken Vili and Mr. Burrows and Benjamin and Jin Lo, all working together, to stop it. What could Jin Lo do on her own?

Doyle was the first to speak, still lounging on the couch. "Holy smoke, you idiots *do* need me," he said. "Sheesh."

Janie looked up at him.

"You don't see it?" he said. "You go to the kid!"

"What kid?"

"The commander's son," Doyle said. "He'll know where his father is."

"He's dead," Janie said.

He rolled his eyes. "You go through your After-lounge!"

Janie finally saw what he meant. "But Benjamin isn't here."

"Benjamin's no use! You told Rocco he couldn't go today, because he'd get sick."

That was true. "So?"

Doyle sighed. "So *you* go."

"Me?" Janie said.

"You took the powder too, right? For your secret love chats? And that's what creates the link?"

Janie began to feel apprehensive. Go to the After-room herself? "I don't think Benjamin would want that," she said.

"Oh, I misunderstood," Doyle said, with a sarcastic smirk. "I thought you wanted to save the world from nuclear war. But what you *really* want is to preserve your boyfriend's morbid attachment to his dead papa, and his condescending ideas about what you can and can't do."

"Stop it!" she said.

"Am I wrong?"

"It's dangerous there!"

"But you don't have the emotional investment that Benjamin has," Doyle said. "So it will be much safer for you. And anyway, I'll talk you through it."

She looked to Vili, whose advice she trusted. "Vili?"

Vili looked conflicted. "He might be right. If you want to go. It might be our only way to help Jin Lo."

"But how would I find the commander's son? There are so many dead people! And he died in China!"

"Oh, for Pete's sake," Doyle said, pushing himself up out

of the couch. "Why is this so difficult? You just try it and see! You found the other dead guy. You have the powder?" He grabbed a water glass.

"Now?" Janie said.

"Now!"

"I'm scared," Janie said. Her lungs felt tight, all of a sudden. She understood why Benjamin couldn't breathe, when he went.

"We'll be right here," Vili said.

"It's like the high dive at the pool," Doyle said, filling the glass from the tap. "You can't think about it too much, and stand there shivering. You just *go.*"

CHAPTER 36

The Afterworld

At first there was nothing but the sound of her own breathing and the fear that she would fail. She kept her eyes closed and tried to push the fear away. She had to think about the apothecary, to make the connection.

She thought about the time Mr. Burrows had taken a dead-looking tree that only bloomed every seven years, and made it burst into a cloud of white blossoms. There had been a pleased, boyish look on his face at the moment when the huge flowers burst forth, and she'd had the strange impulse to tell him he'd done a good job. It was hard to imagine Mr. Burrows as a boy, and she wondered if he had been stubborn and impatient with his own father, like Benjamin was. He was so deliberate and careful, always working out some problem behind his spectacles.

Then she thought about the trip back from Nova Zembla, where Benjamin had almost died, and how upset the apothecary had been. And she remembered the apothecary's own death, how he had struggled with his last breath to tell

Benjamin not to get caught up in bitterness and regret, so that he could carry on their work.

The darkness behind her eyelids changed and deepened, and then she was in another place. She understood why Benjamin had called it a *room*. It had a boundary that surrounded her on all sides, with a feeling of space beyond. The silence was complete—no birds outside, no Rome traffic, no sounds of Vili and Doyle shifting or breathing.

Outside in the distance, there were shimmering particles. They reminded her of glinting snow, or fireflies on a summer night. Benjamin believed that his mother was out there. But he hadn't said how beautiful the lights were. Janie thought with longing of her grandmother, who'd died when she was ten, and whom she'd loved. She felt her mind drawing toward the lights, out of the After-room, and she felt pressure in her lungs, and a hoarse gasp in her throat.

She heard Doyle say her name from a great distance, very sternly: *"Janie! Breathe!"*

Breathe. She couldn't be distracted. That was how Benjamin had got into trouble. She couldn't go chasing her grandmother. *Breathe in. Breathe out.* Her throat relaxed and she stabilized. She listened to the strange silence.

Then she saw the gray figures outside the boundary of the room, much closer than the glinting specks, and drawing nearer. The ghosts knew she was here, just as Benjamin had said. She tried not to panic.

"Mr. Burrows!" she called, with her mind, as in a dream.

What if the apothecary wouldn't talk to her? The ghostly

figures were coming closer. She tried to remember Keats, who had only wanted to see the girl he loved. These people were missing something, that was all. But they still made her shudder. There were so many of them. She began to see individual forms: an old man, a woman, a child.

"Mr. Burrows?" she called. "Mr. Burrows!"

Finally she heard a voice. It was the apothecary, his voice flattened, with no resonance or echo. It wasn't coming from inside a body. It had the effect that Benjamin had described, of a great effort to make speech possible. "You shouldn't be here," it said.

"Sorry," she said. "But we need your help."

There was a silence.

Janie was curious about something. Benjamin said he had called for his father for some time before hearing his voice, too. But that didn't make sense. They were making contact with his father's mind, but that mind didn't notice them right away. It was elsewhere. "Where were you just now?" she asked.

"With my wife," he said. "Almost. If I concentrate very hard, I can just feel where she is."

"Oh," she said. She felt she had touched on something very private. "Where is that?"

"I'm not sure, exactly," he said. "I won't know until I can go. But I know that she's there and I'm going soon." The apothecary's voice was different than she had ever heard it. Happier. Dreamier.

"Um—" Janie said, "is it okay if you don't go yet?"

A silence.

"Because Jin Lo needs our help," Janie said. "She's looking for a man who stole a nuclear shell, but she can't find him. And the reason he stole the shell is that his son was killed. So if I can talk to the son, I think he can help us find the father." Another silence, but Janie took this one as encouragement, and went on. "The son died in the shelling in China three months ago. I just need to talk to him."

"It isn't safe," the apothecary said.

"You told Benjamin we had to help Jin Lo," she said. "So we're trying! You should help us!"

She felt Benjamin's father sigh, and recognized the sound from his arguments with Benjamin.

Then she felt the apothecary begin to search—his mind grown vast and spacious. She remembered Keats dissipating, in the book-lined library, becoming not himself but part of something larger. But this was different, because she was *inside* the apothecary's mind. She could feel him ranging over continents, and also over this strange separate universe. It made her want to hunch down on the ground and cover her head with her arms, but there was no ground, and she had no arms.

After what seemed like a long search, although she couldn't guess how much time had passed, she saw a single misty gray shape moving toward her. It was a young man in an officer's trim uniform. He came through the wall of the After-room and stood looking around, a troubled, summoned presence.

"Hello," she said.

He looked around for the source of her voice. "Who are you?" he asked.

"I came to talk about your father."

"Do you know what he's done?" he asked.

"Yes," she said.

"He's gone mad!" he said. "He thinks he's doing it for me!"

"My friends want to find him and stop him," she said.

"Stop him how?"

"I don't know, talk to him," she said.

"Will they kill him?"

"No!" she said.

The ghost moaned. "He'll be ruined, his reputation destroyed."

Janie tried to make her voice gentle. "I think that's already happened," she said. "It'll be much worse if he sets off the bomb."

He nodded. "I know. So what do I do?"

"Tell me where he is."

"I need to talk to him first."

She wasn't sure how to put this tactfully. "But—you're dead."

"I'm talking to you, aren't I?" he asked, his thin, echoless voice rising. "And you're alive, I can feel that you are!"

"I am, but I—"

"I need to talk to him!" he cried.

"I can send a message," she said, desperate. The powder was going to wear off soon, and she was losing control of the situation. She could feel her hold on the room slipping.

"I have to go," the ghost said, looming toward her. "I can change his mind. I'm going."

"Wait, no!" she said.

"I have to." His spectral arms reached for her.

"No!" she said.

The apothecary's voice joined her, crying, *"No!"* His voice was in her head and everywhere.

But it had already begun. A strange coldness passed through her, so deep that her bones ached. Then a screaming wind blew inside her mind. She couldn't hear anything but the gale. It was a howling alien wind, an otherworldly chill.

Finally the feeling passed, and she was left exhausted. Someone was shaking her, pulling her back into her body.

"Janie!" a voice was saying. "What happened?"

She struggled to open her eyes and saw two worried faces staring down at her. For a moment she didn't know who they were. It was Vili who was shaking her. He looked stricken. And there was the orange-haired magician—Doyle. He was the reason all of this had started. She was lying on the rug in Vili's apartment, shivering and sweating. She must have collapsed onto the floor when the ghost passed through her.

Passed through her. He had used her as a bridge to the living world, like Keats had done. Benjamin hadn't described it as so violent, or so cold. She didn't know how that one hazy figure could have such force.

"Did you find the son?" Doyle asked.

She nodded. Her hair felt damp. She wished the two men wouldn't hover over her, their faces like floating balloons. "He went to his father," she said.

"What do you mean, he *went* to him?"

"To talk him out of using the bomb," she said. She tried to sit up, but a spinning dizziness hit her, and she sank back down to the floor.

"But how could he go?" Vili asked.

She closed her eyes. The light hurt them. "Like Keats did—" she began, but it was too tiresome to explain.

"Janie!" Vili said, shaking her until she looked at him. "Stay awake! Did you find out where the commander is?"

"No! Don't shake me!"

"Well," Doyle said, sitting back on the floor. "*Cherchez le fantôme.* The bad guy'll be the one with the ghost, right? Tell your China girl that if she finds the ghost, she finds the bomb."

"Stop calling her that," Janie muttered.

"Her name is Jin Lo," Vili said. "And I can't *tell* her. I have no way to contact her."

Janie covered her eyes. She wished they would stop arguing. She willed all of this to pass.

CHAPTER 37

The Grand Canal

Jin Lo surveyed the boat traffic at the mouth of the Grand Canal: barges and freighters and sampans and junks, all moving expertly around each other in a kind of waterborne dance. She had to concentrate to avoid collision. She wondered what kind of boat the commander might have chosen. For the first time, she felt that Ned Maddox might be right, that their task was impossible. Thomas Hayes could be anywhere. A needle in a haystack. A sampan in the Grand Canal.

She had hoped for a sign or a push from the apothecary, but none came. So perhaps she had only imagined that he was signaling to her in flashes, sending her inspiration, because she wanted so badly for him to be nearby.

Ned Maddox stood beside her, looking at the traffic. "You know this canal is a thousand miles long, right?"

Jin Lo nodded.

"Any idea what we do now?"

She shook her head. "No."

"Yeah, I was afraid of that," Ned Maddox said.

CHAPTER 38

The Breach

Janie lay on Vili's couch, wrapped in a throw blanket, looking at the ceiling. Vili was at his desk writing a message to Jin Lo about the ghost of the commander's son, even though he didn't know where to send it. He'd said he would try the last telegraph office she'd used. Janie thought he just needed a task, to feel like he was doing something. Doyle was having a drink, the ice clinking in the glass.

There was something on the ceiling, or at the ceiling, and Janie rubbed her eyes, wondering if she were hallucinating. But she wasn't. A mist hovered there. Then tendrils of fog began to emerge and slither down the walls, pooling near the floor and gathering shape.

"Vili?" she said, pushing herself to sitting. "Do you see this?"

Vili looked up from his coding. "See what?"

"These—figures?" she said, because they were becoming figures now. There were five, then six or seven. They began like Giacometti sculptures, narrow and elongated, stretching up from the floor, and then they took full human form. They were identifiably male and female, but transparent and hazy, like the ghosts she had seen in the After-room. They stood about like uncertain guests at a party, confused about where they were.

"Do *you* see them?" she asked Doyle.

"No," he said, setting down his drink. "But I can feel that they're here."

"Do you know what they want?"

"I'm not sure," he said. There was dread in Doyle's voice. He'd been so blithe about talking to dead people when he wasn't actually in their presence. "Their thoughts aren't very clear."

"I think they followed me," Janie said, disentangling herself from the blanket. There were at least fifteen of them now. It was hard to count, the way they drifted.

One of the spectral figures—a tall man in a suit—glided through the closed door to the street, and was gone. The others watched with interest, then moved to follow him.

Janie stood, unsteady on her feet. "Wait!" she said.

The figures paused and looked at her. She was trying to think it through: The commander's son must have opened up some kind of rift, when he came through—a passageway between worlds. That was why it had felt so overwhelming, so violent and cold. But how big a rift? Could *all* the ghosts come through?

"You're not supposed to be here," she said.

A girl in a loose dress shrugged, then passed through the thick plaster wall and was gone. A fat man followed. The others waited for Janie to speak, as if they wanted instructions.

"I think you should go back," she said.

One of the ghosts laughed. It was a bright, brittle sound, and Janie jumped.

"*Già siamo arrivato,*" the woman said.

"Can you hear them?" Janie asked her friends.

"No," Doyle and Vili said together.

"She says they all just got here," she said.

"*Ciao!*" the woman said, waving good-bye, and she disappeared through the wall.

"Um," Janie said, trying to summon her Italian to tell them to go back. "*Dovete—ritornare. Non dovete stare qui.*"

"*Dov'è Mario?*" a man demanded, looming toward Janie. She felt a deep cold coming off him, and stepped back.

"I don't know!" she said. "I don't know Mario."

"Isabella?" another man asked, drawing close. It was ghastly and disorienting to see the others right through his face.

Then they were all shouting names and requests, crowding around her. There seemed to be more of them now. She retreated until she was against a wall, and she could feel their collective breath, like a cold wind.

"*Sonia!*"

"*Giovanni!*"

"*Stanislas?*"

"*Marianne!*"

"I'm sorry!" she said. "I don't know any of your people! I don't know where they are! *Io non so! Perdoneme!*"

There was a disappointed silence.

A stout older woman asked, in a Midwestern accent, "Honey, are we still in Rome?"

"Yes," Janie said.

"Oh, fiddlesticks," the woman said. "I'm from Kansas. I need to get back there."

A nebulous girl in a sundress laughed brightly and said, "That's easy. You just click your ruby slippers together and say, 'There's no place like home.'"

"Oh, of course!" the woman from Kansas said. She clicked her ghostly heels together and vanished.

"She did it! I was only joking!" the American girl-ghost said.

A small boy in shorts stepped forward, shivery and indistinct. He seemed to be having trouble hanging on to his presence in the room. In an English accent, he said, "I want to see my mummy."

"Oh!" Janie said. What had he died of? He was so young. "Where does she live?"

"In Trastevere," he said, deliberately: an important word he had memorized.

"When did you—die?" Janie asked.

"I'm four." The boy held up four drifting fingers.

The girl in the sundress took his hand and said, "We'll find her. Think about where you last saw her."

The boy closed his eyes, and then they were both gone. One by one, the others began to vanish after them.

"They're all leaving," she said to Vili and Doyle. "I can't stop them!"

"Try harder!" Doyle said.

But what was she supposed to do—tackle the ghosts?

Most of them were gone by now. They had plans and destinations. The few stragglers seemed dazed by their return to the living world.

One young man tried to take a book from a table, but his hand passed through it. He swore to himself in English.

"Excuse me," Janie said. "Did you die in Rome?" She thought it would help to understand why they had come.

"Yes," the young man said.

"What happened?"

"I caught a fever on a summer abroad," he said. "Like the heroine of a novel—very romantic."

"Are you looking for someone in particular?" she asked.

He shook his head. "Not really. I just miss the world. I miss reading books. I miss sunshine on my face. All the little ordinary things. I keep thinking of that line from Auden, 'Find the mortal world enough.' Because the mortal world, you see, it's *amazing*!" He gestured with his shadowy arms at the comfortable couch, the floor lamp spilling warm yellow light.

"Do you know when you died?" she asked.

"Two years ago," he said. "It feels like yesterday. My name is Anthony. Would you say it?"

"Anthony?" she said, uncertain.

"Ah, nice," he said. "Thank you. I've missed that. And would you open the door for me?"

"You can pass through it," she said. "The others did." What was the point of keeping one nostalgic ghost here, when he just wanted to see sunshine, and all the others had left? She couldn't force the ghosts back through the ceiling.

"I know," Anthony said. "But just for the pleasure of it. Of walking through a real *door*. I never appreciated *anything* properly while I was here!"

So Janie opened the door, feeling miserable. She'd barged into Benjamin's After-room without permission and brought back a horde of homesick ghosts.

"Thank you," Anthony said, with real feeling.

"You're welcome," Janie said.

He looked up at the door frame as he drifted beneath it, and sighed. "I thought I'd never do that again," he said. And then he was gone.

CHAPTER 39

Death in Rome

Janie went out into the street with Vili and Doyle, to see what damage she had wrought. It was mid-afternoon, and she needed to check in with her parents and tell them that she'd found Benjamin and he was fine. Except that she'd *lost* Benjamin again, and had no idea if he was fine. And now there were ghosts everywhere.

The ghost of a young man was haranguing the old woman who owned the bakery. The old woman could hear him, but not see him, and she protested—she said she had always loved him. To Vili and Doyle, she looked like she was talking to the air. So it seemed to be love or attachment that allowed people to hear the voices. They could hear a ghost they knew. They just couldn't see them, as Janie could.

The transparent young man was complaining that the old woman had married his best friend. The woman said it was thirty-five years ago, and what had he wanted her to do when he died? Starve? She had needed help with the bakery!

Vili calculated. "Thirty-five years ago, he might have died of the Spanish flu," he said. "Millions did."

"I hope they don't *all* come back," Doyle said.

"This was your brilliant idea," Janie reminded Doyle.

The ghosts, single-minded in pursuit of their old lives, didn't move out of the way of people walking down the street. They just passed straight through, causing the living people to shudder with cold and look around in confusion.

"I have to go see my parents," Janie said. "Will you keep looking for Benjamin?"

Vili nodded and hailed her a taxi. On the way to Cinecittà, she passed a car with its hood crumpled against a stone wall. She imagined a ghost in the passenger seat, beginning a conversation with the terrified driver. She looked out the back window of the taxi to see if anyone had been hurt, but it was impossible to tell.

At the movie studio, Janie gave her parents' names to the receptionist in the gatehouse, who told her that a boy had just arrived to see them.

"Benjamin Burrows?" she said, excited.

The receptionist shook her head, confused. "No. Another boy."

Janie made her way back toward the building where her parents worked. At least there were no ghosts here on the outskirts of the city.

Then she saw the boy. He wore a tweed jacket, and looked lost among the soundstages, with a rolled magazine in his hand. His dark blond hair flopped over his eyebrows, and he was taller than Janie. But there was no mistaking him. He was

healthy and handsome now, but the face of the mischievous, underfed pickpocket was still there if you knew how to look for it.

"Pip!" she cried. She ran to hug him and he lifted her off the ground, then set her down.

"I had to read about your parents' movie in a gossip rag!"
he said, brandishing the magazine, *Picturegoer*, which had a
photo of Marilyn Monroe on the cover.

"Seriously?" She remembered Vili talking about the film
news. Had he planted an article there?

"Why didn't you *tell* me?" Pip asked.

"It all happened too fast," she said. "But I'm so glad you're here."

He waved the magazine. "D'you know they've got Clifford Kent starring in this film? He's *terrible!*"

"I think the whole movie might be terrible, honestly," she said. "But it doesn't matter. I have so much to tell you. Come see my parents. You're going to be the perfect distraction."

In a windowless office with the door open, they found her father hunched over a typewriter, her mother pacing the room with her hair piled up on her head. "I think we need another moment there," her mother was saying. "The chaperone gives in too easily."

"Sorry to interrupt," Janie said, knocking on the open door.

Her mother's face brightened, then clouded with confusion. "Oh," she said. "I thought you'd found Benjamin."

"I did," Janie said. "But look who else I found. It's Pip!"

Her parents stared at him, puzzled.

"The kid from *Robin Hood!*" her father finally said.

"And my *friend!*" Janie said.

"Sorry, you're so out of context, Pip," her mother said. "And you've grown up so much!"

"I read about you in the film news," Pip said, with an appealing shyness, holding up the rolled *Picturegoer.*

"No kidding!" her father said, standing and swiping the magazine.

"I just wanted to check in," Janie said. "We actually have to go."

"Already?" Pip said. "Do you know how hard it was to get *in* here?"

Janie shot him a meaningful look. "But we have some more *locations* to scout."

"Oh, good, which ones?" her mother asked, while her father flipped through *Picturegoer*, looking for his own name.

"Um—the Borghese gardens," Janie said. "And . . . that statue you put your hand in to test if you're lying. Maybe the Colosseum." She sounded suspicious even to herself.

But her mother wasn't listening—she was staring at Pip. Then she turned to Janie's father. "Is the girl still here? I'd like to see them together."

"You know we don't get casting approval," he said.

"Just to see it," her mother said. "Humor me. Something might fall on Clifford Kent's head."

"We should be so lucky," her father said.

Her mother ran out of the room and down the hall.

"What girl is she talking about?" Janie asked.

"She's an unknown, but wait'll you see her," her father said.

"Is she Swedish, like the princess?"

"I think half," her father said. "She has hair like corn silk."

Her mother returned with an actress in tow. "This is Evie," she said. "Our princess."

Janie heard Pip, beside her, catch his breath.

"So happy to meet you," the girl said, smiling.

Her skin seemed to be lit from within, golden and dewy. Her eyes were amber, and her hair was much nicer than corn silk. It fell in a single platinum curve to her collarbone, so smooth and shiny that Janie wanted to tug her own hair down into submission. She hadn't even combed it, after sleeping on the balcony. She made her hands into fists so she wouldn't reach up, and felt impossibly scruffy.

"Evie was raised in a convent, and speaks five languages without accent," her father said.

"The press is going to love that," her mother said.

"Five languages?" Pip said. "I barely speak one!"

Evie's laugh was like a wind chime, and Janie thought how irritating wind chimes could be.

"Now, look at them together," her mother said, putting Pip and Evie next to each other, shoulder to shoulder. They looked like figures on a wedding cake. Janie found it oddly nauseating.

"It's good," her father admitted. "It makes me think they should end up together, in the script."

"No!" her mother said. "It has to be bittersweet at the end."

"I don't know," he said. "People like a happy ending."

"Well, we're stuck with Clifford Kent, so it doesn't matter," her mother said. "I just wanted to see that."

"Cliff the stiff!" her father moaned. "He's not worthy of her!"

Janie watched Evie blush and smile through all this, and she felt very confused. Even if she hadn't grown up in Hollywood around preternaturally attractive actors, high school would still have taught her that there would always be someone prettier than she was, just as there would always be someone smarter and taller and better at chess. So what had happened to her calm acceptance of that incontrovertible fact? Was she jealous? She seemed to be *jealous*. Her father liked to point out that "jealous" and "envious" were not interchangeable words. You were envious of something you didn't have, and jealous of something you *did* have, and wanted to keep. Janie was envious of Evie's looks—anyone would be. But she was also jealous that Pip and her parents seemed so taken with her.

While Benjamin was missing! And Jin Lo was chasing a nuclear weapon! And Rome was full of ghosts! So why should this girl's beauty matter to her, let alone be so painful?

"We have to go," Janie said.

"Meet us for dinner at Angelo's," her father said. "I want a full report on your day."

"I think I'll just stay here," Pip said, gazing at Evie.

"No, I *really* need your help," Janie said, taking his arm.

Pip let himself be led out of the building, but he wasn't happy about it. "Why do you need me for location scouting?" he asked. "I'm not a location scout! I have to go find Clifford Kent and drop something on his head!"

"We have bigger problems," Janie said, leading him toward the studio gate.

"*Bigger?*" he said. "Did you see that girl? I *have* to be in that movie!"

Janie searched for any sign of a cab. The street was deserted except for a paper bag blowing along the wall. Taxis didn't prowl out here, so far from the things tourists went to. "We'll never find a taxi," she said.

But then one veered around the corner, black with a wide green stripe on the side, as if she'd summoned it. She waved and the taxi stopped, right outside the studio gate.

"Amazing," Pip said.

The rear door opened and Primo leaped out, gesturing wildly for them to get into the car. *"L'ho trovato!"* he cried.

"Benjamin?" Janie said. "Where?"

Primo grabbed her hand and pulled her into the taxi. Pip climbed in after her, and the taxi pulled away from the curb.

"Dov'è Benjamin?" she asked.

"In prigione," Primo said.

The taxi braked hard. Janie was thrown forward, and caught herself against the front seat with her hands. A pedestrian, nearly flattened, shouted abuse at the driver. The driver shouted back.

"Benjamin's in *prison?*" she asked.

But Primo had already leaned forward to urge the driver on with a string of invective.

"Are you guys ever *not* in trouble?" Pip asked.

"Not really," Janie said, her stomach knotted with worry.

"And who's the kid?"

"Vili found him on the street. He's been very helpful finding people. His name is Primo."

The two boys reached across her to shake hands. Pip looked the kid over: shabby clothes, crooked grin, head shaved against lice.

"Oh, I get it," he said, a little sadly. "He's the new me!"

CHAPTER 40

The Visitation

J in Lo and Ned Maddox made their way up the canal, but it was dispiriting. There were so many boats. Hayes might be hundreds of miles ahead of them. Jin Lo, scanning the boats with Ned Maddox's binoculars, was about to give up when she saw a little girl sitting at the back of a barge, eating something in a red and silver wrapper. Everything else on the canal barges had been washed so many times in the silty water that it had a brownish tinge.

She focused the binoculars on the wrapper. It was torn, but Jin Lo didn't need to read it. It was the same candy she had given to the old herbalist. The girl on the barge was no older than six, and she was utterly absorbed in the chocolate.

"Look," Jin Lo said, handing over the binoculars to Ned Maddox.

He trained them on the barge. "Hey, she's got a Mounds bar!"

"You have them in your navy rations," she said.

"Always."

Another girl appeared on the barge deck, walking on her

hands. A tiny gymnast. She righted herself, spotted the chocolate, and pounced on it, sending up a wail of protest.

"I want to go aboard," Jin Lo said.

"Do you want to hail them first?"

"No."

So Ned Maddox brought the boat silently alongside the barge in the busy canal. Jin Lo slung her bag of supplies over her shoulder—you never knew when they might come in handy—and hoisted herself aboard. The little girls were too absorbed in their fight to pay any attention. Jin Lo saw five juggling pins in a bucket, and a sign in Chinese characters, lying on its side. It said "Xiao Family Acrobats." She had seen small circuses like this, traveling the countryside, with children raised to do tricks as soon as they learned to walk.

She heard voices forward, and moved along the rail. A man in a broad hat and a fisherman's clothes stood with his back to her. He was not Chinese—she could tell by the way he stood, and by his hands gesturing as he spoke. At first she thought he was talking to the air. Then she saw a shimmering disturbance beside him, like heat rising off a road.

"Just let me see you," the man said in English. "Why can't I *see* you?"

"Commander?" she said.

He whirled on her. Beneath the broad hat, he was windburned and unshaven, his face red and his beard full of gray.

"I've been looking for you," she said. "Who are you talking to?"

"My son," the commander said, his eyes wild. "I can't see him, but I hear him. He wants me to turn myself in."

"That's good advice."

"But I can't! I've come so far—"

Ned Maddox had come aboard the barge behind her, and now he stepped forward. "Commander Hayes," he said, in a voice full of military authority, "I'm first lieutenant Ned Maddox, U.S. Navy."

The commander grabbed a boat hook hanging on the rail and held it across his body as a weapon. "Don't come any closer! I'm on an undercover mission!"

"Sir," Ned Maddox said, "I just want to talk."

"Get away from me, lieutenant!" Hayes cried. "That's an order!"

Ned Maddox started to lunge for the hook when a blur came running toward them across the deck. Jin Lo turned to defend herself, and was hit by something very solid and very strong. Ned Maddox went down, too; something flew at his head out of nowhere. She had a moment to think *acrobats*, before there was another blow and the world went dark.

CHAPTER 41

In Prigione

In the taxi, Janie made Primo repeat his explanation of what had happened to Benjamin. As far as she could tell, Sal Rocco had received a tip that the police were coming to the hotel. But Benjamin had insisted on staying, because he'd told Janie he would be there. He'd given his word, a thing Rocco respected. Rocco fled, and when the carabinieri arrived at the hotel room, they found only Benjamin. They could tell right away that he was unprotected, unconnected—*fesso*, Primo said. Benjamin was the kind of guy the police could threaten, and they might get him to talk about Rocco's business. So they picked him up.

"But he doesn't know anything about Rocco's business!" Janie said.

"The coppers didn't know that," Pip said. "They've got the uniforms, and the badges, and the car, and they've gone running out on a mission. They don't want to slump back to the station, all empty-handed."

"But Benjamin is innocent, so they have to let him go, right?"

"They don't have to do anything," Pip said.

They were back in the center of the city, and Janie was starting to see ghosts again. There was so much she needed to tell Pip. As the taxi weaved through crowded streets, she began with the powder and the After-room, and Doyle and Rocco, and Pip listened carefully. A skeptical look never crossed his face, and she loved him for that. He didn't disbelieve what she said just because it seemed far-fetched.

When she got to the ghosts streaming in through Vili's apartment, he whistled appreciatively. "You *have* been busy," he said.

They arrived at a police station, and Primo hurried them out of the taxi and paid the driver. Then they were inside, in a waiting room lined with wooden benches. A hulking uniformed officer sat at a desk.

"*Buon giorno,*" Janie said. "My friend is here."

"*Nome?*" the officer asked.

"Benjamin Bur— I mean, Benjamin Scott," she said.

"*Il americano.*"

"*Sì!*" she said. "*Il americano.*"

"*Venite,*" the officer said. He came out from behind the desk and took her by the arm—a little harder than necessary, she thought. He grabbed Pip's arm, too, and started to lead them away.

"Wait, what's going on?" Pip asked.

"I don't know!" she said.

She saw Primo's shaved head slip out the front door. He wasn't stupid enough to get himself arrested.

The officer pushed them through a door, down a hallway that smelled of mold and disinfectant and soup, past what looked like an officers' break room with no officers in it.

The next door took them to a room divided into four cells, two on each side of a passageway down the middle. The cells had barred doors, but only one was occupied: Benjamin sat on a cot with his head in his hands, a ghost standing on either side of him.

"Benjamin!" Janie said.

He jumped up. The ghosts started shouting at the officer, making accusations, asking questions. But the officer didn't hear them. With brisk efficiency, he unlocked the empty cell across from Benjamin's and shoved Pip and Janie inside. Janie stumbled and caught herself, and the barred door clanged shut behind them.

"Wait!" she said. "What have we done?"

But the officer left them there.

Benjamin came to the bars of his cell. "Pip!" he said. "What are you doing here?"

"I read about the movie," Pip said, brushing off his jacket. "I thought I might get a part. I forgot about the way you two attract disaster." They had first met Pip in circumstances much like this, in a juvenile lockup in London. But at least this time her cell was across from Benjamin's, so they could see each other.

"They brought me in to ask me questions about Rocco," Benjamin said. "At least I think that's what was going on. But then the ghosts showed up with complaints about their treatment here. Two of the cops could hear them, and they panicked. They decided I had something to do with the haunting, because I could see the ghosts, and they locked me up. And then they ran away, leaving that big guy, who can't see or hear the ghosts. He's not afraid. And he's mean."

"The ghosts are my fault," Janie said. "I'm so sorry. Jin Lo is chasing a bomb, and I was trying to help her."

"A bomb?" Benjamin asked.

"Oh, boy," Pip said.

"I had to go to the After-room," Janie said. "And they followed me back."

"You *had* to go?" Benjamin asked angrily.

"Everyone thought it was a good idea!" she said.

"What say you have this fight later," Pip said. "After we get out of here." He jiggled the lock on their cell. "You don't have that stuff that makes you a bird, do you?"

"I wish we did," Janie said.

"I do," Benjamin said.

"You *do*?" Janie and Pip said together.

"But there are three closed doors between us and the street," Benjamin said. "At least one of them is locked."

"Wait, how do you have the avian elixir?" Janie asked.

"I made some."

"When were you going to tell me that?"

"I'm telling you now."

Janie stared at Benjamin, and thought how little she'd known him, in the last months. She hadn't thought he was capable of such planning and energy.

"Well, let's have it!" Pip said.

"There are three closed doors!" Benjamin said.

"Someone will open them," Pip said. "And then we'll be ready."

So Benjamin untucked his shirt and tore the stitching on the hem. He'd sewn three small vials into his shirt, like Jin Lo used to do. Janie hadn't even known Benjamin could sew. He forced the vials out of the fabric and got ready to toss one underhand across the passageway.

"Wait!" Janie said. "If I miss, it'll break."

So Benjamin crouched and rolled the vial across the stone floor toward her cell, but the stones were uneven. The vial caught on an edge, spun, and stopped halfway between the cells. They all stared at it. Janie remembered the telegram and the straw, and tried to pull the vial toward her with her mind, but it didn't budge.

"Okay, throw the next one," Janie said.

Benjamin held it out between the bars and hesitated.

"Dai, dai, dai!" one of the ghosts said, encouragingly.

Benjamin tossed the vial, and Janie held her hands out and willed the vial toward her. It dropped into the palm of her hand, the glass cold and smooth.

"You're sure you made it right?" she asked. She was thinking of the white foam all over her parents' kitchen in Ann Arbor.

"I'm not sure of anything," Benjamin said.

The door opened at the end of the hall, and the burly officer came in. He wore heavy shoes, and Janie watched his big

feet approach the vial on the floor between the cells. If it broke, then only two
of them would be able to get out.

"Pull it toward you!" Benjamin said.

She tried again to move the vial with her mind, but it
didn't budge. She was too nervous. "I can't!"

The officer's foot missed the glass tube by an inch. He
turned toward Benjamin's cell, reached between the bars, and
grabbed Benjamin by the throat.

"We have to get out of here," Pip whispered.

Janie uncorked her vial. She had once jumped off a building while still human, trusting that she would transform before she reached the ground. This should be easier. She drank
the elixir down. It had the familiar bitter, mossy taste.

Then her throat felt too constricted to speak. Her head
felt light, and her arms and legs began to shrink. Her skin
prickled all over. She tipped forward at the waist, and her
nose grew pointed and hard. Soft feathers grew down her
chest, and her arms became delicate wings. Her bones light-
ened and her skull thinned.

She darted out easily between the bars. The vial on the
floor was so huge now! She didn't think she could get her
beak around it. She felt the looming officer notice her on
the ground. He let Benjamin go and swiped at her with both
meaty hands. She jumped free, into the air.

Benjamin uncorked his own vial and drank the contents
down. The policeman tried to grab Janie again, almost crushing

the vial with his foot. Out of
the corner of her eye she saw
Benjamin begin to shrink and tilt and
sprout feathers. She sang out with happiness. The policeman stared at the diminishing boy.

The ghosts were shouting again in Italian, which
made everything more confusing. As soon as Benjamin became a skylark, he flew out through the bars directly at the
policeman's eyes, and Janie swooped down to the vial while
the cop swung his hand at the bird. With her beak, she pushed
the vial laboriously across the floor toward the cell where Pip
was still trapped. Pip reached out his arm and snatched it up.

The policeman saw the vial in Pip's hand, and stuck his
arm between the bars, lunging for it.

Janie flew to the policeman's head and took a hank of his hair in her talons, pulling hard. He shouted, snatching at her, but she flitted free.

Pip drank the elixir down, and the policeman grabbed his shoulder. But Pip was shrinking, tilting, changing, slipping out of the policeman's grasp.

The ghosts were chanting, *"Uccelli! Uccelli!" Birds! Birds!* But the policeman couldn't hear them.

Pip became a swallow and shot out between the bars. He and Benjamin dived for the policeman's eyes, and the policeman screamed and ran away, throwing open the door at the end of the cells to escape.

The three birds flew after him, darting out through the door before it slammed shut. He threw open the next door, and they made it through that one, too.

Now they were in the police station waiting room, where they'd first arrived. The officer caught up a wire letter tray and held it over his head like a cage.

Benjamin tried to fly at him, to herd him toward the door to the street, but the policeman was more confident behind his wire basket. He grabbed a broomstick and started to swing it at the birds. They dodged away, but they were trapped in the waiting room, hovering near the low ceiling. Janie felt the *whoosh* of the broom come dangerously close.

Then the door to the street opened, and Vili strode in, wearing his rumpled white linen suit and his green scarf. He looked at the man with the wire basket on his head and the broomstick in his hand like a sword, and then up at the three birds. Pip the swallow shot out through the door Vili had come through. The skylark followed, but then the door swung shut. Janie tugged on Vili's scarf and sang out a warning.

"Ah yes," he said. "The door."

He opened it again, and Janie shot free into the fresh air. A heavy bench stood beside the door, and Vili dragged it over to trap the policeman inside. Then he looked around, brushed off his hands, and walked quickly away, swinging his walking stick, attended by three small birds circling his head.

CHAPTER 42

The Pharmacopoeia

Janie thought she had remembered what it was like to fly, but now she realized it was impossible to hang on to the true feeling. The majesty of it, and the freedom and vulnerability, were so overwhelming that she only retained a shadow of the experience when she was back in human form.

But now here it was again—she felt every passing air current in her wings, and knew how to ride it up or down. She swooped and whirled. Benjamin flew through the air beside her. Pip made a great plunging dive, then shot back up for another.

"Excuse me," Vili called from the ground. "Would you all come down here for a moment?"

The three birds descended reluctantly. Vili could have become an albatross and joined them—except that they had drunk all of the elixir. And it was useful to have someone to open doors. They hovered over his head.

"I need to consult the Pharmacopoeia," Vili said. "There might be some way to help Jin Lo that we haven't considered. The book is at your flat?"

The skylark nodded.

"I assume you prefer to fly," Vili said. "I will meet you there." He hailed a cab.

A warm column of air lifted Janie's wings as Vili climbed in, to travel along the ground like an insect. The Pharmacopoeia! She had forgotten it existed. What did a bird need with a book?

The churches and monuments looked like models in a toy city, from above. There was the Pantheon, with its smooth domed roof. The people were tiny, walking the streets. One or two even looked transparent, from so high. Then Janie remembered—they *were* transparent. They were ghosts. But where her human brain would have worried, weighing her guilt and wondering what to do, her robin's brain only lighted on the thought for a moment, then took off again.

Worms! She would like some worms.

Ordinary birds gave them a wide berth. There were no American robins in Italy, and the other birds knew there was something unnatural about the three of them.

They neared Cinecittà with its matching buildings, which looked more like a bunch of cardboard boxes than ever from the air. She wondered if her parents were still at work. She was supposed to meet them for dinner, and they would be upset if she didn't show up. But she was sixteen years old, and perfectly responsible, and a *robin*! There was no reason for them to worry.

Except that she had let some ghosts into Rome.

And there was a nuclear bomb missing in China.

Worms! Fat, glossy ones. She wondered if Benjamin and Pip were hungry, too. She hadn't even had breakfast.

Outside the apartment, she stopped in a tree, wobbling a little as she perched. Braking was still the hardest part of flying—not enough practice. Her parents weren't home, and all the windows were closed.

Vili went inside the building, and Janie followed. He knocked on the landlady's door and began speaking beautiful, courteous Italian, asking to be let into his dear friends' apartment. Janie perched on a light fixture near the ceiling and admired how reassuring and convincing the count sounded. The landlady was smitten, and took Vili upstairs. She unlocked the door to the flat. Easy as that. The three birds flew inside as soon as the landlady turned her back.

Benjamin led Vili to his room, and tapped his beak on the bottom drawer. Vili pulled it open and dug through the clothes. Janie had a moment of panic that the book was gone—stolen!—but then she saw the weathered leather cover.

Vili had just tucked the Pharmacopoeia under his arm when Janie heard a high-pitched alarm from Pip, a rapid-fire cheeping.

She flew to the windowsill and saw her parents walking down the street below, on their way home. They were deep in conversation and she could see, in the way they stood a little taller than usual, with their shoulders back, how happy they were, working on the movie. Happy! So coming to Rome had been a good thing. Something to celebrate.

Vili, still carrying the heavy book, looked out and saw them, too.

"Oh dear," he said.

CHAPTER 43

Discovery

There was nowhere for Vili to run, with the heavy Pharmacopoeia in his arms. Janie's parents were on their way into the building. Vili was good at smoothing things over, but how would he explain why he was there in the apartment with the book and three small birds?

Stress and fear always sped up the reverse transformation, and Janie felt the prickling in her scalp that meant that her feathers were retracting. The main door opened downstairs, creaking on its old hinges. Janie's legs stretched and grew, and her talons became toes again. Her feathered wing tips stretched into fingers, and her bones grew dense and strong. The tiny feathers on her head disappeared, and she felt the familiar weight of her hair spilling down her shoulders.

There were voices downstairs. The landlady was trying to explain, in slow, careful Italian, that she'd let an eminent, distinguished gentleman friend into their flat to wait for them. But Janie's parents didn't understand what she was saying.

Pip and Benjamin were still changing back into their human forms. The skylark's crest became Benjamin's wavy hair. Pip's long wings became arms. Her parents' footsteps climbed the staircase. Janie thought they were taking the stairs more quickly than they usually did, in their brisk new happiness. Why couldn't they dawdle? The landlady called something after them, from her apartment below.

The black feathers on Pip's face had just disappeared when her mother pushed open the door and saw the four of them standing there, staring at her. "Oh!" she said, surprised. "*That's* what the landlady was saying. You're all here!"

Janie saw a tail feather vanish under Benjamin's jacket. She touched her nose—it was soft. She was pretty sure her beak had become a mouth again, but she didn't trust herself to speak. Luckily, her parents, in their cheerful mood, could keep the conversation going on their own.

"Your Excellency!" her father said. "Hello!"

"I came to borrow Benjamin's book," Vili said.

"He lets you borrow the *book*?" her father said, with mock awe, but then he noticed Pip. "Hey, we were looking for you!" he said. "Clifford Kent is sick!"

"Sick?" Pip said. His voice was still high-pitched, with the hint of a swallow's call.

"Or maybe you poisoned him," her father said. "With Benjamin's big book of potions."

"Dad!" Janie said.

"We didn't!" Benjamin said, horrified.

"He's joking," her mother said. "Clifford came down with pneumonia."

Her father dug in his briefcase. "How quick a study are you, Pip?"

"The quickest!" Pip said, his face radiant, his voice normal.

Her father handed over a pile of loose script pages. "Maybe look at the first scene, to read for Tony tomorrow."

"Yes, sir!" Pip held the pages with reverence, as if they were the manuscript of *War and Peace*.

Then Janie's mother rounded on Benjamin. "*You* have some explaining to do, young man. Why didn't you come home last night?"

"I'm sorry," Benjamin said, hanging his head. "I—fell asleep in the ruins. I didn't mean to."

"In the ruins!"

"I'd just gone for a walk. I was really tired, I guess from the time difference. I'm not sure how it happened."

Janie's mother seemed unconvinced.

"Is it a good location?" her father asked.

"Not really," Benjamin said.

"Can we go to dinner?" Janie asked, to head off this conversation. "I'm starving."

Pip said, "I'm not hungry. Can I stay and read the script?"

"We'll bring you something back," her mother said.

"And I have a great deal of work to do," Vili said, patting the Pharmacopoeia's leather cover. "So I'll excuse myself, if I may."

• • •

On the walk down the street to Angelo's trattoria, her parents talked about their day, about Clifford Kent's sudden illness, about the director's panic and his relief when they told him they had another actor in mind. Janie tried, in whispers, to explain to Benjamin about Jin Lo and the commander's son, but her father was soon waving them through the restaurant's door.

They chose a table in the corner, and Angelo himself came to take their order. *"Buona sera!"* he said.

"Come stai?" Janie's father asked, winking at Janie and looking very pleased with himself for having formed an actual question.

In response, Angelo launched into a long complaint in Italian about his dead sister. She had been talking to him all day. She was full of criticism. She didn't like what he'd done with the restaurant. She didn't like the garlic knots. He'd told her *fine*, if she had so many ideas, then she should come back to life and take over.

When Angelo had gone, Janie's father said, "Did you catch any of that?"

"Something about his sister," Janie said. "Complaining about the restaurant."

"I thought I heard the word *morta*," her mother said. "Doesn't that mean *dead*?"

"Mmm—I dunno." Janie popped a big piece of garlic knot into her mouth.

"Maybe she thinks the restaurant is dying," her mother said. "But I don't think it is. It seems very popular."

"Mmm-hmm," Janie said, through the oily bread. She caught sight of a bosomy middle-aged ghost—the sister—scowling at the food being served to another table.

"Do you feel something weird in here tonight?" her father asked. "Like something's kind of off?"

"Unh-uh," Janie said, still chewing.

"Nope," Benjamin said.

Janie got the bread down. "So—how's the script going?" she asked.

"Oh, you know," her mother said, unfolding her napkin. "It's a little like doing surgery, with the new scenes. Sometimes I'm afraid we're losing blood flow, killing the patient."

"Do you think they'll really cast Pip?" Janie asked.

"If Tony likes him," her father said. "And I don't see why he wouldn't."

"Pip would be thrilled," she said. "He's in love with Evie."

"Terrific!" her father said. "That'll be good press. Young stars in love."

"Who's Evie?" Benjamin asked.

"She's our princess," Janie's father said. "Wait'll you see her. *Mamma mia.*"

Janie glanced at Benjamin, who didn't seem interested. Maybe it was better that he didn't care about anything except the After-room. If he were fully in the living world, he might fall for Evie, as everyone else had.

Angelo brought a large pizza, and everyone reached for the hot slices, with tomato sauce and basil and rounds of melting mozzarella. There was a silence as they fell to eating. When Angelo came back to see that everyone was happy, Janie could see his transparent sister standing beside him with her arms crossed over her chest, judging his table-waiting skills.

"Angelo, this is the best pizza I've ever eaten!" her father said, wiping his hands on his napkin. "*Magnifico, delizioso, fantastico!*"

"Please tell your sister we *love* this place," her mother said. "We love everything you've done with it."

Angelo bowed, deeply moved, and the shade of his sister frowned.

CHAPTER 44

The Tiger's Back

When Jin Lo woke up, she heard water hitting something hollow. The hull of a boat? She was thirsty, her tongue dry and swollen. She tried to remember where she was. The sun was beating down, and her wrists were tied behind her back. She remembered an attacker flying at her, out of nowhere. Was Ned Maddox still here? Her head hurt when she turned to look for him. Then she saw him on the deck beside her, unconscious, his wrists tied, his shoulders slumped against the barge's rail. He had trusted her, and abandoned his post, and this was what she had brought him to.

A small, bow-legged, sun-weathered man stood over her. In Cantonese, he asked, "Why are you on my barge?"

So this was Xiao, of the circus. She saw her bag of supplies spilled out on the deck. Someone had pawed through it.

Xiao followed her eyes to the bag. "Are you an opium addict?" he asked.

"Medicines," she croaked.

"Are you a doctor?"

She shook her head.

"A thief?" he said. "Sneaking aboard. We do not tolerate thieves!"

"Water," she whispered.

The captain seemed to consider, then barked a command.

Footsteps on the deck, and a small woman lifted a tin cup to Jin Lo's mouth. The water was faintly metallic. Jin Lo thought she had never tasted anything so sweet. If the barge captain was Xiao, of the family of acrobats, then perhaps this was his wife. And the flying attackers would be his sons, the little girls who stood on their hands his daughters. Jin Lo didn't see the commander.

When she could speak again, she asked, "Where is your passenger?"

"That is not your concern," Xiao said.

"You know nothing about him," she said. "He is a dangerous criminal."

Xiao frowned, but seemed ready to hear more.

"He has stolen a bomb from the Americans," she said, because she had no strength to invent a lie.

"You see?" Xiao's wife said. "I told you it was something bad."

Xiao looked pained.

"Please untie us," Jin Lo said. "I must find him."

"He is gone," Xiao said.

Jin Lo struggled to sit up straight. "Where?"

"He took your boat."

Jin Lo looked to the rail, and indeed, Ned Maddox's boat was gone. "Please go after him!" she said.

Xiao shook his head. "One should not climb on a tiger's back," he said. "It is hard to get off."

It was a proverb from Jin Lo's childhood that had always infuriated her. It told people to stand by, in a bad situation, and do nothing. "But you're already *on* the tiger's back," she said. "You took that man aboard. He will kill people, and start a war."

"I will not put my children in danger," Xiao said.

"They are already in danger! The whole world is in danger! You can help!"

She thought the captain's wife looked uncertain. But Xiao's face was impassive. He was determined not to get involved. Jin Lo struggled, but her wrists were chafed raw, and she couldn't get them free.

PART THREE

CHAPTER 45

A Portal

Janie couldn't sleep. She rolled back and forth until the sheets twisted into a rope beneath her, wondering how to help Jin Lo when they didn't know where she was. Her parents were up late talking to Pip about the script, and she heard their murmuring voices.

Then it was morning. Her father was calling, "Breakfast! Come an' get it! Can't work if you don't eat! Can't eat if you don't work!"

Janie pulled the pillow over her head. But the clanging of dishes and the smell of cooking made their way into the room. She dragged a brush through her hair, remembering her mortifying meeting with Evie the actress, all uncombed. Then she pulled on a pair of yellow capri pants and a white button-down shirt.

At the table, Pip looked chipper and rested. Janie slumped into the chair beside him. "Morning," she mumbled.

"My audition is today," he said.

"Mmm-hmm," she said.

"Wish me luck?"

"No!" Janie's mother said. "You're supposed to say 'break a leg.'"

"Or *merde*, if you're French," her father said.

"I thought that was just for dancers," her mother said.

Benjamin shuffled out and dropped into a chair, looking as exhausted as Janie felt. Her father dropped a plate of eggs in front of him, but he pushed it away.

"Eat!" her father said. *"Mangiare! Coraggio!"*

"I'm not hungry," Benjamin said.

"You two clean up the kitchen before you go out," Janie's mother said.

Janie groaned.

"You have no other responsibilities!" her mother said. "The least you can do is some dishes."

"Dai, dai, dai, ragazza!" her father said jovially.

Janie made a face at him.

When her parents finally left, bundling a suddenly nervous Pip out the door, Janie was alone with Benjamin for the first time since they'd sat together in the chair in Rocco's hotel room.

"I *wish* we had no responsibilities," she said.

"I wish we knew what to do about the ones we have," he replied.

"I've been thinking about that."

"Me too," he said. "A fat lot of good it's done me."

She took a breath. "The commander's son went through the After-room to get to China," she said. "At least we think that's what he did, to find his father."

Benjamin said nothing, and she could tell he was still angry that she had gone to the After-room without him.

"So," she said, "I thought maybe we could do that, too. Go through it."

Benjamin frowned. "But he was a ghost."

"Yes," she said.

"And we're not," he said. "So we're not really *in* the After-room, when we go. We're just connecting to my father's mind."

"But it seems to be possible to use the After-room as a portal," she said. "To travel through it."

"Yeah, possible for a dead person!" Benjamin said.

Janie knew that his anger at her was making him resist the idea, but she didn't know how to make it go away. "I'm sorry that I went to the After-room without you," she said quietly. "We didn't know what else to do."

"It was so dangerous, Janie!" he said. "You could have died!"

"But I didn't."

They stared at each other. Was it really fear for her safety that had upset him, or was it, as Doyle had said, his condescending ideas about what she could and couldn't do? Finally he said, "Okay, so *theoretically*, if I went through the portal to China, how would I get back?"

"I don't know," she said. "But maybe you could use the connection to me, since I just took the powder. It would be like a rope you could follow back."

He shook his head. "It's a crazy idea."

"We might be on the verge of a nuclear war," she said. "Wouldn't you do anything to stop that?"

"That's not a fair question."

"Why not?"

"Because it doesn't matter if you would do an *impossible* thing, to keep something terrible from happening. It's still impossible!"

Janie turned a fork over, on the table. "Do you remember the trip on the icebreaker?" she asked. "With all the stars overhead and the white bow wave churning under the rail of the boat? The first time we ever kissed?"

Benjamin nodded.

"Well, that's what I used to think about," Janie said, "when we used the powder to communicate, and I had to think about you to make the connection. But it was a long time ago. So much has happened. I think we should have a fresher memory to work with, in case you need it to get back from China."

He shook his head. "I don't think I can get to China."

"Benjamin," she said.

"What?"

She leaned toward him and kissed him, and an electric current seemed to pass right through her body, and to ground itself in the floor beneath her feet. She had waited for this moment for so long. His lips were warm and soft, and she could feel the heat radiating from his face, in the morning light through the balcony window. She had a feeling that a transformation was taking place, a chemical reaction, and the touch of his skin was the catalyst. It was like the moment of taking flight, the moment of becoming invisible, the moment the flowers all burst into bloom in the Physic Garden.

She pulled back and looked at him. "Did you feel that?" she asked.

He nodded, and she didn't know how to read his expression.

"I think that would bring me back from anywhere," she said.

"You're not *going* anywhere," he said hoarsely.

Janie stood up, disappointed, and gathered plates from the table. Maybe he didn't feel the way she did. Maybe he never had. It probably *was* crazy to think they could travel through the After-room, or that a kiss could bring them back together. A kiss didn't change anything. How could it? She ran water in the sink.

"*What?*" he asked.

"You were supposed to say it would bring *you* back from anywhere, too," she said.

"How was I supposed to know that?"

She shook her head.

"Anyway, I don't know that it *would* bring me back," he said.

Janie started to laugh, and pressed her fingers against her eyes to chase away the tears that were welling up. If he hadn't felt it, then he hadn't felt it. And there was no chemical reaction if it wasn't there for both of them. The connection was everything.

"Okay," Benjamin said. "I'll ask my father if your idea will work."

She nodded, and ran water in the greasy frying pan.

"Do we really have to do the dishes?"

"My parents asked us to," she said. "And we should try to get rid of the ghosts, too."

"I don't know," he said. "It's not the worst thing ever to happen in Rome."

Janie turned on him. "Your father always said there are unintended consequences, when you start altering the natural world," she said. "And that our job is to try to limit them."

"That was *his* job," Benjamin said. "And mine."

Janie stared at him in disbelief. Benjamin was so sure that he was alone in the world, with his burden and his talent and his grief. "Do you think I haven't become *involved* in your work?" she asked. "Do you think I'm just some—cheerleader, on the sidelines?"

"No."

"So it's my job, too! The ghosts are my fault, and I have to fix it."

Benjamin scowled. "I don't know what you want from me," he said.

"I want you to let me in!" she said. "And I want you to care about the world. About anything!"

"I do care!"

"Well, then show it!" she said.

CHAPTER 46

Another Telegram

They cleaned the kitchen in silence, Janie's face flushed with anger and embarrassment. She wished she hadn't kissed Benjamin. She wished he had kissed her back. She didn't know what she wished. It was all too confusing.

They took a cab to the center of the city. They still weren't speaking to each other, but at least the ghost problem didn't seem too bad. Janie saw one or two shadows pass fleetingly by.

Outside Vili's apartment, they knocked, and he opened the door. "Were you followed?" he asked.

"I don't think so," she said.

He shut the door behind them. The Pharmacopoeia was open on the table, and a low hum of voices came from a small radio. "I've been listening to the BBC," Vili said. "To see if there's any word of the bomb. There's nothing so far."

Doyle was asleep on the couch, his mouth slightly open, snoring. An uneven scattering of orange stubble had grown in on his chin. Janie wondered if he would feel her disgust and wake up.

"I received another telegram," Vili said.

Janie's heart leaped. "From Jin Lo?"

"I don't think so," Vili said. "But it's in our code." He spread the paper on the counter. It was written in typed letter combinations that didn't mean anything to Janie. But above each combination was Vili's handwriting working out the code. She leaned over to read the penciled-in words:

GREETINGS KIDDIES LONG TIME
BEATI POSSIDENTES

Janie felt as if a cold hand had reached in and grabbed her heart.

"It's from Danby," she said. She could hear his lazy English drawl even in the telegramese. And he was the only person she knew who communicated in Latin tags. She had assumed Danby was dead by now, sunk somewhere in the China Sea.

Benjamin seemed too choked with anger to speak. Danby was the real cause of his father's death. He had threatened to kill Benjamin, and forced the apothecary to make the uranium immune to their methods. So a bomb made from it would be unstoppable. It went against everything they stood for, and Benjamin had devised the smokescreen to escape.

"I'll kill him," Benjamin whispered. Janie had wanted Benjamin to care, but now she was afraid of the look in his eye. His nostrils flared. "I really will."

She looked at the telegram and dredged up her Latin from where it was buried in her mind. *"Beati possidentes,"* she said. "Blessed are those who possess. Does that mean that he has the bomb?"

"It might refer to the uranium," Vili said.

"Or to Jin Lo," Benjamin said. "He must have found her, if he has your code."

"He could have obtained the ticker tape from the telegraph office," Vili said. "But I don't know why he would write to us."

"Because he loves an audience," Janie said. She had first known Danby as a charming Latin teacher. "There's no point in doing what he's doing if no one knows."

"I'm going to China *now*," Benjamin said, almost spitting the words. "And I'm going to strangle him."

Vili looked puzzled. "Going how?"

"I had this idea," Janie said, "that we could go through the After-room, the way the commander's son did."

Vili frowned and waited for more explanation.

"It's some kind of portal between worlds that Benjamin's father is keeping open," Janie said. "Or the ghosts couldn't keep coming in. Right? At first it was just for communication, but then the commander's son passed through it."

Vili rubbed his temples, thinking. "In a sense."

"But Benjamin pointed out that we're not actually *there*, when we go," she said. "We're only connecting with his father's mind."

"Exactly," Vili said. "You only have access to that world as *his mind* has access. And if he is keeping the After-room open, then it would collapse if he took you to China. There would be no way back here."

There was a silence while they all considered what that meant. *Benjamin could get to China, mentally, but he couldn't come back.* His body would still be in Rome, but Janie had seen how quickly his body started to shut down when his mind wanted to leave it.

"Okay, I take it all back," she said. "It's a really bad plan."

But Benjamin's breathing was harsh and uneven. "I'm going."

"No!" Janie said. "I didn't understand what it would mean!"

"I'm *going*," he said. He grabbed the jar of powder off Vili's shelf and drew a glass of water from the tap. "I'll just talk to my father. I won't do anything stupid."

But the look on his face made Janie worry. She was afraid Benjamin *liked* the idea of going to China with his father and never coming back. It would be like their old days on the run, forever. *I have been half in love with easeful death.*

"You're too upset," she said. "You won't be able to control your breathing." She reached for the jar of powder, but Benjamin pulled it away. She turned to Vili. "Don't let him go!"

Vili looked uncertain. "It might be our only way to help Jin Lo."

"And stop a nuclear war," Benjamin said, staring her down. "Because we care about the world. Right?"

Janie shook the sleeping Doyle on the couch. "Wake up!" she said.

The magician snorted and jerked out of sleep.

"We need you!" she said.

Doyle swung his long legs down to the floor, knuckled his eyes, and saw Benjamin with the glass of water. "Oh, not this again," he said.

"Be ready to help him," Janie said. "And bring him back."

Doyle scratched his head and yawned. "All right," he said, in a bored, singsong voice. "Remember to *breathe*."

"This is serious!" she said. "Be serious!"

Benjamin tapped the powder into the glass and swirled it around. Janie could see him drawing air deep into his lungs, preparing.

"You know, there are nicer places to visit," Doyle said. "Paris. Morocco. Venice!"

"Be quiet," Janie said. She wished Doyle wouldn't take everything so lightly. What if the After-room collapsed, and Benjamin couldn't get back? What if it was too late to help Jin Lo anyway, and there was going to be another world war?

"Sweetheart, you worry too much," Doyle said, rubbing his temples. "Stop thinking. You're making my head hurt."

Benjamin lifted the water glass. But before he could drink, Primo came tumbling in through the door, sweating and dirty-faced. He was talking so fast and so frantically that Janie couldn't understand. Something about *gli amici*, something about *il libbro*.

Vili translated: "Rocco's men are on their way here. They want the Pharmacopoeia."

"How does Rocco even know about the Pharmacopoeia?" Benjamin asked.

There was a silence.

Doyle looked sheepish. "Well, I maybe—told him."

All of Benjamin's formidable rage at Danby transferred to Doyle. "You did *what?*"

"He wanted to know about your powers!" Doyle said. "He was making an investment, he needed to know your bona fides! Due diligence, you know? I had to assure him that this wasn't just some kid. That you have this special book that's been passed down through your family, that tells you what to do."

Benjamin jumped up. "We have to go."

"Where?" Janie asked.

"I don't know!" he said. "Somewhere else!" He swept the Pharmacopoeia off the counter and stuffed it into his satchel, then dumped the glass of water into a potted plant.

In her mind, Janie ran through the places they knew in the city. Where would they be safe from Rocco, a man with so much power? They were strangers here. There was only one place where they had connections and allies: a city within the city, with a wall around it, and many places to hide.

"Cinecittà," she said.

CHAPTER 47

Captives

Jin Lo had stopped trying to work her hands free. The skin on her wrists stung. The sun was relentless, and she closed her eyes against it, and against the sight of Ned Maddox bound beside her. The captain's wife had suggested moving the captives into the shade, but Xiao had refused.

"They are thieves!" he said. "Pirates. They deserve no sympathy."

"We are not pirates," Jin Lo said weakly.

One of the two little girls crept forward, when their father wasn't looking. "You don't look like a pirate," she said.

Jin Lo opened her eyes. "I'm not."

"What are you?"

"A friend," Jin Lo said. She edged her hands out from behind her back to show the little girl. "Do you know how to untie knots?"

The little girl nodded, but her mother called, "Ming!" and the girl scampered off.

Jin Lo sank back against the rail. There was another child somewhere. Jin Lo scanned the deck. There: watching from behind a bucket of juggling pins. Wide, dark, frightened eyes. The shy sister. She wouldn't be any easier to convince.

Ned Maddox struggled back to consciousness and sized up the situation. "Can't you do something?" he whispered. "One of your tricks?"

But her tricks were just that. A cloud of orange smoke, an immobilized cricket. None of those was good theater, outside in daylight. They were all designed to be seen close up, indoors. Her bag of supplies from the herbalist still lay spilled on the deck, but she couldn't reach it. She searched in her mind for the apothecary, for guidance, but she felt nothing.

Her shoulders ached, and she shifted on the hard wooden deck.

CHAPTER 48

Catastrophe

Benjamin left Vili's apartment with the Pharmacopoeia in the satchel slung across his chest. Janie and Vili and Doyle ran out onto the pavement after him. Primo was edging away. He had brought them the warning, but Benjamin guessed he would vanish and save himself if Rocco's men actually turned up.

The important thing was to protect the book. Salvatore Rocco claimed to be a man of honor, and in some ways he was, but he was also a criminal. It was very clear to Benjamin how his own mistakes had led him here, but his mind was fogged about what to do next. Janie said they should go to the movie studio. Would they be safe there?

"There's a taxi stand this way," Janie said. She stepped into the street, and looked back to see that Benjamin was following.

The fog in his mind cleared, and in colors bright and clear as after a rainstorm, he saw a red car come careening around the corner. The driver had a petrified look on his face, and the filmy shape of a ghost in his passenger seat. Before Benjamin could call out a warning, the car picked Janie up like a rag doll. She hit the windshield with a sickening *thump*, then flew over the top of the car. The driver raced on as if he hadn't noticed. Janie rolled to a stop in the cobblestone street, her arms up around her head.

Everything moved in slow motion after that. Benjamin's feet seemed to be trapped in deep mud, and his voice caught in a cry of protest. Then somehow he was beside Janie, throwing off his bag, trying to remember what to do.

He knew he shouldn't roll her over without stabilizing her spine. He cradled the back of her head with one hand and found her chin with the other, pressing his trembling forearm to her sternum, and eased her over carefully. Her forehead was marred by a bloody red sunburst.

"Janie!" he shouted. "Do you hear me?"

He'd told Janie that it wouldn't matter if the ghosts stayed—that it wasn't the worst thing ever to happen in Rome.

The worst thing ever to happen in Rome. Had just happened.

He heard the clanging bell of an ambulance. Who had called it? What were Roman doctors like? Shouldn't he and Vili use the Pharmacopoeia to heal her? But there was no time. Janie's white shirt was stained with blood and her eyes were closed.

"Stay with me!" he cried.

Then the ambulance was there. Men gave commands in

Italian. They were annoyed with Benjamin for moving her. But her face had been in the gutter. He couldn't leave her like that. Had he hurt her?

They lifted her gently to a stretcher, and put her in the back of the ambulance, while Benjamin hovered. He tried to climb in after her, but one of the men put a hand out to stop him, and closed the door.

Then the ambulance was pulling away. Benjamin ran a few steps after it, shouting. He became aware of Vili standing in the street, trying to hail a cab. Two went by, agonizingly, before one screeched to a stop. They climbed in.

The streets went by in a blur.

At the hospital, when Benjamin scrambled out, Vili stayed in the taxi. "I'll collect her parents," the count said.

Her parents! What was he going to tell them? Benjamin sprinted into the hospital, through the halls.

Janie's room, when he found it, was so full of white coats that Benjamin couldn't see the bed. When he tried to go inside, a nurse pushed him out: polite but firm. He stamped his feet quietly on the linoleum floor in the hallway to try to keep his body from shaking.

He waited, and waited, and then Vili came down the hall with the Scotts. They looked stony-faced, but when they saw Benjamin, their composure melted. They'd been keeping horror at bay with disbelief, and now they believed.

"Where is she?" her mother cried.

"How could you let this happen?" her father shouted.

"I'm sorry," Benjamin said. "The car came out of nowhere." He was shaking again: a full-body tremor.

"It wasn't anyone's fault," Vili said.

"Janie's always so careful," her mother said.

"I know!" Benjamin said.

Then he remembered Janie saying that they could go through the After-room to help Jin Lo. And his insistence that they couldn't, because they weren't ghosts. So had she stepped in front of the car on purpose? But no, he had seen her turn her head, just before the ghost-ridden car came flying around the corner. She'd been hit only because she was checking on him, looking back to see if he would follow.

"Have the doctors told you anything?" her father asked.

Benjamin shook his head.

Mrs. Scott collapsed on a bench against the wall. "Oh, God."

"Where do I give blood?" Mr. Scott asked, rolling up his sleeve. "Nurse! How do you say *nurse*?"

"You're not her blood type," Mrs. Scott said.

"I'm not? What's my blood type? She's my daughter!" Mr. Scott pointed a finger in Benjamin's face. "If she dies, I will *murder* you."

"Davis!"

"I will!"

"It's not his fault!"

A passing nurse with a clipboard gave them a warning look.

"I feel as bad as you do," Benjamin said quietly.

"Oh, no, you don't!" Janie's father said.

Her mother began to sob.

Vili looked at his watch. "They'll tell us something soon."

As if on cue, a doctor came out of Janie's room. *"Siete la famiglia?"* he asked.

"Sì," Benjamin said, stepping forward, taking advantage of the Scotts' hesitation, and calling on every bit of Italian he had picked up. *"Siamo la famiglia."* Because he *was* Janie's family. He had no other. "Is she okay? What's happening?"

"The blood pressure," the doctor said. "It drops too much."

"So give her more blood! Take mine!" He held out his arm.

The doctor shook his head. "It is too dangerous, with this trauma. There is too much pressure on the brain."

"Can't you do something about that?"

The doctor looked pained.

"Can we see her? I have to see her."

The doctor frowned. "For one minute. And no agitation."

Benjamin crept into the room, afraid of what he might see. A nurse stood between him and Janie, and then the nurse moved away. Janie's eyes were closed, with purple bruises growing beneath them, and her head was bandaged in white. He thought of how she had looked with the sun in her hair at the kitchen table that morning—only that morning!

He sat and picked up her hand. He could feel the Scotts' presence behind him, and their anguish at seeing her bruised and broken. He only had a few seconds to say what he needed to say. Was Janie in the After-room now? Was she headed for Jin Lo?

"Janie," he said, squeezing her hand. "Listen. Whatever you're doing, I need you to come *back*."

There was no sign from her motionless face that she had heard.

CHAPTER 49

A Decision

There was pain, so much of it, so sudden. A blow to her body, and then to her head. A feeling not of flying as a bird, but of being flung: her human body airborne and twisting out of control. A view of sky. The world distorted. Then cold, wet stone and darkness.

Next was a hospital room, with a lot of people. Blinding pain again. Then numbness flooding her body, and soft voices. Benjamin's voice. He seemed to be very far away. She was too tired to open her eyes.

Next she saw the ghosts. They were all around her, like people waiting for a train. Janie could feel their readiness to leave. They knew she had let them in to the living world, and they were ready to go back with her. They had gotten the thing they had wanted so badly, and most of them had said what they needed to say.

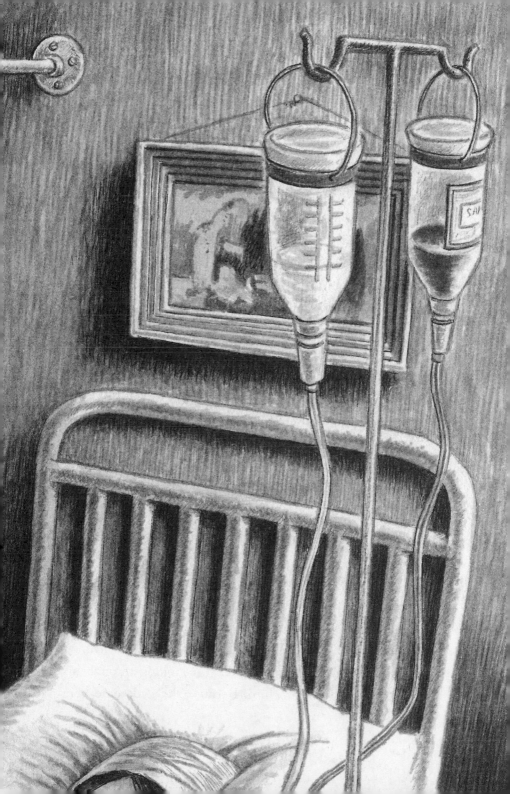

A little boy took her hand. He might have been seven. She felt him tug at her arm, but there was no pain. It was a relief to be out of her broken body.

"It's time to go," he said.

What language was it? She didn't know. The thought simply came into her head: Time to go.

So she began to walk, holding the child's hand, in a crowd of figures stretching out into the darkness. It wasn't anything like the rush of wind she had felt when the ghosts came into the world. This journey was slow and deliberate, a procession. The little boy told her it was going to be all right.

They walked down a green grass path, with trees all around, and Janie had the sense that the boy was *making* the path with his mind. It was the place he wanted to be. Beyond the leafy branches, beyond the springy grass, she could feel the great distance of space.

"*Ciao,*" the little boy said, and he vanished.

And Janie was alone in the After-room.

Back in the living world, Benjamin was holding her actual, physical hand, and he was talking. He was telling her to come back. But she was here, and there was something she needed to do.

"Mr. Burrows?" she called.

At first, nothing. Was he with his wife again?

"Mr. Burrows!"

Then he was there, in front of her. She was overwhelmed with joy at seeing him. She wasn't just looking through his mind now; she was *with* him. Because she had come here not with the powder but the old-fashioned way: by an unexpected blow. The apothecary was hazy like the others, but she knew his kind face and his serious manner.

"Mr. Burrows, I'm here!" she said.

"I know," he said sadly. "That wasn't supposed to happen."

"But it means I can help Jin Lo!"

"It might be too late," he said.

Janie imagined what it would mean to be too late—Beijing destroyed, tens of thousands dead, China humiliated, Russia outraged, a nuclear war. It all flashed through her mind as a serial horror.

"I *have* to go to her," she said. "Like the commander's son went. Now that I'm really here, I can do it."

"The tether to your body would be stretched too far," the apothecary said. "You wouldn't be able to go back."

Janie felt, as a distant dream, Benjamin and her parents sitting by her bedside in Rome. Her mother weeping. Her father raging about incompetent doctors. There was so much pain there. She turned her mind away from it. "This place is a portal," she said. "You'll keep it open for me, so I can try. And I know you know where she is. I *need* to go."

"Your parents will suffer every day of their lives if they lose you," the apothecary said. "So will Benjamin. It will deform their existence."

Janie felt impatient. "Were you with your wife again, just now?" she asked.

"In a way," he said. "Almost."

"Do you know where she is?"

"I don't," he said. "But I can feel the edge of it, with my mind."

"And you'll go to her, when you're through here," she said.

"I will," he said, and there was elation in his voice.

"I need to go to China, Mr. Burrows," she said. "If I can't get back to Benjamin and my parents, I'll find them later, like you found your wife. It's better that I die now than that thousands of other people's children do. You *know* that."

The apothecary was silent. Then he said, "You won't be able to touch anything, you know. And no one but Jin Lo will see or hear you."

"That's enough," she said. "I'm ready."

The apothecary bowed his head. "It's your choice."

So Janie pulled her mind away from the hospital room, leaving her lifeless body there. She thought about Jin Lo, their brilliant, impatient, orphaned, self-reliant friend. And she stepped out of the dark After-room onto the deck of a boat, late in the afternoon, in the waterborne world of China's Grand Canal.

CHAPTER 50

The Vessel

The first thing Janie saw was Jin Lo tied up against the barge's rail. She wanted to rush to her side, but she hesitated, afraid someone might see her. Then she remembered that no one could see or hear her. It was like being invisible again.

Someone had dumped out a bag of bottles and packets on the deck. And a man was tied beside Jin Lo. Janie remembered Vili saying that Jin Lo had an ally in the U.S. Navy.

She willed herself across the deck. Movement was a strange sensation. There was no friction beneath her feet, because she had no mass. So she floated, more or less. She had the sense that she could sink down through the wooden planks of the deck into the barge's hold, if she wanted to. She could stay underwater, because she didn't have to breathe. It was almost thrilling. She was invincible, invisible, bulletproof—

Dead.

She pushed the thought away, and crouched at Jin Lo's side. Her friend's eyes were closed against the late afternoon sun, and Janie wondered how long she had been here without water. Long enough for the people on the barge to get bored and leave her alone, clearly, because no one was guarding her, or the man tied up beside her.

"Jin Lo, it's Janie," she whispered.

Her friend looked up and scanned the air. "Janie," she croaked.

"Can you see me?" Janie asked.

"Only a little. Like heat in the air. Like the commander's son."

"I came to help you."

"Oh, no!" Jin Lo said. Tears sprang to her eyes.

"I'll try to go back," Janie said. "But I'm here now. I want to help you."

"I can't get loose." Jin Lo slid her wrists over to show Janie, then winced. The skin on her wrists was rubbed red. Janie reached to untie those awful ropes, and get them off, but her hands passed right through the knots, like Keats reaching for the book.

Jin Lo shuddered. "You're so cold."

"I can't touch anything," Janie said. "My hands just go through." What good was being invincible if you couldn't untie a piece of rope? If you couldn't pick up so much as a piece of paper?

A piece of paper!

She had only moved very light things before, with any control. But Doyle could juggle oranges in the air. If Doyle could do it, then she could. She began to focus her mind. She tried to determine which way the loose ends went through the knots, and which direction to tug. It was the friction of the fibers that she needed to overcome, more than the weight of the rope. She tugged with her mind and felt nothing. The knot didn't budge.

"Leave me and go find the bomb," Jin Lo whispered.

"Just hold still," Janie said.

"You must stop the commander."

"Shh," Janie said, concentrating on the rope.

"You can go across water, yes?" Jin Lo said.

"I haven't tried." There was a slight give in the knot. Had she imagined it? She pulled harder with her mind, and the rope end slid a fraction of an inch; she could see it move.

She missed having fingers. She wished she could just grab the stupid knot and untie it. *If beggars were horses,* her father would say.

She renewed her concentration, and the knot gave. She pulled the loose ends through.

"It's done!" she said, and she looked up to see a little girl standing beside her, looking curiously down at Jin Lo. Janie froze, but of course the little girl couldn't see her. She was about five or six, and she asked Jin Lo something in Chinese. Jin Lo answered, slipping her hands secretly from the loops behind her back.

Janie moved to the side of the captured man, who was slumped over, asleep or unconscious. She started the process over again, and it was easier now. She imagined the knot that bound his wrists coming loose, and slowly it began to obey. He stirred as the knot loosened, and he struggled to sit up. He had a bruise on his forehead, and he blinked in confusion.

"Ming!" a man's voice barked, and the little girl looked in that direction, but didn't run away.

Jin Lo spoke in English. "Ned Maddox," she said, "catch the girl. Make a distraction."

Ming looked interested in the strange language Jin Lo was speaking, and unafraid. But the man had his hands free, and he lunged forward and tucked the little girl under his arm like a football. She screamed. He ran for the other side of the barge.

Jin Lo sprang to her feet and gathered the spilled bottles and packets. "Janie," she said, "find the commander. He went north."

"I don't know what he looks like!" Janie said.

Jin Lo's voice had some of its old impatience. "White man in small boat with ghost," she said. She scooped the scattered supplies back into the bag. "I will follow."

CHAPTER 51

Teatime

Jin Lo heard shouting, as Ned Maddox, on the other side of the barge, held the little girl in his arms and fended off the barge captain and his sons. She heard the captain say that Ming couldn't swim. What an absurd fact, on a boat, and what good luck. She hoped this would not be the moment when Ming's childhood ended, her life forever divided into *before* and *after*. But the little girl was clearly brave, and Ned Maddox would manage it all right.

She crept with her bag down to the barge's deserted galley and put a kettle to boil on the swinging stove. She had once argued with Marcus Burrows about mind control, about the idea that you could administer some concoction that would render people malleable and suggestible, so they would do what you wanted them to do. The apothecary said it would not be ethical. You could not rob human beings of their free will.

But Jin Lo had experienced too many frustrating situations in which she knew she was right, and the people thwarting her were wrong. Right and wrong were not always subjective terms. Xiao, the barge captain, would not go after the commander, even knowing that the commander planned to kill many innocent people. She only wanted to help this stubborn man make the ethical choice. The ends justified the means.

She sorted through the packages she had bought from the herbalist and took out a bundle of fresh green leaves and a packet of dried brown ones. She added both to a teapot, guessing at the right proportion. The kettle boiled, and she poured it into the pot.

She heard footsteps on the ladder, and turned to face the captain's wife, whose face was red with fury.

"That man has my daughter!" she cried.

"I'm sorry," Jin Lo said. "He won't hurt her."

"What are you doing in my galley?"

"Making a calming tea. We've had a misunderstanding."

"He will drop her overboard!" Mrs. Xiao said.

"I promise we only want to help you. Here, please." Jin Lo held out a cup.

The woman frowned. "Where did you get it? Tea is scarce."

"In Xiangshan," Jin Lo said. "At an herbalist's shop."

"It smells like mold."

"It's a special blend."

She sipped. "It's not bad. But Ming cannot swim!"

"Your daughter will be fine," Jin Lo said. "It's very important that we go after the foreigner."

The woman took another sip of tea. "My husband doesn't want to be involved."

"But you have great power over your husband," Jin Lo said. "You can help me. We could save many people."

Mrs. Xiao frowned into her teacup, and Jin Lo could feel her willpower softening. She looked up from the cup, astonished. "You're right. We have to find him!"

"Let's take some tea to your husband."

They carried a tray up to the wheelhouse. Xiao was at the wheel, trying to keep the barge from a collision in the crowded canal. He looked at his wife standing with Jin Lo in surprise.

"Captain," Jin Lo said. "I brought you some tea, to apologize for my friend's rudeness."

"Tell that madman to set my daughter free!" Xiao said.

"I will," she said. "But first I bring a peace offering."

The captain swore vividly about her peace offering.

"Please," Jin Lo said.

"Have some tea," his wife said. "It's very calming."

He scowled, then took a cup from the tray, drained it, grimaced, and returned his eyes to the canal. "I don't feel calm. Set my daughter free."

"We need to go after your passenger," Jin Lo said.

"I told you, that's not my business."

"It became your business when you took him aboard," Jin Lo said.

"We aren't safe, with him out there," his wife said. "And we could be punished for helping him."

The captain looked uncertain.

"Have some more tea," Jin Lo said.

"It smells like mold," he said, but he drank down another cup.

"You should increase your speed now," Jin Lo said.

The captain nodded, docile now, and pushed the throttle forward. The old engine whined in protest, then settled in at a higher revolution. They moved faster through the water.

"Thank you," Jin Lo said. "I'll go get Ming."

Ned Maddox had the little girl on his shoulders, near the stern rail. He kept her brothers at bay by threatening to throw her into the churning wake if they advanced, but Ming thought the whole thing was a tremendous game, and taunted her brothers from her perch.

"You can give her back now," Jin Lo said.

Ned Maddox started to lift the girl down, but Ming shrieked, "No!" and clung to his head, arms wrapped tight around his face so he couldn't see.

Jin Lo got her first good look at the fierce and nimble creatures who had overpowered her. They were two teenage brothers in silt-brown clothes, one a little taller than the other, with pimples on their foreheads. They looked confused and disgusted when their mother told them they were going after the foreigner after all.

"Father just changed his *mind*?" the younger one asked. "Out of nowhere?"

"Have some tea," their mother said dreamily. "Our new friend will explain."

CHAPTER 52

Grief

The doctors sent Benjamin and Janie's parents out of her hospital room, and a nurse arrived with long silver scissors. Benjamin's first thought was that they couldn't cut off her hair! It was too much a part of who Janie was—always getting in her face, looking a little wild. But of course her hair didn't matter, not really, not if they could save her.

Still, the whispering sound of the scissors made him shiver. He watched through the door as a tangled lock fell to the floor. Janie's mother sobbed.

"What does it mean?" Janie's father asked. "Are they going to operate? Why don't they have an interpreter in this place?"

The scissors whispered and snipped.

A doctor—a surgeon?—arrived and frowned at Benjamin and the Scotts. *"Perché siete qui?"* he asked.

Benjamin pretended not to understand. They were here because they were not leaving Janie alone, that was why they were here. The surgeon went into the room and blocked Benjamin's view, examining Janie's head. Then he felt her pulse, studied her chart. He left, ignoring Benjamin, and returned with another doctor.

And all the time the scissors went *whisper, snip*. The hair fell to the pillow, and to the floor.

The two doctors stood over Janie in intense conversation that Benjamin could barely hear, let alone understand. He wished he'd eaten those mushrooms of his father's. The first doctor said something sharp to a nurse approaching with a razor and a bowl of water to shave the last of Janie's hair, and sent her out of the room. Then he sent away the nurse with the scissors. Neither of the women looked at Benjamin. After another moment of consultation, the two doctors left, too, avoiding Benjamin's eye as if he were a beggar on the street. He understood: They considered the case hopeless. They were giving Janie up for dead.

"Wait!" Benjamin said. He stared after them, the professionals who were supposed to save Janie's life, as they walked away.

Her parents understood too. "An American doctor wouldn't give up so easily!" Mr. Scott shouted. "I'm going to go find one!"

"Davis!" his wife said. "This might be our last time with her!"

"It's not! I won't let it be!" He stormed away down the hall.

Mrs. Scott looked to Benjamin. "I can't lose her," she said, and he had never seen anyone so desolate. They went into the room.

Janie lay unmoving in the bed, with her strange shorn hair around the white bandage, and Benjamin picked up her hand. She seemed to be eighty percent of her usual size. He felt no pulse in her wrist.

The two people he loved best in the world were Janie and his father, and disaster had struck them both, through his mistakes. It was intolerable. He should have knocked her out of the car's path. But it had come around the corner so fast! It had hit her before he knew what was happening. He should never have shown Doyle what he could do. That was where it had all started. If he had kept the secrecy his father had always insisted on, then they wouldn't have come to Rome in the first place. "I could have kept this from happening," he said.

"You're not superhuman," Janie's mother said, through tears. "None of us are."

"But I kind of am!" he said.

She looked at him with incomprehension.

"And I've done everything wrong!" He grabbed Janie's cold hand. "Listen to me, Janie," he said. "I need you here to argue with me, and tell me when I'm doing something stupid. You were right, it's your job, too. We're supposed to do it together!"

"Be careful with her," Mrs. Scott said.

"I need her back!" he cried.

"So do I!"

He squeezed his eyes closed and thought of Janie turning to look at him in the street—but that just led back to the car racing around the corner. He reached back further in time, and thought of Janie at the dance in Ann Arbor, with her smooth bare shoulders and her hair piled up in stiff, sprayed curls, the unfamiliar smell of her borrowed perfume. She had seemed so far away from him then.

Come back, he pleaded, with his mind.

Her hand was cold. Her mother wept.

"Janie!" he said aloud.

Then the sound of Mrs. Scott's sobbing faded into the background, and Benjamin knew what was happening. The white room was gone, and he was in the deep, familiar dark. He breathed deeply.

If she wouldn't come back, then he would have to go to her.

CHAPTER 53

Negotiations

Janie floated over the surface of the canal looking for a white man in a small boat with a ghost. But most of the boats were small, and the men all wore wide-brimmed hats that hid their faces. How was she supposed to pick out one, and a solitary ghost, in the bright sunlight?

Then she saw a transparent figure on a small boat. The light almost washed him out, but as she drew closer, she saw that it was the young officer from the After-room. He was waving his diaphanous hands in argument with an older, living, unshaven man who crouched at the stern. A white man, a small boat, a ghost.

She glided nearer. She could hear the ghost's thin, echoless voice, saying, "You can't do this! It's all you'll be remembered for! You'll be a murderer!"

Then she saw the shell. It was matte silver, pointed at one end and flat at the other, with a shiny copper band at the base. Very simple and beautiful and sinister. The commander must have made some kind of detonator for it. He was fumbling with wires. She realized with a shock that he was not going to Beijing. He was just going to set the thing off here.

She wondered what the blast radius might be. All the boats she could see would be gone, of course. And the towns on both sides of the canal. The radiation would poison people

for miles, and the surviving fish would travel farther and people would eat them. The poison would spread. Cancers and sickness, hair falling out, burns.

She hovered over the deck of the boat. "He's right," she said to the commander. "You have to listen to your son."

But he didn't even look up. It was so disorienting to be a ghost. Janie Scott of Ann Arbor, Michigan, didn't mean anything to the commander, so he couldn't hear her voice.

His son heard her, though, and looked up, his face drifting and agonized. "What do I do?" he said. "How do I stop him?"

"You can't," his father muttered.

"Dad, please!" the ghost said.

Janie had said exactly that so many times to her own father. It was impossible to keep your dad from doing embarrassing things. This was just a million times worse. But the truth was, her father never *meant* to embarrass her. When he'd pulled up at the dance and started calling out stupid things about Lord Figment, he was just trying to protect her. When he made dumb jokes, he was trying to make her laugh. When he spoke his weird hybrid language, he was trying to impress her. He was infuriating, she realized for the first time, because he loved her.

"Listen," she said to the ghost, who hovered around his father. "He doesn't care about his reputation. He only cares about you. Tell him you love him."

"We don't—say that to each other."

"Now's the time!" she said.

The ghost looked unsure, but said, "Dad, I love you."

The commander looked up, startled.

"Tell him you know he loves you, too," she said. "And that's why he's doing this."

"I know you love me, too," the ghost said. "I know that's why you're doing this."

The commander blinked. "Of course it is."

"Now tell him it won't bring you back," she said.

"This won't bring me back," the ghost said.

"But I'll be where you are!" the commander said, with great, pathetic hope on his face.

"No!" Janie said. "Tell him that's not true. If he dies like this, you won't be able to see him. You won't be able to talk to him. You won't have anything to do with him." It was manipulative, but she thought it was the kind of threat that might work on her own father.

The ghost repeated her words. "I won't be able to talk to you, Dad," he said sadly. "Ever again. If you do this, we're done."

The commander sat back on his heels, still holding the wires. "You don't mean that."

"I do," the ghost said. "I would have no choice. I would be too ashamed."

"That's good," Janie said. "Keep going."

"I know you want revenge for my death," the ghost said, warming up. "But I'm asking you to give that up. If you love me, don't kill all these innocent people in my name. Be magnanimous, and generous, and good—all the things that I know you are. Let *that* be my legacy."

The commander's face was tormented. His deranged eyes filled with tears. "But you're my only son," he said. "And they took you from me."

"They didn't," the ghost said. "I'm here with you now, see? I've stayed with you. So push it overboard."

The commander, his mouth working strangely, put both

hands on the smooth satiny surface of the shell. Janie could see his fingers trembling. She waited for him to shove the shell into the water, where it couldn't hurt anyone.

"Wait!" a voice called.

Janie turned, and saw the barge drawing near, with Jin Lo's handsome friend leaning over the rail as if he might jump in and swim.

"That's U.S. Navy property!" Ned Maddox called.

Janie had a moment's hesitation. Was sinking it the right thing to do? Jin Lo hadn't given her clear instructions—

But it was too late. The commander shoved, and the sleek shell disappeared with a splash into the murky canal.

CHAPTER 54

Orpheus

Benjamin wandered in the darkness. He wasn't sure where he was. He felt cold figures pass by and he shuddered, but he couldn't make them out.

"Janie!" he called, with his mind.

She didn't answer.

He thought of Orpheus. Benjamin had carried a book of Greek myths in his knapsack, when he was on the run with his father, and he'd read it in train compartments and borrowed safe houses. In the myth, Orpheus was in love with Eurydice, but a snake bit her on their wedding day, and she died. So Orpheus went to the Underworld and played his lyre for Hades, the king of the dead. The music was so beautiful that Hades said Orpheus could take Eurydice. She could follow him out of the Underworld. But there was a catch— Orpheus couldn't look back at her until they were in the land of the living, or his beloved would have to stay in the Underworld forever. Orpheus agreed, but it was a long way out. He tried as hard as he could not to look, he tried to follow the rule, but suddenly he was sure Eurydice wasn't behind him anymore. He was afraid, and he looked back. She was there, and she gave him a heartbroken look and vanished, back to the land of the dead.

Benjamin had first read the myth on a train on the opposite side of the world from Janie. His father had drugged Janie and her parents so they would forget about Benjamin, forget everything that had happened. He had understood that the myth was about being sure of someone. If you loved them, then you couldn't distrust them and be afraid they would abandon you, or you would lose them. So he'd tried to believe that he would find Janie again, and she would remember who he was, before she fell in love with someone else.

But back then it was just a metaphor. He hadn't been thinking he might really *go* to the Underworld. He hadn't thought of the myth as a guidebook.

And now that he was here, he saw that it wasn't a very good guidebook. There was no boatman, no river to cross, no three-headed watchdog. There was no Hades to charm with his lyre, if he'd had a lyre. The only instrument Benjamin had ever played was the recorder in school, shrill and off-key, so it was probably a good thing that no one was expecting music.

He sent his mind out, groping for Janie's mind, as if reaching for her hand in the dark. Was she too far gone to hear his voice, or to feel his presence? Had she already moved on to the place of the glinting particles in the darkness, where his mother was? And if so, could he ever get her back?

He felt his heartbeat speed up in his body, in the hospital room, in protest. She couldn't really be gone. *Maybe* he could let his father go, but he couldn't lose Janie. He called her name again, in the darkness.

Nothing. *Breathe in. Breathe out.*

The message of the myth was that he had to be sure of her. He had to *know* that she would come back with him.

Finally he saw the dim walls of the After-room around him and his father's voice came into his head. "Benjamin," it said. "You shouldn't be here."

"Where's Janie?" he cried.

"Helping Jin Lo."

"I need her back!"

"I'm trying to wait for her," his father said. "But you need to leave. I can't keep this up much longer."

Benjamin looked around, and saw that the walls of the After-room were slowly dissolving. He could feel the vastness of the universe beyond, glinting with light. It was pulling at him. He wouldn't be able to breathe soon. "What happens when you go?" he asked.

"This place won't exist anymore," his father said.

"And I won't be able to find you."

"No," his father said.

"Will you be with my mother?"

"I will," his father said, and again Benjamin heard that unfamiliar joy in his voice. "You have all her best qualities, Benjamin. I'm so proud of you. Our love still exists in the world, because of you."

Benjamin thought of the lifeless body in the hospital bed. "Janie has to come back!" he said.

"I'm trying," his father said. "But Benjamin, whatever happens, you have to live. You have to go."

He could feel his hold on the After-room slipping. His body was stubborn, and didn't want to die. It needed air. But if he left, he would never see his father again. "Listen!" he said. "It was my fault that you died! I'm sorry!"

"You were trying to do the right thing," his father said. "You were braver than I was."

"So you forgive me?" Benjamin asked.

"There's nothing to forgive," his father said.

"But there is!" Benjamin said. "Please!"

"Of course I forgive you," his father said.

Benjamin felt a flood of relief and happiness, a burden lifting from his heart, but also a fear that now he was really losing his father. It was time. "Wait!" he said.

There was darkness again, and the pulling sensation. A roaring wind. He could feel that the After-room was disappearing. Ghosts rushed by him, and he felt the bone-chilling cold as they were pulled back through the portal by which they had come. The door was closing, closing.

Benjamin felt the heaviness of his body, and the disorienting electric light behind his eyelids. The walls of the hospital room appeared around him. He was clutching Janie's hand so tightly that her fingertips should have been purple, but they weren't. She'd lost too much blood. He rubbed her pale, lifeless hand in his.

The image of her sitting at the kitchen table that morning, in a shaft of sunlight, came into his mind. He thought of her leaning toward him, and how warm and soft her lips had been. He thought of the apple smell of her hair, and the electric jolt he had felt when she kissed him. The feeling that something had shifted, that they had acted on each other as separate substances, and become something new. It had scared him at the breakfast table, and he had wanted to think about it some more. Because if they really were so connected, then what would happen if he lost her? And now he was losing her. He heard her voice in his head: *I think that would bring me back from anywhere.*

He leaned forward to kiss her dry, cold lips. It was there again, that sense of transformation, but he wasn't afraid. They had already become something different than they were before. The kiss had only made him aware of the magic of it, the way everything became possible. He smelled apples, and felt the morning's sunlight.

Janie gasped, and coughed.

CHAPTER 55

Coercion

From the circus barge, Jin Lo thought she saw the moment when Janie and the commander's son vanished. The look of heat rising from a road was gone. It happened so quickly after the shell sank into the canal that there were still ripples on the surface of the water. She wondered if Janie had survived.

Commander Hayes seemed meek and drained of energy, and allowed himself to be led aboard the circus barge without protest. His eyes were hollow, and Jin Lo wondered when he had last slept, and if he had been running on pure rage and vengeance this whole time. She wondered, too, how Janie had persuaded him to push the shell overboard, but it didn't matter: It was done.

Buried in muddy silt at the bottom of the canal was not a bad place for the shell. The titanium casing would stay intact a long time. So she directed Xiao, still under the influence of the tea, to take the barge south toward the sea. They could come back later to recover the shell.

"But we have to dive for it now!" Ned Maddox said.

She shook her head. "It cannot fall into Danby's hands."

"That skinny Englishman? Seriously?"

"And the pirates. They are looking for us."

"They'll never find us," Ned Maddox said.

Jin Lo did not want to argue with him. Janie was quite likely dead, along with Marcus Burrows, and Jin Lo felt as exhausted as Hayes looked. Grief was tiring. "Danby will find us," she said.

"But we have to return the shell to the navy," he said.

"It is a weapon to kill civilians."

"It's my job to return it," he said.

"But it is not *my* job."

He was exasperated. "Do you know how many more of those shells we have?"

Jin Lo looked at him, weary with sadness. "This is your reason to give it back?"

"I'm just saying it won't matter if we do!"

"It always matters," she said. "Everything we do, it matters."

"Well, I have to return it," he said. "We need diving equipment. And a winch—it's too heavy to bring up without a winch. Or serious floats."

"We have no winch," she said. "And it would not be safe to draw attention now. We must get out of the canal."

"I will not leave U.S. nuclear technology in enemy hands!"

"It's buried in silt, underwater. No one knows it is there."

"Someone might find it!"

"One moment," Jin Lo said. She went looking for the abandoned teapot and the cups, and found them stowed in the wheelhouse. The tea had gone cold. She had not had time to explain about the tea to Ned Maddox, and he had not seemed to wonder why everyone on the barge had done her bidding. She poured him a cup. Marcus Burrows would advise her not to do this, but he was not here. She took the cup to Ned Maddox.

"You are dehydrated, I think," she said. "Have some tea."

"We need to find a salvage barge," he said.

She nodded.

"And we need to anchor. I have to take very specific bearings."

"The tea will help you think."

He sniffed. "It smells disgusting."

"It's my special blend."

He gulped it down and then began to argue with her again, about winches and floats and where they could get them, but she could see the tea taking effect. And worse, she could see that he understood what was happening. He felt the tea melting his willpower away, and heard himself agreeing with her. A look of profound betrayal came over his face.

"We will leave the shell," she said, "and leave the canal. Now."

He stared at her, horrified. "You *drugged* me."

She turned away. Her regret for having given him the tea was swallowed up in all her other sadness. What she regretted was that she had *needed* to give it to him.

She gave the last cup of cold tea to Commander Hayes, but only because there was some left. She didn't think he would give them any more trouble. He drank it down as obediently as a child. Then she dumped the sodden leaves overboard, imagining the fishes becoming biddable, offering themselves up to bigger fish, or to the hook, and she carried the pot and the cups down to the galley.

She should have kept arguing with Ned Maddox, without resorting to the tea. She should have explained to him why salvaging the shell and risking it falling into Danby's hands would be the worst thing for the United States. Danby would sell the shell to his North Korean buyers, their nuclear program would leap forward, and the Americans would have a powerful new enemy in the world. But Ned Maddox would not have listened.

Maybe Marcus Burrows was right, and mind control was morally wrong, but the Wine of Lethe was just as bad, taking away people's memories. And Marcus Burrows had given that to people he cared about—for their own safety, and for the greater good. Would it have been acceptable, if she'd had some of the wine, to make everyone on the barge *forget* what had happened and where the shell was?

But she would still have had the problem of Ned Maddox. To drug him or not to drug him. There was no good answer. And why should someone she loved be different from anyone else? The ethics should be the same. She should treat all people as she would treat a loved one. Or was it different?

She wasn't sure. She wished she could talk to Ned Maddox about these questions. But he wouldn't be himself until the tea wore off. He would be someone who was bound to agree with her.

She put the cups away and thought about what to do

next. She would ask Xiao for food and water and fuel, and he would give them to her. They would take Hayes into Ned Maddox's boat, say good-bye to the little girls, and head out of the canal. Ned Maddox could return the commander to the navy, if he was so desperate to return something to them. She went back out on deck.

Night was falling fast, and Jin Lo hadn't even noticed. They were heading south, toward the mouth of the canal, past sailing junks and coal barges. The banks above the canal walls disappeared into the twilight.

Little Ming came walking on her hands across the wooden deck. When she got to Jin Lo's side, she dropped her feet in a backbend and stood up, as if that were a normal way to get around. She was like a human Slinky toy.

"Where are we going?" she asked.

"South," Jin Lo said.

"Are you in love with that foreigner, the younger one?" Ming asked.

Such a good question. "Perhaps."

"Will you stay with us?"

"Not for long."

"Why not?" Ming asked.

"Because I need to go out to sea."

"But why?"

"I'm looking for someone."

"Another foreigner?"

"Yes."

"Are all your friends foreigners?"

Jin Lo reflected on that. "Not you," she said.

"I've never been out to sea," Ming said. "Is it far?"

"It can be. It depends on how far you go."

"Are you going far?"

"I don't think so," Jin Lo said. "The man I'm looking for is looking for me, too."

"Are you in love with *him*?"

"No," Jin Lo said, appalled by the idea of loving Danby. "I just mean it won't take long, if we're moving toward each other."

Ming considered this idea. In the fading light, Jin Lo watched the concepts of time and distance play over the girl's mobile face. Jin Lo's own childhood in Nanking was hard to access, in her memory. It was on the other side of that great gulf formed by catastrophe. She watched Ming for signs of what she herself might have been like, back then. But had she ever been so open and so innocent?

"Jin Lo?" the little girl finally said.

"Yes?"

"Is that the man who's looking for you?"

Jin Lo followed Ming's pointing finger and saw a barefoot, black-clad figure climbing over the side of the barge, followed by another, and then another. They were swarming aboard. Jin Lo only had time to push Ming behind a barrel before the boarders had the captain facedown on the deck. Jin Lo heard a short scream from Xiao's wife.

Someone grabbed Jin Lo from behind, and she caught his wrists and threw him over her shoulder. He landed on his back with a heavy thump and lay there with the wind knocked out of him. He was upside down and gasping like a fish, but still she recognized the sharp features, the long straight nose, the white lock of hair at his forehead.

She was surrounded by pirates, and she stood up slowly with her hands in the air. They were on all sides of her, men in black clothes, with long curving knives. She tried to contain her fear, and to remember that she had *wanted* to find Danby—just not under these circumstances. She had not expected the pirates to come all the way into the canal. Their leader was either very brave or completely mad.

She tried to make her voice clear and steady. "I demand to see Huang P'ei-mei," she said.

The pirates locked Hayes and Ned Maddox and the circus family into the hold before their leader came aboard the circus barge. Even the captain's nimble sons had been overwhelmed, un-ready for the attack. But Jin Lo had not seen the pirates take Ming, only her sister. So maybe Ming was still hiding. Again, she found herself hop-ing that this would not be the catastrophe that would divide the girls' lives into *before* and *after*

Huang P'ei-mei surveyed Jin Lo with a skeptical expression, by lantern light. The pirate queen was about sixty, her black hair streaked with silver and pulled severely back. She wore the same simple black cotton clothes as her crew. She didn't look like a legendary pirate.

Danby had brushed himself off and recovered his dignity. "Jin Lo," he said, "may I present the illustrious Huang P'ei-mei." Jin Lo was surprised to hear him speaking Cantonese. He had the same lazy, supercilious, school boy drawl as he did in English—it was not respectful.

She sensed that a show of courtesy and deference would be her best strategy, so she bowed. "Madame Huang," she said.

"Where is the bomb?" Huang P'ei-mei asked.

"It sank to the bottom of the canal."

"Take us to where it sank," the pirate queen said.

"I don't know the place," Jin Lo lied.

"Of course you do!" Danby said.

"I don't."

Ming stuck her head out from behind a barrel. "I do!"

They all turned to look at the little girl.

"I remember where it is!" Ming said. "It's that

way!" She pointed north, up the canal in the direction from which they had come.

Danby began to laugh.

"The bomb is worth nothing, Madame," Jin Lo said. "The water and silt will have destroyed the mechanism."

"Perhaps," Huang P'ei-mei said. "Perhaps not. Catch up that little brat. And turn this barge around!"

A black-clad pirate grabbed Ming, who looked at Jin Lo from under his arm.

Jin Lo pleaded with her eyes: *Don't tell them.*

One of the pirates took the wheel and began the slow process of reversing course.

"And seize the Englishman!" the pirate queen said.

"What?" Danby said, as two pirates grabbed his skinny, wasted arms.

"You are rude, and it makes me weary," Huang P'ei-mei said. "Tie him up. I will deal with him later." Then she turned back eagerly, to watch their progress up the canal.

CHAPTER 56

Primo

P rimo kept seeing Janie fly through the air, in his mind, like a film playing over and over. He had seen many things, but he had never seen a car pick someone up and *toss* them like that. Benjamin had thrown his satchel down as if it meant nothing to him so he could run to Janie. She lay in the street, unmoving, and then there was the ambulance and Benjamin was trying to argue with the medics. Primo was too stunned to step forward. He had slipped the bag over his shoulder, for safekeeping. Couldn't let the book that everyone wanted lie there in the street. He thought that Benjamin would ask for it back, and he would hand it over.

But Benjamin and the fat count were crazed with worry, they weren't thinking. They flagged a cab and they were gone, and Primo was left with the strap hanging across his body, the heavy book weighing it down.

He could take it to the hospital. That was where they were going. They would thank him, give him coins, and say, "Oh, Primo, what would we do without you? *Grazie*, Primo. *Grazie mille.*"

That would be a nice moment. He liked these people. They were free with money. But they were foreigners, and foreigners always went away. Once, Primo's cousin Gina had thought an American boy was going to marry her. She was going to move to America and be rich. She told everyone, bragging and prancing around. But then the American went home from his trip, and left Gina behind. He had come to Rome for the beautiful things, but he had never meant to take her. Gina had sobbed and sobbed. She threw herself into the river with a broken heart, and had to be fished out, puking water, by a man working on the dance boats.

But she'd been foolish to trust the American and his promises. Primo could do every single thing for these people, and they would still leave, and he could end up back in the orphanage. With the soup that was like glue, and the cruel older boys, and the matron who pushed his head into a bucket of freezing water to shave him when he got lice from the filthy beds.

No. He was not going back there. He had his whole life to think of.

There was blood on the cobblestones, Janie's blood. It would be on the car, too. Should he go find the car? It had a broken windshield; it would be easy to find. But what then?

Maybe the count would give him some more money and the driver would go to jail. It wouldn't help Janie. It wouldn't help Primo.

Salvatore Rocco, on the other hand, wanted the book. And Sal Rocco could be a useful friend. He wasn't going anywhere. He was rich, he was powerful, he was respected. It could take a long time to earn his gratitude and protection—unless you had something he wanted badly.

If Sal Rocco's men found Primo and took the satchel away from him, which was likely to happen any moment, that would do Primo no good. The giant himself might come. Primo was fascinated by the giant, and a little afraid. What had that man eaten, as a little boy, to grow so big? Not glue soup, that was certain.

Primo had a nagging feeling that he owed the foreigners his loyalty, but why? He barely knew them. They had left him here, protecting their precious book, all by himself, against someone as powerful as Salvatore Rocco. What did they expect? They could hardly blame him if the giant came and took it away.

The far better thing was to find Sal Rocco and offer the book as a gift. *Here, I took this for you. I think you were looking for it. Your men couldn't find it, no—they searched the apartment. They looked everywhere. So maybe you need some new men, perhaps? A small assistant can be as useful as a big one. He can get in small places, pass unnoticed.*

He and the giant could be a team.

Primo looked once more at the bloodstained cobblestones.

He saw Janie again in his mind, flying through the air like one of his sister's dolls. A person wasn't supposed to fly through the air like that. A blow could come from any corner, at any time, and you wouldn't see it coming. You had to protect yourself as well as you could.

Primo blinked away the image of the flying girl, hoisted the strap higher on his shoulder, and turned and ran.

CHAPTER 57

Mutiny

It was dark night when little Ming directed the pirates to a meaningless point in the canal, far from where the bomb had sunk. She was very convincing, detailing in her high, piping voice the method she had used to mark the place in her mind. Her father had taught her how to take bearings, with two pairs of landmarks lined up in two different directions.

"The tall tree and that tower," she said, pointing her small hand in one direction. "And the buoy there and the triangle rock. Where the two lines crossed is where he dropped it." She lied with a practiced smoothness, better than any adult.

The pirates had an old-fashioned hard-hat diving suit for salvage work. A diver climbed into heavy wool clothes, and then into an oiled canvas suit and lead shoes. He put a round metal helmet over his head, with a thick hose attached to a compressor with a diesel engine on the deck. Then they lowered him down on a tether. The whole operation seemed dangerous, and Jin Lo watched the boy disappear into the water with apprehension. She knew, and Ming knew, that there was nothing down there. And three boats anchored and rafted together—the pirates' boat, the circus barge, and Ned Maddox's little boat—were bound to draw attention. Soon word would make its way up and down the canal, and people would want to know what they were looking for.

Ned Maddox and the others were still locked in the hold, but Huang P'ei-mei had commandeered Jin Lo as a sort of assistant. The pirate queen seemed to think that another woman in charge of a boat was to be trusted, at least in a subservient role, and she sent Jin Lo to raid the barge's galley for food and drink for her crew.

Jin Lo made another pot of tea, and took it out on deck.

She offered it to the pirate queen first, but Huang P'ei-mei scowled at the teapot. "Dirty water," she said. "I never drink the stuff."

So Jin Lo carried it away to the two skinny teenagers manning the noisy compressor that sent air down to the diver below. They were grateful—it had grown cold on deck, and

they didn't even complain that the tea smelled like mold. They clutched the hot tin cups to warm their hands, and sipped.

"Tea is hard to find," one said.

"It's good and hot," said the other.

"It's dangerous to look for this bomb," Jin Lo said, under the noise of the diesel engine.

The young pirates glanced to where their leader stood looking over the rail, out of earshot, then sipped and looked back at Jin Lo, ready to hear what she had to say.

"You have a good life, a good business," she said. "Why take the risk with this bomb?"

"Huang P'ei-mei says it will make us rich," one of the boys said.

"It will only bring the U.S. Navy down on you," she said. "You will spend your lives in prison. You're too young for that."

The boys looked concerned.

"We should abandon the search," Jin Lo said.

They nodded.

Three more of the pirates came over, drawn by the sight of the steaming cups. She poured the hot tea, and waited long enough to see the first two explain the situation for her, spreading dissent.

Then she carried the teapot and the tray of cups to the hold where Ned Maddox and the circus family had been locked up. Two older pirates were guarding it, their faces weathered by sun and salt water, their hands rough as claws from hauling ropes. One had a thin white beard and a scar on his forehead. The other was missing an ear.

Jin Lo sat beside the men on a locker and poured them some tea. "How long have you sailed with Huang P'ei-mei?" she asked.

"Nearly thirty years," one said.

"That's a long time," Jin Lo said.

The men nodded their wary agreement and slurped some tea.

"I fear the power has corrupted her mind," Jin Lo said.

The earless pirate glanced around for eavesdroppers. "She's gone mad," he whispered. "She was so close with that Englishman, and now she's going to kill him."

"Is she?" Jin Lo asked.

The earless man nodded.

"Do you fear you might be next?" Jin Lo asked.

He hesitated, then nodded again, solemnly.

"Why is she taking this risk, with the American bomb?" Jin Lo asked.

"She wants more money," the bearded man said.

"To retire from the sea," the other said. "To buy a farm, and raise vegetables and pigs."

"And what will happen to you?" Jin Lo asked. "Her followers?"

"Pfft," the bearded man said. "Left to scatter and starve."

"We could continue without her," the other said hopefully.

The bearded man shook his head. "Everyone is afraid of Huang P'ei-mei," he said. "They know she is ruthless, and so they stay away. We have many enemies and rivals. If she goes to raise pigs, those enemies will come after us."

The earless man sipped his tea and eyed Jin Lo with growing interest. "Not if we had a new leader," he said. "A woman. Then no one would know we had lost Madame Huang."

Jin Lo was aware of a strange sensation in her chest. It was not ambition—she did not want to be a pirate queen. And she knew these men were drugged, their minds searching for someone to follow. But still she felt an odd surge of pride that they might choose her to be their leader, and obey her orders even after the tea's effects had worn off. She started to say that she did not want to be a pirate, but she stopped herself. Replacing Huang P'ei-mei might be an efficient strategy.

"I'll take some tea to the others," she said.

She stood with her tray, and felt the pirates' appraising eyes on her. She tried to look seamanlike, balancing the tray of cups on one arm. But halfway down a dark passageway she nearly tripped over Danby, tied up like a forgotten package. The tin cups clattered to the floor.

"Set me free!" he hissed.

"You killed my friend," she said.

"I wasn't even there!"

"You forced the apothecary to do a terrible thing. You threatened his son's life. This is how he died."

"They made their own choices," he said.

She was too angry and exasperated to answer. She picked up the cups.

"Give me that stuff that makes you a bird!" Danby said.

"There is no stuff."

"*Stop* playing dumb!" he said. "I know you can do it. I

grabbed Janie Scott's scarf as she changed into a robin. I *need* what was in that bottle."

"I do not care what you need."

"That woman's going to kill me!" he said.

"She won't be in power much longer," Jin Lo said.

"Then her men will kill me!" he said. "They've always suspected and disliked me."

"You made your own choices," she said.

"Please," Danby begged. "All I want is a quiet life. I'm sorry about the apothecary. I'm sorry about everything. Just let me fly away, and I'll disappear. I give you my word."

Jin Lo looked at her battered old enemy, his cheeks hollow and worn, and tried to find mercy in her heart. "You don't know what kind of bird you will be," she said. "You might be too small to fly to safety."

He raised an eyebrow. "Do I seem like a canary to you? A goldfinch?"

"No," she admitted.

"I'll take the chance."

She heard the anchor come up with a clanking of chain, and felt the barge begin to move, sluggishly.

"Please!" Danby said. "There isn't much time! They will throw me to the sharks, in little pieces!"

Jin Lo thought of the kind apothecary. He might have been able to forgive this man. But she could not. She had a mutiny to supervise. She felt the barge bump against the side of the canal.

Jin Lo ran out on deck, and saw Huang P'ei-mei being

carried off the barge by two of the pirates. They were gentle with her. Her face was contorted with fury.

"Let me go!" she screamed. "I have given you my life!"

"It's all right, Madame," one of the pirates said, in a coaxing voice. "You can do what you want now."

"How *dare* you presume to know what I want?"

"You can raise vegetables and pigs," he said.

Huang P'ei-mei spotted Jin Lo on the deck of the barge. "*You* are behind this!" she cried, spitting with rage. "You want to replace me!"

"You don't want to be a farmer?" Jin Lo asked.

"Not—*yet*!" the pirate queen said.

"Sometimes we are afraid of our destiny," Jin Lo said. "We need a little push."

"I don't want a push!"

"I'm sorry, Madame."

The barge pulled away, and left Huang P'ei-mei standing on the side of the canal in the dark, screaming for them to come back. But they all knew the pirate queen was resourceful. She would land on her feet.

Jin Lo told the pirate at the wheel to steer the barge south for the open sea, and was watching the slow rotation when a voice cried, "The Englishman!"

Jin Lo turned.

Danby was standing on deck brandishing something small as a weapon, keeping the pirates at bay. In the lamplight, she could see that his skinny wrists were rubbed red where he must have worked the ropes free. Then Jin Lo recognized the thing in his hand. It was an amber vial of the avian elixir, and it was empty. How had he found it in her supplies? His pale face looked a little green, and the whites of his eyes were yellow. Had he swallowed the liquids at random?

"I found it!" he said to Jin Lo. "I feel it starting!"

"Seize him!" one of the pirates shouted.

One of them grabbed Danby from behind and locked an arm around his neck.

But then Danby began to shrink. His tall, thin body contracted, and his shoulders narrowed, and his skull shrank and slipped from beneath the pirate's crooked elbow. His captor jumped back in surprise. Danby's eyes grew smaller and darker, until they were black buttons. His long, straight nose lengthened into a curved beak. His white forelock spread down his face and chest in a cascade of snowy down, and black glossy feathers sprouted from his shoulders and head.

His arms became wings, but they hung at his sides. They weren't wings that would carry him into the sky. He lifted them to peer at each one. They were more like flippers.

Danby had always looked like a man who was comfortable in black tie, and as a bird he wore an elegant tuxedo. He gazed down at his smooth white belly and his long flat feet. It was not a body designed for flying. The pirates stared in astonishment.

"Catch the bird!" one of them cried.

The penguin looked up at Jin Lo with his shiny black eyes, as if for advice or explanation, but she was as surprised as he was. The pirates stepped forward again—uncertain how, exactly, to seize a creature they had never encountered before—and he waddled to the rail of the boat. As the pirates lunged, he dived under the rail, disappearing into the canal. Jin Lo could see the bubble trail he left, and the path of his sleek body through the dark water. Then he was gone, swimming effortlessly, headed for the open sea.

There was a shocked silence. One of the men muttered, "Sharks'll get him."

Jin Lo wondered if that was true. They were a long way from native penguin grounds. But sharks and seals were travelers, and would know what looked like dinner. Still, maybe Danby would climb ashore somewhere on the mainland, and disappear into China. He was a survivor. He had done it before.

"Did you *do* that to him?" one of the pirates asked Jin Lo, with wonder.

"She's a witch," another whispered.

"As long as she's *our* witch," a third said.

CHAPTER 58

The Quintessence

Everything hurts," Janie said, in a tiny voice.

"You're alive!" Benjamin said. He didn't know if he was crying or laughing, or both. Mrs. Scott, standing next to him, was definitely crying, making a strange animal-like noise as she sobbed.

Janie moaned and closed her eyes.

"May I come in?" Count Vili asked. He was standing at the door in his rumpled linen suit, with a young man beside him.

Janie turned her eyes to them. "Osman!" she said weakly.

Benjamin recognized the cook from the Malayan island where Janie had been held captive. Osman had helped them escape—Benjamin's father had known he would, based only on seeing the garden Osman had planted. He had looked at the garden and looked into Osman's soul. That made the young cook seem like a living connection to Benjamin's father, here in the world. He was slight, with warm brown skin and a shy smile.

"Hello!" he said. "I came as fast as I could."

"Osman has been working as my chef, at my house in Luxembourg," Vili said. "He came on the train, bringing me this." He uncorked a small amber bottle and the sweet smell of the Quintessence filled the room.

Benjamin's chest ached at the smell, it evoked his father so clearly. "You have a whole bottle?"

"The last," Vili said. "I sent for it on a hunch. The situation seemed dangerous."

"*What* situation?" Janie's mother demanded. "What danger? We trusted you!"

"I apologize and will explain," Vili said. "May I?"

Mrs. Scott stepped back, awed by his composure.

"Would you help me, Benjamin?" Vili asked. He gently lifted the blood-soaked bandage on Janie's head. Together they poured a little of the Quintessence onto the star-shaped contusion. Benjamin winced to see it.

Then Mr. Scott burst into the room. "I found a doctor who speaks English!" He was followed by a confused-looking man in a white coat and wire-rimmed glasses. "This is Dr. Patel!"

"But I'm not a trauma physician," Dr. Patel said in a clipped accent. "I'm a dermatologist!"

The two men stared at the strange scene at Janie's bedside: the portly count in his rumpled white suit lowering Janie to the pillow, Benjamin holding the amber bottle, Mrs. Scott watching them, wringing her hands, and Osman standing by.

"What are you *doing*?" Mr. Scott cried.

"May I examine her?" the dermatologist asked. He moved to Janie's bed and carefully unwrapped the bandage from her forehead. Her hair was so strangely short, unevenly chopped. But where a moment ago there had been a scary contusion the size of a child's fist, there was now a small red mark. Dr. Patel looked at the bloody bandage in his hand, then around at the watchers. "When was the accident?" he asked.

"A few hours ago," Mr. Scott said.

"I'm okay, really," Janie said.

Dr. Patel looked at the chart hanging on her bed, then peered again at Janie's forehead. "You say the patient was thrown over a car? The head wound is described as severe, life-threatening."

"These Italian doctors gave up on her!" Mr. Scott said. "They left her for dead!"

"I've never seen a wound heal like this," Dr. Patel said, touching her skin gently. "I will have to study it further."

Benjamin caught Vili's eye. "Um—that won't be possible," he said.

"Why not?" Mrs. Scott asked.

"She's leaving the hospital," Benjamin said.

"*What?*" Mr. Scott said.

"No, no," Dr. Patel said.

"We'll go get a cab," Vili said, and he and Osman left the room.

Janie's mother seemed to be in shock. Benjamin thought she might need a doctor more than Janie did, at this point, and he helped her to a chair.

"You must stay!" Dr. Patel said. "I will write a paper on this marvelous recovery. And the patient must remain under observation, of course. Because you see, this chart says that she was dead."

They all turned to look at Janie, who was pushing away

the hospital sheets. She didn't look like she'd been flung over the top of a Renault. She had pink cheeks and a distracted air, in her white hospital gown. The red mark on her forehead looked like she might have bumped her head in the night. She spotted a lock of hair on the floor and reached up for the exposed back of her neck. "My hair," she said, with wonder.

"What is going *on?*" Mr. Scott demanded.

"She's better, that's all," Benjamin said. "I think Mrs. Scott might need a drink of water."

"No, you will *explain* first!" Mr. Scott said.

"Davis," Janie's mother said from her chair. "Water."

"All right," he said. "But then an explanation!" He left the room.

"I must consult my colleagues," Dr. Patel said.

"Maybe you should go find them," Benjamin said.

The dermatologist ran out, and it was just the three of them in the room again: Benjamin, Janie, and her dazed mother in the chair.

"Do you think you can walk?" Benjamin asked Janie.

"I think so."

"We have to get you out of here, or they're never going to let you go. You're a medical miracle now."

"I am?"

"A few minutes ago you were dead."

"Oh, right."

He found her crumpled yellow pants. Down the hall he heard her father shouting, "Cup! I need a cup! *Taza! Agua!*"

"That's Spanish," Janie said weakly, to no one in particular.

Benjamin struggled to pull on her pant legs, which seemed ridiculously narrow for her feet and ankles. "Do these really go on?" he asked.

"They're capris," she said, in the same far-off voice. "Audrey Hepburn wears them."

She stood and tugged them on under her cotton gown. Benjamin didn't think Audrey Hepburn would have worn the pants so streaked with dirt.

"Do I have a shirt?" Janie asked. Her bare feet looked cold and vulnerable on the linoleum floor.

Benjamin spotted the blood-soaked shirt in a corner. "Just tuck the gown in," he said.

"Should we wait for my husband?" her mother asked.

"No," Benjamin said. "We'll go to the flat. He can follow."

A nurse came in and cried out in astonishment, seeing the dead girl up and dressed, in her dirty yellow pants and her tucked-in hospital gown. The nurse placed her substantial form in front of the door and let loose a flood of Italian, pointing toward the hospital bed. The meaning was clear: *No* dead patients were to be up and walking.

But Benjamin was in charge now. *"Signora, mi scusi,"* he said, and he gently moved past the astonished nurse, helping Janie out the door. Her mother followed. The three of them walked down the corridor, toward the main entrance, and turned a corner. He hoped Vili had found a cab, but Vili always came through. He'd come up with a whole bottle of the Quintessence! They would apply it to all of Janie's bruises and abrasions when they had more time.

There was a cry behind them, from someone finding Janie's room empty.

"Can you walk a little faster?" he asked Janie.

"What was in that bottle?" her mother asked.

"Some medicine," Benjamin said. Seeing Janie fly over the car must have erased everything he had memorized in the Pharmacopoeia. He'd forgotten, even, that the Quintessence had healing powers. He reached for the satchel at his side, to make sure the book was still there.

But there was no satchel.

No book.

He remembered throwing the strap off over his head and kneeling beside Janie in the street. But had the satchel still been there when the ambulance came? Surely he would have seen it on the ground. Or Vili would have.

They were heading out through the main hospital doors, and Vili and Osman were waiting beside a shiny black green-striped cab.

Vili beamed at Janie. "You look excellent, my dear," he said. "The picture of health."

"It's so good to see you both," Janie said.

"I came as fast as I could!" Osman repeated, beaming.

"Vili," Benjamin said, and his voice sounded slow and distorted in his own ears. "The Pharmacopoeia."

The count looked to his hip for the satchel that wasn't there.

"It's gone!" Benjamin said.

CHAPTER 59

Tung Shing

The pirates, convinced now that Jin Lo was a witch who might turn them into flightless birds at any moment, were ready to obey her in all things, tea or no tea. It was an efficient arrangement, and she gave brisk commands. She wanted to get as far as she could before dawn.

Her first order was to let the prisoners out of the hold. They filed out in lantern light, Xiao and his family first.

When she saw Ned Maddox emerge, she had the strangest feeling. It was as if an ice dam had melted in her chest, letting a blocked river tumble downstream. It was difficult to breathe, in all the tumbling. She had never experienced such disorienting fullness around another person, or such a troubling need to be near him. She threw her arms around him. "I shouldn't have given you the tea," she whispered.

"No," he said, into her hair. "You shouldn't have. You can argue with me, and you can fight with me—"

"I'm sorry."

"But never do that again."

"Never."

He held her at arm's length. "I thought they were going to kill you."

"Me too."

"What happened to your Englishman?"

"He's gone."

"Gone where?"

"I'll explain later," she said. "They put Huang P'ei-mei ashore. I'm in charge now."

"So *you're* the pirate queen," he said, with an odd expression on his face.

"It is convenient," she said. "For now."

"I saw the diving suit," he said. "We can go pick up the bomb."

Jin Lo's heart sank. This argument again. "Not yet. It is safe where it is."

"You said it couldn't fall into Danby's hands," he said. "Now he's gone."

"We can't return it to your navy," she said.

Ned Maddox was silent a long time, his breathing unsteady. She could feel the pirates watching them in the dark. It was unsettling, the way she felt about Ned Maddox. And it made no sense. Was she so foolish and lonely that she would fall in love with *anyone* whose island she washed up on? Like the fairy queen in that English play, falling in love with a donkey, because he was there?

"All right," Ned Maddox said. "But you have to marry me. I want to be your husband. Not just as a cover story."

Jin Lo frowned. "This is not a customary proposal," she

said. But of course a customary proposal would involve their families discussing the match, and they had not a single parent between them, not even a brother or sister.

"Take it or leave it," Ned Maddox said.

It had been easier when her heart was frozen. Then she could have dismissed the demand and moved on. They needed to get off this slow barge and out of the canal while it was still dark. But she found she wanted, more than anything, to step back into his arms. "All right," she said. "We will make arrangements."

"No, now," he said.

"There is no time."

"That's the deal." He stood like a statue in the lantern light. "Otherwise I don't leave the bomb."

So she turned to Xiao, the barge captain, and asked him if he would perform a wedding, very fast. He nodded and grinned, and the pirates cheered. It seemed that everyone had understood the conversation, and had only been waiting for her answer. The two little girls grabbed Jin Lo's hands and asked if they could be in the wedding, too, please.

"It must be *fast!*" she said, over the clamor. "Very fast!"

The captain's wife touched her shoulder and said, "But where is your mother?"

Jin Lo shook her head.

"Then I will stand for you," the captain's wife said.

The pirates' clerk produced the *Tung Shing* to see if Jin Lo's and Ned Maddox's stars aligned. He paged through the book beneath a lantern, checking their birthdates, but neither of them knew what time they had been born. While the clerk studied the almanac, the captain's wife unbraided Jin Lo's hair and took a brush to it. Jin Lo tried to protest, but Mrs. Xiao was unstoppable. She tugged Jin Lo's hair swiftly into tight new braids and coiled them high on her head. Finally the clerk announced that today was an auspicious day for marriage, and the outcome would surely be favorable.

A red silk scarf from the Xiaos' juggling props was draped over Jin Lo's face, that she might not see anything unlucky, and the little girls, giggling, tied two more scarves together as a sash around Ned's waist. The pirates produced a package of first-quality oolong for the tea ceremony, and the kettle was set to boil again.

Commander Hayes stood on the groom's side, since he was a naval officer. Jin Lo bowed and served him a cup of tea, then bowed and served some to Xiao and his wife. She felt vaguely ridiculous, but the pirates all beamed at her with approval, and Commander Hayes seemed very moved.

Xiao asked her to bow to her ancestors and her elders, and Jin Lo did, thinking of her father and mother and baby brother. She thought how happy they would have been to attend her wedding, even if she was surrounded by strangers and wearing a red juggling scarf on her head. Her eyes filled, and she was glad no one could see her behind the veil.

Then Xiao asked the bride and groom to bow to each other.

"Can I take that thing off your head now?" Ned whispered. "If you're giving me a cup of tea, I want to look you in the eye."

She nodded, blinking the tears away, and he lifted the silk from her face, and let it drape over her coiled braids. She offered him the ceremonial tea.

"It's not your special blend?" he said.

"No," she said. "But it's probably stolen."

"And I have to drink it?"

"It's our tradition."

His eyes never left her face as he drained the cup.

Next it was Ned Maddox's turn to offer the tea to Jin Lo. She took it and hesitated. Was she really going to do this? To put her heart in this man's hands? She looked into the cup for a sign, but saw only the brown liquid and the rising steam. She drank it down. It was smoky and strong.

Xiao, looking very pleased, pronounced them married. Ned Maddox kissed Jin Lo, and held her tightly. He said, into her hair, "That's from my tradition, Mrs. Maddox."

The pirates cheered.

The scarf slipped to the deck and Ming picked it up, delighted. "Can I be the next pirate queen?" she asked. "If you're leaving?"

"You'll have to ask your parents," Jin Lo said.

Commander Hayes stepped forward and asked if he could stay with the Xiaos. He could help with the circus, and with the running of the barge. Xiao had arthritis in his hands and could use help hauling on ropes.

"You tried to kill all of these people," Jin Lo said.

"I was not myself," Hayes said. "I was deranged by grief."

Jin Lo looked at him closely. He seemed humbled,

sorrowful but calm. She no longer felt the apothecary's presence in her mind, pushing her in one direction or another. But she had a strong sense of her own that Hayes would cause no more trouble.

"Mao's army will arrest you as a spy if they find you," Ned Maddox told Hayes.

"They won't find me," the commander said. "I give you my word."

Ned sighed. "If I'm not returning the shell, I guess it doesn't matter if I return the thief."

Jin Lo gathered her supplies, which had been ransacked and diminished by Danby, who must be one sick penguin right now—if he was still alive, and still a penguin. Ned Maddox gave the pirates his faster boat in exchange for theirs, with the uranium in its hold. And Jin Lo and Ned Maddox climbed aboard.

Commander Hayes stood with the little girls at the rail of the circus barge. Jin Lo thought that Ming would not make a terrible pirate queen. The little girls, who should have been in bed hours ago, waved good-bye.

It had been a long night, and dawn would come soon. But Jin Lo had been searching for the uranium too long not to see it now. She went to the pirates' hold and shone a flashlight on the barrels.

"Is this your idea of a honeymoon?" Ned Maddox asked.

She smiled at him over the spooky beam of light. "Help me open one," she said.

Ned Maddox found a crowbar and they pried off a lid.

There was a white crust on top of the uranium: some kind of precipitate. She reached out to touch it, but Ned caught her wrist.

"Let's be a little careful here," he said.

With the end of the crowbar, she scraped a little of the white crust away. It was not very thick, and it fell to the side like coarse salt. The orange-yellow color of the uranium was rich beneath it. With a piece of paper she scooped up some of the coarse crystals, then folded the paper around them before sealing up the barrel. If she could analyze them, she could discover exactly what the apothecary had done.

They went back up on deck, away from the poisonous barrels and into the clear air. It was still dark, and Jin Lo stood with Ned Maddox at the wheel, in the light wind of their forward movement. Was this more like a honeymoon? It was better than being down in the stuffy hold, at least.

"The pirates said you turned Danby into a *penguin*," Ned Maddox said. "Is that true?"

"Not exactly."

"But sort of?"

"He stole the avian elixir," she said. "He hoped to fly."

"Can you do that?"

"I cannot be a penguin."

"What can you be?"

"A falcon," she said.

Ned Maddox began to laugh. His eyes crinkled with amusement. "Of course," he said. "Because you're fierce and ruthless."

"I am not ruthless."

"No, you just incited a mutiny against a pirate queen who's been at sea since before you were born. And you drugged me when you thought I would disagree with you."

"When I *knew* you disagreed with me," she said.

He looked up at the dark sky, the scattered stars. "It must be spectacular, to fly."

"A man once became a cormorant," she said. "He was caught by a fisherman, who sent him to catch fish with a metal ring around his neck to keep him from eating them. When the elixir wore off, and he became a man again, he strangled." She could feel the ring tightening around her throat, just telling the story. "There are many dangers, for birds. It is no game."

"What do you think I would become?" he asked.

"A peacock," she said. "You are so proud, and your eyes are that color."

"That's a joke, right?"

"I have heard that jokes are useful," she said.

"Not if they aren't funny."

She yawned and shivered. "Okay, I think you will be a hummingbird."

"Come on."

"Hummingbirds have the largest hearts," she said.

"They have tiny hearts."

"Not for their size."

Ned Maddox put his arms around her, and his arms were strong and warm. "I'm asking you a serious question, Mrs. Maddox."

"It is not for me to guess," she said. "You will be what you are."

With her head against his chest, she could hear his large heart beating slowly in her ear. In the other ear she heard the canal water churning against the bow.

CHAPTER 60

Book Thieves

D oyle watched everyone disappear, as if he'd invented a new magic trick. First Janie vanished in the ambulance. Then Benjamin and the count went off in a taxi, and the Italian brat, Primo, ran in the other direction with the book.

Abracadabra. Now you see them, now you don't.

But it was Doyle who was invisible. Because no one on earth cared if he lived or died. He was so irrelevant to their hopes and plans that they simply forgot he was there. Even the wary street kid, taking the bag, failed to register Doyle as a witness to his theft.

Doyle stood alone on the sidewalk, wondering if Janie would die. Then he wondered if another car would jump the curb and take him out. To be safe, he went back inside Vili's empty flat.

"Hello, ghosties?" he called, but he felt no angry dead thoughts in the room.

He lay down on the couch. It was a good couch, long enough that he could stretch out his whole length. He folded his hands on his chest, but every time he closed his eyes he saw Janie sailing through the air, and his eyes flew open again.

He hoped she wouldn't die. He sat up on his elbows. Maybe he should go to the hospital, where he could tell Benjamin what the doctors were really thinking, and not saying. But what if it was something Benjamin didn't want to know? He lay back down again.

He took a quick inventory of people who might care what happened to him. Not his brother, who was sick of him, or his brother's wife, who thought Doyle was a bad influence on her family. Possibly the twins, who were still young enough to be warmhearted and forgiving. What about his old assistant, April? She might once have cared. No one had ever matched April at being sawed in half. She was a genius at the comic, surprised look. But he hadn't treated her well, and she had left. Sweet April, with her soft brown eyes.

He must have drifted off, finally, because a loud knock at the door took him by surprise. He staggered up from the couch and opened the door to see yet another kid, about Janie and Benjamin's age. Floppy hair, good cheekbones, not tall. Where did these kids keep coming from?

"I'm Pip," the boy said. "Benjamin's father's book is missing."

"I know."

"What happened to it?"

"Primo took it," Doyle said. He started to close the door.

Pip put a foot out to stop it. "You have to help me get it back."

"No, I don't."

"Janie almost died, and you're *napping?*" Pip said. "Aren't you their friend?"

Doyle narrowed his eyes at the kid to see where *he* had been all this time. "I might ask the same of you—running lines with the pretty blonde. Preparing for your close-up."

Pip flushed. "I didn't know what had happened! I came running as soon as I knew!"

Doyle pushed the door closed again, but it stuck against the kid's shoe. "Your foot's in the way," he said.

"Don't you care about *anyone?*" Pip asked.

"Not really." But Doyle saw Janie flying through the air again in his mind, and flinched. "Is she all right?"

"They took her home from the hospital, and sent me to find you. They said that if the book wasn't here, then you were the only one who could find it."

"Oh, *now* they need me," Doyle said. He heard the petulance in his own voice. He thought, suddenly, of choosing baseball teams on the playground, getting picked last because he couldn't hit the ball, even though he could catch anything. The humiliation of standing there on the field when everyone else had been chosen.

Pip must have heard the sulkiness in his voice, because now he eyed him. "I used to feel left out by Janie and Benjamin," he said. "Like you do."

Doyle stiffened. "I don't feel left out. They're children."

"We're all friends, of course," Pip went on. "But they're in love. And they've got this important responsibility, the book and all. So it's always going to be Janie-and-Benjamin and then—whoever. The sidekick."

"I am no one's *sidekick*."

"You keep telling yourself that, mister."

"I'm not!"

"We both are, to them," Pip said. "But we have our own stories, too, where we're the main players, you know? So how about you start acting like a hero, right now, and not like a rat?"

Doyle blinked. "A rat?"

"Janie and Benjamin have a lot of faith in you," Pip said. "They say you can do real magic."

"Well," Doyle said, tucking in his rumpled shirtfront.

"They say you can move stuff. And read minds."

Doyle shrugged. That was supposed to be a secret. But he could do a few things.

"So where did Primo take the book?" Pip asked.

"To Sal Rocco," Doyle said. "The mob boss."

"And do you know where Sal might be?"

"Oh, you're on a first-name basis now?" Doyle asked. But his sarcasm sounded pathetic, even to him.

"The book could be halfway to Naples by now," Pip said. "While you pretend you don't want to help me."

Doyle sighed. "Let me get my coat."

They climbed into a taxi, and wound through the narrow streets. Doyle looked out the window and concentrated on getting a signal: anyone thinking about the big leather-bound book. If he could find *two* people thinking about it, that would be even better. He could start to triangulate.

"Why would Primo steal it?" Pip asked.

"Because he knows that foreigners always leave Rome," Doyle said. "While Salvatore Rocco will stay here. The kid felt *left out*, as you put it. And for him, that means going back to a miserable orphanage. Which he wisely wants to avoid."

Pip nodded, and Doyle received a flood of images and sensations from Pip's mind: an empty belly, a stinging slap to the head, chilblains from the cold. Beneath the tweed coat and the posh haircut and the actor's accent, there was an undersized London pickpocket here, who knew something about hunger and want.

"Are you getting anything?" Pip asked.

"Not with you thinking so much," Doyle said. "Your miserable childhood is distracting."

"I don't know how to stop."

"Concentrate on the sky," Doyle said. "How blue it is. How soft the clouds. That will fade nicely into the background."

"Can't I help you?"

"I just told you how."

Pip sighed, gazed out the window, and filled his mind with blueness and clouds.

"Perfect," Doyle said. "Just like that."

They had crossed the river into the neighborhood of Trastevere. Doyle was hoping Pip had cash for the taxi, if they were going to drive around like this all day. But then he got a brief flash of the leather cover, the embossed circle inside the star.

"Slow down," he said to the driver, and he looked up at the buildings around him. "Is there a hotel near here?"

The driver turned down a side street, toward a red awning. Doyle closed his eyes and focused. He could see flashes of the book in people's minds, but he also thought he could feel the book itself, as an object, in the way he could feel the oranges when he summoned them across the room. The pull was strong in a seven-hundred-year-old book, because it had been held by so many human hands. It had been coveted and treasured.

Pip had started *thinking* again, wondering how to get into the hotel room, and how many bodyguards Sal Rocco might have.

"Stop that!" Doyle said.

"Sorry."

"We can't overpower them," Doyle said. "And we can't steal the book. You have to talk to Rocco, and get the book back."

"*Talk* to him?"

"You're a good talker," Doyle said. "You got me here. You'll think of something."

Pip frowned. "What about the kid?" he asked.

"What about the kid?"

"If he doesn't do this favor for Sal Rocco, then he goes to the orphanage?"

Doyle sighed. "Our mission is to get the book. Not rescue the kid."

Pip looked at him for a long moment, his mind opaque. "All right," he said, and he opened the cab door and climbed out, straightening his jacket and shooting his cuffs in a way he must have seen someone do in a film.

Doyle walked the hallways of the hotel until he found the room where the signal from the book was strongest. Pip rapped smartly on the door.

After a long moment, the enormous Gianni answered. Doyle was inordinately happy to see the great slab of the giant's face, and to feel the blessed silence of his mind.

"Gianni!" he said.

"I need to talk to Rocco," Pip said. "I have a business proposition for him."

The giant closed the door in their faces.

Pip blew all his breath out. "Great," he said. "Now what?"

"Just wait," Doyle said. "Think of this as a performance. Yours, theirs. It doesn't happen all at once. It requires patience."

After a long moment, the door opened again and Gianni led them inside. Salvatore Rocco sat in the corner of the room with his fingers tented in front of his face. He was not happy to see them. He was trying to decide what to do with them, in his cold and calculating way.

Pip stepped forward and thrust out a hand to shake.

Rocco looked at the hand as if it were a rat that had just scuttled into the room, but Pip left it there.

"Sal," he said. "I've got a proposal for you."

CHAPTER 61

Intercepted

J in Lo worked in the boat's galley, peering through a microscope the pirates had stolen from a hapless research vessel, trying to reverse what the apothecary had done. She thought she had found a microbe that, with a little encouragement, could be coaxed to eat the uranium, and render it nonradioactive.

They were in the open sea now, trying to steer a course just far enough from shore to avoid Mao's patrol boats, and not so far as to run into water patrolled by the Americans. The waves tossed them so that she had to lash her equipment down.

She heard Ned Maddox call her name, and she ran on deck to see him training his binoculars on the horizon. It was a gray day, unseasonably cold.

"U.S. Navy patrol boat," he said, passing her the binoculars.

She studied the distant boat through them. "I'm not ready," she said.

"Can you make another storm?"

She shook her head. Danby, searching for the avian elixir,

had drunk her storm-seeding solution. "How soon will they reach us?" she asked.

"Depends on if we run or not."

"If we run, they will chase," she said.

"Yes."

"But if we don't run, they will take us."

"Probably. There's a slight chance they'll ignore us."

"I need time," she said.

Ned Maddox made a considering face. "They've got twin screws—double propellers. If we run, we might have an hour or two. If we stay on course and play innocent, and they don't buy it, then we've got maybe twenty minutes."

Jin Lo calculated. She hadn't cultured enough of the bacteria yet to devour all of the uranium. She needed the hour or two. "Okay," she said. "Run."

Ned spun the wheel and the boat responded, heeling over to change course. Jin Lo put a hand out to steady herself as she staggered back to the galley.

In her makeshift lab, she put her eye to the microscope. Beneath it, her bacteria were happily eating the uranium, excreting a harmless, dull orange substance. But how to make the microbes multiply and thrive? She tried not to panic, but to think—or not to think, but to let her mind wander. *The universe is doing its work. We are the vessel through which it flows.*

She rummaged through the little bottles and packets from the herbalist. She didn't have exactly what she needed, but she might be able to improvise.

"They're gaining!" Ned Maddox called from the deck, over the wind.

She wished he wouldn't interrupt. Of course the patrol boat was gaining. Unless it sank or capsized, it was going to gain.

She tapped a few grains of saltpeter into her culture, and then a small amount of sulfur. If the bacteria liked uranium so much, maybe they would like the makings of gunpowder. The bacteria seemed perfectly content with the addition, but they weren't multiplying. An anxious feeling fluttered in her middle, and she willed it down. She added the extract of a variety of nightshade, thinking it might act as an accelerator. But nothing happened.

The boat lurched, and she lunged for her materials, to keep them from flying in all directions. Her hands were cold, and she thought Ned Maddox must be freezing on deck, in the wind and the spray. It was hard to work or to think when you were cold. Warmth was essential to life.

Warmth. Was essential to life.

She turned on a flame on the galley stove, and held the glass dish high over it with tongs, just enough to warm it. Her hands felt less stiff and clumsy already, in the rising heat.

And as she watched, the bacteria began to divide, and divide again. She made another culture, and another, in every available cup and bowl the pirates owned. Then she heated a bucket of water on the galley stove. When it was warm enough, she rinsed each of her dishes into it, making a happy bacterial soup.

She carried the bucket, sloshing, to the hold. She pried open the first barrel of uranium, and poured the warm solution over the top. The microbe-rich liquid reached out like damp fingers to devour the white crust, reversing the apothecary's transformation. They feasted on the orange uranium, changing its valence, leaving it inert and nonradioactive. She opened the next barrel, and the next, and poured the solution over the top of each one. Then she clamped the lids back on, to let her little friends eat.

She ran up to the galley and dismantled her lab, sweeping the remains of her supplies into her bag. When she emerged on deck, the patrol boat was much closer. She could see the tiny shapes of the men on board.

"You should go now," Ned Maddox said.

Jin Lo had spent most of her life alone, but now the prospect of separation from Ned Maddox was painful. They hadn't been apart since she'd washed up on his beach.

"Come with me," she said.

He shook his head. "I can't just go AWOL. I need to resign my commission, and leave the navy in a way that's honorable for me."

"But you left your post," she said. "How will you explain?"

"I'll find a way," he said.

"You won't betray me?"

He shook his head. "Of course not."

"So how will it be honorable, if you lie?"

There was a struggle on his face. "I don't know yet," he said. "I'll meet you in Seoul, at the Chosun Hotel. I'll get there."

Jin Lo nodded, trying to hide the despair she felt.

Ned Maddox turned away, to watch the approaching boat.

She held her bag of supplies at the rail. She couldn't take it with her, and couldn't leave it behind, but it was hard to let it go. She would be diminished without it. She might not find someone like the old herbalist in Xiangshan for a long time. She forced her hand to open, and the bag dropped and disappeared beneath the waves.

She had kept out a small vial, but she couldn't bring herself to drink it. Why was this so difficult? It never had been before.

Ned Maddox caught her around the waist and kissed her, which didn't help. She fit so neatly against his body—her husband. How could she leave him? How would they treat him?

"I can't let you be taken," she said.

"I'll be fine. You have to go."

He dropped his arms and she felt the cold air between them. She uncorked the vial and drank, and Ned Maddox watched her closely.

It didn't take long. She felt her skull lighten, and her bones began to shrink. Her skin grew a layer of feathers, and her mind gained a protective distance from human concerns. Her feet became sharp talons, and her heart became the heart of a predator, hardened and remote.

By the time she lifted off the fishing boat, the ache in her chest was gone. She could see Ned Maddox grow smaller, looking up at her. His eyes were filled with concern, but human eyes were puny, underpowered things, always leaking tears. The patrol boat leaped into focus, every detail clear and sharp. The men on board were very young. One had chicken pox scars on his chin, the other had cut himself shaving. She was not afraid of them.

She could see everything for miles. Nothing sentimental or soft or foolish was left in her. The wind lifted her wings and she soared.

CHAPTER 62

Shooting Script

Benjamin sat beside Janie in a director's chair, watching the filming. The costume designer had found a warm wool shawl for Janie, and she had it wrapped around her shoulders even though it was August. It had been two months since she'd walked out of the hospital, and she was stronger every day, but she was always cold, as if she had caught a chill in the land of the dead. She said the back of her neck got especially cold, and she was always reaching to push away the hair that wasn't there. The hairstylists had cleaned up her haircut and cooed about how chic it was, but sometimes her own parents looked around the set and didn't see her, not recognizing this short-haired girl.

The caterers brought her hot honey and lemon drinks as she sat wrapped in the shawl, and generally doted on her. They knew she had been hit by a car, and they were apologetic on behalf of the notorious drivers of Rome.

"People should stop making such a fuss," Janie said. "It's embarrassing."

"You don't want hot drinks?"

"I do like the hot drinks," she admitted.

As Janie's parents had rewritten the movie, it became clear that it would cost more to shoot than Tony had in the original budget. But that was all right, because the film had a new backer.

Salvatore Rocco had come on board as an executive producer, thanks to Pip, bringing with him an influx of cash. Rocco had his own canvas chair with his name on it, and he sat watching the filming through tented fingers. He'd traded his tailored suit for a cashmere sweater and a silk scarf tied at the neck, to look more like movie people. He still had the look of a coiled snake, with hooded eyes, but most of the time he seemed satisfied with his first film.

His giant bodyguard, Gianni, was given the boom mike to operate. Gianni could hold the long pole so high and so effortlessly that the microphone in its fuzzy cover never crept down into any of the shots. Tony kept asking, "Where has he been all my life?"

Primo stood by the director's side, ready to run messages

or relay demands. He conveyed a sense of great urgency, and people jumped when he called. The actors came straight from their dressing rooms without complaint, and the makeup girls materialized with powder and brushes. The caterers had stuffed Primo with food, and his face had filled out. His head was covered with soft down.

"*Silenzio!*" he shouted now, and everyone on the set went silent. "*Suono,*" Primo said, and Gianni nodded in response. "*Camera,*" Primo said.

"*Velocitá,*" the cameraman said.

Primo clapped a slate in front of the camera and scurried out of the frame.

"*Azione,*" Tony said, and Pip climbed in through the princess's bedroom window, on the set.

Evie, as the princess, turned to see him, looking anxious and beautiful in an embroidered nightgown and a white robe.

Pip had become an actual actor, since his *Robin Hood* days. Evie was beautiful, but everyone agreed that you couldn't take your eyes off Pip. Everything he said rang true, except when you knew his character was lying, and then you wanted him to get away with it.

When the shot was finished, Pip flopped down in the canvas chair next to Benjamin, with an exasperated sigh.

"Evie's supposed to have her hair cut short," he said. "When she's in the hospital with the head injury. And she won't do it, she's pitching a fit."

"Short hair's not so bad," Janie said.

"She says she'll look like a boy," Pip said. "I told her, 'Who cares? It'll grow out again!'" He looked from Benjamin to Janie. "I see from your faces that was the wrong thing to say."

"Tell her she won't look like a boy, and she'll be even more beautiful with short hair," Janie said.

Pip made a face. "You think that'll work?"

"You got Rocco to finance the film," Janie said. "You can get Evie to cut off her hair."

Janie's father leaned forward in his chair and lowered his voice. "I still don't understand how you got Rocco to cough up so much money," he said.

Pip looked to Benjamin, who shrugged. They might as well tell the truth. They had to start sometime.

Pip said quickly, "I just told him I knew that the coppers were after him, and his best friend was dead, so he might be looking for a change."

"But how did you know all that?" Mrs. Scott asked.

Benjamin studied his fingernails.

"Word gets around," Pip said. "I told him I was a thief once, a bloody good one, but I still got myself nabbed sometimes. And there's nothing worse than being locked up. It just kills your soul. So I told him that what saved my life was finding this other thing I wanted to do, making movies. And I thought it could save Rocco, too. It was a real business he could invest in, but it had plenty of risk and danger and excitement just like his current work. I offered to make some introductions. I said I was going to be in a film that had real possibilities—brilliant screenwriters."

Mrs. Scott laughed. "Flatterer."

"But that the script needed some work."

"Oh, here we go," Mr. Scott said.

"And the budget was too low for what these brilliant writers wanted to do."

"So—are we laundering mob money?" Mrs. Scott asked.

"Don't think of it that way," Pip said. "You're making art!"

"The crew all knew who Rocco was," Mrs. Scott said. "I think they're a little afraid of him."

"He's not a bad guy, really," Pip said. "And he got us a permit to film at the Trevi Fountain. He's very connected, and he understands business. It's going to be a good thing all around."

Mr. Scott nodded. "All right," he said. "Go work your magic and get us the haircut."

Pip pushed himself out of his chair and headed off to Evie's dressing room.

Rocco had returned the Pharmacopoeia to Benjamin as part of the deal with Pip, and Benjamin had offered to make Doyle a new filter, but the magician didn't want one. Doyle said he was going to live in such a way that people wouldn't think terrible thoughts about him. It would be an experiment, and the only way to monitor his progress was to know what people were thinking. He was going to consider his ability a gift and not a curse. If it didn't work out, he would take a rain check on that filter. For now, he just wanted to go home.

He bought passage to New York on an Italian ocean liner, the SS *Cristoforo Colombo*, and said he was going to rediscover

America. A sister ship, the *Andrea Doria*, was leaving earlier, but Doyle had a bad feeling about that one. He took a train to Genoa to meet the ship, to set out on his voyage of discovery.

Benjamin and Janie had been back to the Trevi Fountain one warm Roman night, with the streetlights all softened in the foggy air, and the horses leaping, and the pool of water lit from below. They had each tossed a coin in, to make sure they'd come back to the city. Then Benjamin took the little gold death's head from his pocket and rolled it between his fingers.

The charm had set them on their course, and started everything that had happened, when the magician stole it and then dropped it back into Benjamin's hand. It had taken them to Rome, and to the After-room. It was supposed to remind you that you were going to die someday, but Benjamin didn't need to be reminded of that. He threw the little skull into the fountain, and it dropped with a tiny splash into the glowing pool at the horses' feet.

CHAPTER 63

The Brig

B oy, am I happy to see you!" Ned Maddox told the two
officers on the patrol boat, grinning like an idiot.

The squids were nervous and young, and seemed
taken aback by his cheerfulness.

"I didn't know who you were!" Ned said. "Sorry to lead you
on a chase like that. I've been hoping to run into you guys—
I've got this cargo that's a pain in my ass."

So they went together back to the aircraft carrier *Ulysses*,
and Ned turned over the useless uranium, and his debriefing
began.

He was taken to a small office where a bullet-headed intelligence officer named Richardson made careful notes as
they talked. Richardson wanted to know when, exactly, Ned
Maddox was taken prisoner, and why he hadn't sent word to
the navy of his movements, and what the uranium barrels had
to do with the hunt for the missing bomb.

"I found them when I was looking for the bomb," he said.

"Found them how?"

"I ran into these pirates who had them."

"Pirates?"

"Yes, sir."

"And can we contact them?"

"I'm afraid I lost track of them, sir."

"And why didn't you send word?"

"I didn't think it was secure to transmit by radio."

"And where did the pirates get the uranium?"

"From a British subject named Danby. I think he was a spy."

Richardson made a note in his file. "We're aware of Danby," he said. "Where is he now?"

"He went overboard," Ned said. "His mind seemed altered, I think."

"Altered?"

"Yes, sir."

"There were reports of a woman who might know Danby," Richardson said. "A Chinese national. A source puts her in the telegraph office in Hangzhou not long ago."

"Oh?" Ned tried to control his breathing. *Don't sweat. Don't show surprise.*

"We know she sent a telegraph to Rome," Richardson said. "But the ticker tape is missing. Do you think she might be in league with this Danby?"

"I couldn't say, sir."

Richardson eyed him with cold blue eyes. Ned looked steadily back. *Breathe in, breathe out.* He hadn't thought he would have to answer direct questions about Jin Lo.

"So this Danby," Richardson said, after a while. "He had the uranium. But he was after the shell?"

"Yes, sir," Ned said.

"Do you know where it is?"

"I don't," he said, which was more or less true. He had not taken bearings.

Richardson made another note in the file, then closed it and stood up.

Ned thought he'd done as well as he could. He'd kept his story consistent, hadn't betrayed his nervousness, hadn't indicated any knowledge of Jin Lo. But then two burly sailors came into the room, and at a nod from Richardson they transferred him to the brig. So maybe it hadn't gone so well.

The brig had been scrubbed, like everything on a navy ship, but it still retained a faint smell of vomit, from drunken seamen sleeping off binges ashore. The floor was steel, and the cot narrow. The bars on the door formed a grid, with holes about four inches square, just big enough for a man's fist.

The two sailors left Ned there with Richardson.

"I've told you everything I know," Ned said.

"Not about the Chinese girl. Our patrol says they saw a girl on the boat with you, from a distance."

"But they searched the boat," Ned said.

"I think you know something," Richardson said. "I just don't know what it is."

"I only want to get my discharge papers and move on with my life," Ned said.

"Yeah, I'll bet you do," Richardson said. "I'm putting you on a plane to Guam, and then to Hawaii, to face a court-martial."

Court-martial! He had given his life to the navy, and now they were going to put him on trial, and discharge him or lock him away. "I haven't done anything wrong," he said. And in his heart, he believed it was true.

"You left your post without leave," Richardson said. "We'll start with that. And you lost your boat."

"The pirates took it."

"Right. The pirates."

Richardson shut the barred door of Ned's cell with a clank and walked away.

Ned sat alone in the vomit-smelling cell, then untucked his shirt and found the hard glass vial Jin Lo had sewn into the hem. He ripped open the stitches with his teeth, pushed the vial out, and pulled loose the tiny cork. Then he hesitated. If his personality did make him a peacock, or a penguin, then he would be stuck.

But he had a feeling he would become something that flew. He was betting everything on that possibility. He drank the liquid down. It tasted bitter, like tea strained through moss.

At first nothing happened.

But then he started to feel light-headed. His head was shrinking, his skull growing thin and fragile. His skin prickled all over, and then feathers burst out of his arms and his chest as he stared down. His feet grew hard and bony, long talons emerging from his toenails. His hands were replaced by wing tips, and he dropped the vial with a clink to the steel floor of the brig. His shoulders narrowed, but they felt very strong. His body tipped forward, and he found himself much closer to the floor than he had been before. He looked down at his chest, on which light feathers grew, dappled with horizontal black bars.

He held out his wings to see them better, and joy surged in his chest. He was a peregrine falcon. The fastest bird on earth. Jin Lo's mate.

But he was distressingly big.

He considered the grid of bars on his cell, and stuck his beaked head out through one of the holes. Both folded wings wouldn't fit through at once, so he eased his left shoulder through, then scrabbled at the steel floor with his talons to try to push himself forward. He felt claustrophobic, caught in a snare. He remembered Jin Lo's story of the cormorant, enslaved by the fisherman, with a ring around its neck. His falcon's heart began to beat faster.

Calm down, he told himself. Jin Lo had warned him that fear made the stuff wear off more quickly. He got his talons around one of the bars and pushed. He had some leverage now, in spite of the awkward angle. With his left wing nearly free, the right shoulder popped through, painfully. Then the rest of his body followed it.

He was in the passageway, surrounded by the other cells,

all empty. He took three quick steps, talons clicking noisily on the steel floor, then spread his wings, hoping to lift off—

And fell flat on his face.

He remembered his brief stint in pilot training, and how quickly he had washed out. He'd never had the knack for flight. But he wouldn't wash out now. He tried again, and fell again, but his wings caught a little air and he understood how they should move. One more time, he took the three launching steps. And this time he lifted, and sailed two feet off the floor.

Then he was in a new corridor. Left or right? He wasn't sure. He let his bird's brain take over—*sky, air*—and turned left. He heard footsteps coming toward him and pressed himself against the bulkhead to one side. He watched two sailors clomp past him in their heavy, navy-issue boots, which now seemed enormous.

As soon as they were past, he skipped into flight. He

was getting better at the takeoff. He was up a deck, down a passageway, and up another deck before he heard more men coming. This time he perched on an exposed pipe in the ceiling while they passed beneath him. They didn't look up, and he resisted the temptation to let loose a white nitrogen-rich stream on their heads.

Up another deck, and now he could smell fresh air, close by. An alarm sounded—had someone found his cell empty? He turned a corner and saw sunlight ahead, a blinding bright rectangle, some kind of hatch. He aimed himself at it. But just as he reached it, the door slammed shut. He hit the steel plate with a thud, and it knocked him to the ground. The corridor went dark.

He woke to the sound of the alarm again and looked down at his feathered belly, his taloned feet, and remembered: He was a falcon. But he didn't feel fierce or ruthless. His head hurt. He was hungry, and had a vague hankering for the rats he knew were hiding in the shadows. The idea of tearing a rat apart, all fur and bones, turned the part of his stomach that was still human, but was thrilling to his falcon brain. He struggled to his feet and shook his head to clear it. Then he looked up at the sealed door he'd drilled his head into. Freedom was on the other side.

He would have to find another hatchway. He flew back the way he had come, willing himself toward the fresh air, ignoring the pull of the rats on his mind and the blare of the alarm. He banked down a corridor that seemed promising, and flew smack into a young seaman, with another behind him.

The man he'd hit cried out in surprise, and the other threw his jacket over Ned's head. The world grew dark again. He tried to attack with his feet, but the canvas jacket was all around him. He was being carried like a bundle of laundry. His captors' voices were excited, but he couldn't make out what they were saying. Would they tether him on deck as a mascot? He thought of the unlucky cormorant with the ring around its neck. He tried to fight his way free, but was only pinned more tightly.

"A peregrine, sir!" he heard the boy say. "He got stuck on board!"

The voice, resonating inside the boy's ribs, was bright and eager—still a teenager, probably. With quick reflexes.

And then the jacket was off, and the boy hurled Ned from the rail of the ship. The world turned very bright all at once, and the sea came up surprisingly fast. Ned did some ineffectual backward-pedaling with his feet, but some part of his brain also made him spread his wings, and he caught the air just as the wet spray hit him in the face. He rose off the ocean's surface, back up to the level of the carrier's deck.

"Look at that!" cried his rescuer. "Lookit him go!"

Others had gathered at the rail, watching. Ned spotted Richardson's wind-reddened cheeks, his bullet head tilted up to stare. Would he put it all together? Ned found that his falcon's brain didn't care.

"Wouldn't it be something to *fly?*" the kid said. "To see *everything?*"

And it was. It was *something*. Ned flew higher and higher, up over the carrier, over the whole fleet. The wind was in his feathers, the ocean vast and blue below. So he'd washed out of pilot training—so what? *This* was the way to fly. He circled over the carrier, a victory lap, and then caught a thermal air current, warm and lifting, and headed north.

CHAPTER 64

A Screening

J anie's parents held an advance screening of their movie at the Michigan Theater in Ann Arbor. A red carpet was rolled out beneath the lights of the marquee, and the Scotts invited their colleagues and students from the university to a black-tie reception in the lobby. The Doyle twins arrived, Nat in his white tuxedo and Valentina in the robin's-egg blue dress she'd worn to the dance, with their parents in tow.

Janie was wearing her yellow dress from the dance, and it was disorienting to be in the clothes they'd all worn months ago, before Benjamin told her that he'd contacted his father. Clothes from another life. She looked around for her parents—her mother would want to see the Doyles—and saw them on the other side of the lobby.

"Don't worry, we'll go say hello," Mrs. Doyle said, taking her husband's arm and heading off.

Janie felt shy with the twins, their friendship not yet re-established.

"Our uncle said he saw you in Rome," Valentina said.

Janie had been through so much with the magician, but didn't know what to say about it. And she wished she didn't feel so awkward and they could just pick up where they'd been before. "He did," she said.

"That's so weird," Valentina said.

"It was," Janie agreed.

"When are you coming back to school?" Nat asked.

"Soon, I hope," Benjamin said. And he sounded like he meant it.

"Your parents don't want to move to Hollywood?" Valentina asked.

Janie shook her head. "They miss their students. They want to finish out their teaching contract, and they say they'll write their next project here."

"This kid has been trying to get in touch with you," Nat said. "He has a science team in Ohio and he's looking for other schools to have meetings and competitions with. He wondered if we have a science team. His name is Sergei Shiskin."

"Sergei!" Janie said, remembering the lonely Russian boy from her school in London, and how desperately he had wanted friends.

"Do you know him?" Valentina asked.

"We do," Janie said. Sergei's father, a Soviet diplomat, had defected to the United States, and the last she'd heard, they were living in Florida. "He's really nice."

"So would you join a science team?" Nat asked.

"If you guys were doing it," Benjamin said.

"We'll get it started," Valentina said.

Everything was just starting to feel normal again, when Doyle the Magnificent came up the red carpet in his full magician's tails and top hat. A woman in turquoise sequins like a sparkling mermaid walked beside him. "May I present my lovely assistant, April," Doyle said, sweeping off the hat.

"I've never been to a movie premiere," April said, glittering in the lights and gazing around the lobby.

"That's the only reason she took me back," Doyle said. "But you have to start somewhere, right?"

"April's *so* good at getting sawed in half," Valentina said. "Way better than I was."

"I'm not sure that's a compliment," April said with a sweet smile. "May you develop other skills."

"How was the Atlantic crossing?" Benjamin asked Doyle.

"Excellent!" Doyle said. "I mean—terrible. Rough seas. I was seasick the whole time, just turned myself inside out. I had a steward who brought me consommé every day and was full of self-righteous advice. Wouldn't let me order a brandy. I loathed him. But by the time I staggered off the ship, I hadn't had a drink in a week. The worst of the cravings were over and I felt awfully good. So I kept it up, I stopped drinking. I might be the only person ever to dry out on an ocean liner. And you'd be surprised how much friendlier people have become. So the experiment is going well!"

"That's funny," Benjamin said. "I thought people liked their kids' magicians to reek of alcohol."

Doyle raised an eyebrow. "Don't ruin my mood," he said. "Things are good!"

Benjamin laughed, and there was a lightness and happiness in his laugh that made Janie's heart lift.

A very short old man in a tuxedo walked up the red carpet, with a tall young woman in a long purple gown on his arm.

Doyle saw them and his eyes widened. "Joey Rocco is here?" he said.

"Sal asked if we would invite him," Benjamin said. "As a favor."

Janie studied the little man. So that was Joey the Haberdasher. He didn't look anything like his cold-blooded cousin—he looked like an ancient tailor.

"I'm going to pay my respects," Doyle said. "I want to tell him no hard feelings, and all that."

"Don't let him invite you to a poker game," Benjamin said.

"Of course not!" Doyle said, as he took April's arm. "I'm reformed!"

"He really is a different person now," Valentina said, when they were gone.

"Does he still do the trick where he steals stuff?" Janie asked.

"Yes, but it's not so mean," Valentina said. "He might take a watch that needs winding, but he doesn't make fun of everyone."

Pip and Evie were posing for a photographer from the *Detroit Free Press*. The Italian papers, promoting the movie, had been full of the stars' fairy-tale romance, and Evie wore a white silk dress with a gauzy, layered skirt, calculated to suggest princesses and weddings. Her short hair was very fetching: platinum curls around her ears.

In real life, Pip and Evie had started to fight before the shooting wrapped, and now they weren't talking to each other. They spoke only through Janie: "Tell Pip not to wear that awful aftershave, I can't stand the smell a minute longer." "Please tell Evie to stop flirting with the reporters interviewing us, it's embarrassing."

"Are those the movie stars?" Nat asked.

"Come on, we'll introduce you," Janie said, and she took Valentina by the hand to weave through the crush of the crowd. Pip was talking to a reporter in a pink trenchcoat, and he leaned close to hear the woman's questions over the noise of the crowd, with an attentive and respectful look on his face.

"He's really cute," Valentina whispered.

"You think so?" Janie said.

Valentina nodded, watching Pip.

"It's funny," Janie said. "He was just this infuriating kid, the first time I met him. And then he became my friend, and now he's grown up and handsome and kind of famous. I can't get used to it. He's *amazing* in the movie, wait'll you see him."

Pip wore his thoughtful, talking-to-the-press expression as he turned from the reporter. But then he saw Janie and Benjamin waiting, and their friends. His smile spread across his face like sunshine, and it was Valentina who got the full dazzling effect.

CHAPTER 65

A Letter

The Los Angeles premiere felt like an anticlimax, after Ann Arbor. Janie's yellow dress came out of the suitcase looking like a wilted daffodil, but there was no time to find anything else. She had seen the movie too many times to be excited about sitting through it again. She was freezing, as usual, and Benjamin had given her his jacket to wear around her shoulders. They were standing in a corner of the crowded lobby, Benjamin gazing into the distance with his hands in his pockets, when a couple slipped in late, through a back door.

Jin Lo wore a close-fitting Chinese cheongsam, bright green, and her long black hair hung loose and shining. She outshone every actress who had come down the red carpet. A camera flash went off, but Jin Lo had already turned her back, showing the camera only a silken curtain of hair. The man behind her had ducked his chin, hiding his face.

Janie couldn't stop herself, she shrugged off Benjamin's jacket and ran over and hugged Jin Lo. "You came!" she said.

"I forgot about cameras," Jin Lo said, wincing at a distant flash.

"That dress is going to attract them," Benjamin said.

Jin Lo flushed. "We were trying to blend in. Ned said I had to dress up."

Benjamin turned to Ned. "So she does what you say?"

"Almost never," Ned said, smiling easily.

"We didn't meet properly before," Janie said, putting out her hand. "I'm Janie, and this is Benjamin."

"My husband, Ned Maddox," Jin Lo said.

"Husband!" Janie said.

"Congratulations," Benjamin said, shaking his hand.

Jin Lo flushed deeper.

Ned Maddox was tan against his white shirt collar, and his eyes were blue-green. "I've heard a lot about you two," he said.

"That we're a pain in the neck, always doing things wrong?" Benjamin asked.

"No, that you're the hope for the future—something like that."

"She *said* that?" Benjamin said.

"Not in so many words."

Ned looked kind, and Janie was glad of that. She hoped Jin Lo would be kind to him, too, and not too impatient.

A green silk bag hung from Jin Lo's arm, and she took out a small package wrapped in brown paper and handed it to Janie. "Open it only in the dark," she said.

Janie nodded and clutched the package tight.

Jin Lo turned away from another photographer's flash. "Will the film start soon?"

"Let's go inside," Benjamin said. "There aren't any cameras in there."

There were so many things Janie wanted to ask that they tumbled over each other in her mind. "Where's the uranium?" she whispered as they walked into the theater.

"The U.S. Navy has it, but it is harmless now," Jin Lo said.

Ushers were directing them down toward the front rows. "And Danby?"

"He became a penguin," Jin Lo said.

"A *penguin!*"

"He escaped in the water," Jin Lo said. "I don't know if he survived."

Janie imagined a dark shadow looming up from the ocean's depths. A frantic paddling of feet and flippers. A shark's white teeth. They slid into their seats.

Pip and Evie came into the theater, clearly furious with each other, but Pip broke into a glorious smile when he saw Jin Lo. He kissed her hello and shook Ned's hand. Evie, whose now-famous pixie haircut had been discussed in magazines and requested endlessly in salons, flounced off to her seat. Evie had turned into a *real pill*, as Janie's mother would say.

But Pip had taken Valentina Doyle's address, and Janie had high hopes. When the two of them met, Janie had felt an odd sense of the future stretching out ahead, almost visible in the distance.

The little brown paper package rested on her lap, and she wondered what was inside it. It was nerve-racking to have Jin Lo here. The police officer standing near the emergency exit seemed to stare at them a little too long, but that could have been because of the green dress.

The lights went down, and the heavy red curtain parted. Janie knew the movie by heart and kept her attention on Jin Lo and Ned Maddox beside her—they were holding hands!—but still she missed the moment when they slipped out. When the lights came up, she turned to see what Jin Lo had thought, and they were gone.

The applause after the movie was thunderous, and Janie's parents were mobbed. It wasn't until Janie was squeezed between Benjamin and her father in a chauffeured car on the way to the hotel that her mother turned from the front seat and asked, "Who were those people you were sitting with?"

"What people?" Janie asked.

"That fabulous-looking couple," her mother said. "The girl looked Chinese."

Janie shook her head, feigning confusion.

"Green geisha dress," her father prompted.

"It was a cheongsam," Janie said, before she could stop herself. "Geishas are Japanese."

Benjamin elbowed her from one side, and her father grinned.

"Gotcha," her father said. "You *do* know who we're talking about."

"Are they actors?" her mother asked.

"Sort of," Janie said.

"Help us out, here, Figment," her father said. "She's hiding something."

Benjamin laughed. "Maybe, but you won't get it out of her."

"I wonder who their agents are," her mother said, settling back against the front seat in her silk wrap. Janie could see her parents beginning to imagine a movie starring Jin Lo and Ned Maddox. Janie settled back, too, close against Benjamin's side, and let them imagine it. They wouldn't be able to track down the Chinese actress and her date, and something else would distract them in the meantime.

Back in Michigan, Janie opened the little package in her bedroom's dark closet, and felt an unspooled roll of slick film inside. As soon as her fingers touched it, she understood: It would have been exposed if someone had taken the package and opened it in the light.

She got the keys to the photography lab, and after school, when no one was around, she and Benjamin developed the film in the darkroom and hung it up to dry. Then they made prints, sinking the paper in the trays of chemicals to develop and fix them.

When Janie needed a pair of tongs from across the darkroom, she held up her hand and the tongs slapped satisfyingly into her palm. She had to remember not to move things with her mind when anyone except Benjamin was watching. The other day she'd been reading at the kitchen counter and wanted an apple from the fruit bowl. A moment later it was in her hand, before she'd realized she'd summoned it.

In the low red light, they saw that some of the photographs Jin Lo had sent were maps and overhead views of buildings. One was a list of names. A few were blurry images of faces, taken from a distance. There was a mailing address for Jin Lo in Seoul, with instructions on how to code letters.

There was also a three-page letter. It wasn't in code, having been put into Janie's hand on the unprotected film. It was written in neat cursive on lined paper. Janie switched on a lamp, and she and Benjamin read the letter in the locked darkroom:

Dear friends,

I wanted to tell you some things, because we might not see each other again for a long time.

I have sent you what information I have about the North Korean nuclear program. Please keep it safe. China, too, will have nuclear capabilities soon. Vili will continue tracking the Soviet project. He believes he can recruit a promising physicist there. There are also France and Pakistan to consider, and of course England and its Commonwealth.

The two of you are uniquely positioned to grow up with the program in the United States, to enter its ranks as the scientists you will surely become. Even if war does not break out, the possibility for accidents to occur is great. Human error is inevitable, and you can help protect against it.

Such a course may require lies and deception, and lies erode our sense of self. Dishonesty can become a habit of mind. It will help that you have each other, someone with whom you can be truthful.

I am putting all of this in a letter, in spite of the risk of discovery, because I want you to have time to think and consider. If I asked you face-to-face, you might simply agree, out of friendship or a sense of duty, and then you would feel an obligation. Ned says that I fail to consider other people's wishes, when I think that I am right. (He is helping me with my English spelling here, so that I do not embarrass myself.)

I do not wish to sway your decisions. You may choose to lead a less dangerous life. You might find some other vocation that calls to you.

You have a gift for this work, but that does not mean that you have a calling. You might owe your loyalty or your love to your friends, but you do not owe them your talent. You have to determine if this work is the thing you want most, or only something

that was forced upon you by an accident of birth,
or an accident of circumstance.

 You are still very young. And you may each make
separate decisions, when the time comes. You must
destroy this letter now, but I hope you will keep these
questions in mind. And we will remain in contact.

Your friend,
Jin Lo

Janie looked up when she finished reading, and again she had that odd feeling of the future as a visible plane, stretching out in front of her, ready to be filled with people and events. The sharp smell of the developing chemicals was in her nose, and she knew she would always associate the smell of a darkroom with this moment.

Benjamin stood over the counter, reading the last of Jin Lo's words. "What do you think?" he asked.

"About which part?"

"Well, would you want to be a nuclear physicist?"

"I don't think it's that specific," she said. "I think I could still be a chemist, like Jin Lo. It's just about trying to keep people safe."

"She says we don't have to decide yet," Benjamin said, stacking the pages of the letter and lining up the corners. "There's still time."

Janie had become better at deciphering Benjamin's

expressions and moods than she used to be, even though mind-reading skills hadn't come along with the telekinesis. Right now, for example, he was afraid to hear her reply, afraid she might not join him in what was, without question, his destiny.

"I've already made my decision," she said.

Benjamin's face was uncertain, his eyes anxious, the light revealing those copper flecks that she loved. "About which part?" he asked.

"About everything important," she said.

TURN THE PAGE FOR A PEEK AT THE
START OF JANIE AND BENJAMIN'S
ADVENTURES IN *THE APOTHECARY*

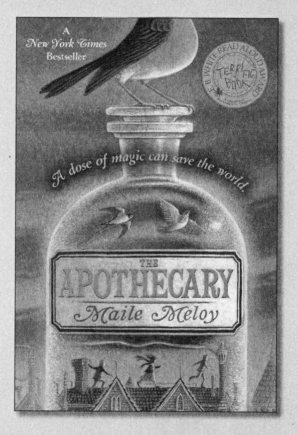

"Think of a cross between Harry Potter and Nancy
Drew…The magic of this book is dazzling."
—*New York Journal of Books*

CHAPTER 1

Followed

I was seven and living in Los Angeles when Japan surrendered at the end of World War II, and my first vivid memories are of how happy and excited everyone was. My parents took me to a parade on Fairfax Avenue, where my father hoisted me onto his shoulders and sailors kissed girls in the streets. In school we made little paper flags to wave and learned that an evil force—*two* evil forces—had been defeated. We weren't going to have wars anymore.

Some of my parents' friends said it wasn't true that we had ended war for all time.

"People said that about the *last* war," they said, sitting on our back patio, surrounded by tall green hedges, drinking wine or lemonade, which is how I remember all of my parents' friends from that time: the women with their hair up in French twists, the men with their ties undone, on the back patio with a drink in hand. "And look where we are."

Others said that such terrible things had happened that the world would never be the same again. But my parents gave those friends hard looks when they knew I was listening.

My father said gasoline wasn't going to be rationed anymore, and we could drive to Kings Canyon, which I imagined was populated with kings, to see the giant trees. My second-grade teacher said we would get real butter again, not white oleomargarine with the yellow color capsule you could add to it. I didn't remember real butter, and I liked the white oleo on toast with sprinkled sugar (my mother never added the yellow coloring because she hated fakery of all kinds), but I did believe that life was going to be better. We would have real butter, whatever that was like, and I might get a baby sister out of the deal. I would name her Lulu. The war was over and the bad guys had lost. A golden era had begun.

For a while, it actually seemed true. I never got a baby sister, but I had the smartest, funniest parents I knew, and they had friends who were almost as smart and funny. They were a writing team, Marjorie and Davis Scott, and they had started in radio and worked together on television shows, first on *Fireside Theater*, then on *I Love Lucy*. They had story retreats in Santa Barbara, and the other writers' kids and I would run through the avocado fields, playing elaborate games of tag and kick-the-can. We would gather avocados that fell from the trees, and eat fat, green slices with salt right out of the shell. We swam in the ocean and played in the waves, and lay in the sand with the sun on our skin.

In my parents' front yard, there was an orange tree, with blossoms that made people on the street stop and look around to see what smelled so sweet. I used to pick myself an orange when I came home from school and eat it over the sink to catch the juice. In school we read a poem with the line "Bliss was it in that dawn to be alive, / But to be young was very heaven!" It was supposed to be about the French Revolution, but I thought it was about my life.

But that was before I started being followed.

First the whole world changed. Another war started in Korea, against the Chinese, who had been our allies in the last war. The Russians, who had also been our allies, had the atomic bomb and seemed inclined to use it against us. The Communist threat was supposed to be everywhere, though my parents thought it was exaggerated.

In school, at Hollywood High, we watched a safety film in which a cheerful cartoon turtle named Bert explained that when a nuclear bomb came, we should get under our desks and put our heads between our knees. It had a little song that went like this:

There was a turtle by the name of Bert
And Bert the turtle was very alert

When danger threatened him, he never got hurt
He knew just what to do!
He'd duck—and cover
Duck—and cover!
He did what we all must learn to do
You—and you—and you—and you—
Duck—and cover!

Our teacher, Miss Stevens, who had been born deep in the last century and wore her white hair coiled up like a ghost's pastry on the back of her head, would lead us in a bomb drill. "Here goes the flash," she'd say. "Everyone under the desks!" And under we'd go—as if our wooden school desks full of books and pencils were going to protect us from an atomic bomb.

The important thing, the films emphasized, was not to panic. So instead, everyone maintained a constant low-grade anxiety. I was only in the ninth grade and I might have managed to shrug off the worry, except that I'd started to think that someone was watching me.

At first, it was just a feeling. I'd get it walking home: that weird sensation that comes when someone's eyes are on you. It was February in Los Angeles, and it was brisk and cool but not cold. The tall palm trees by the school steps were as green as ever.

On the way home I practiced walking like Katharine Hepburn, striding along with my shoulders back. I wore trousers whenever I could, and my favorites were bright green sailor pants, with four big buttons and flared legs. They were worthy of Hepburn as the cuffs swished along. She was my favorite movie star, and I thought if I could walk like her, then I could feel and *be* like her, so sure and confident, tossing her head and snapping out a witty retort. But I didn't want anyone to see me practicing my Hepburn walk, so at first the sensation of being watched only made me embarrassed. When I looked over my shoulder and saw nothing but the ordinary traffic on Highland Avenue, I hugged my books, rounded my shoulders, and walked home like an ordinary fourteen-year-old girl.

Then there was a day when I had the watched feeling, and looked back and saw a black sedan cruising more slowly than the rest of the traffic. I could have sworn it was driving at exactly the speed I was walking. I sped up, thinking that Kate Hepburn wouldn't be afraid, and the car seemed to speed up, too. Panic rose in my chest. I turned down an alley, and the car didn't follow, so I hurried along the side of the buildings, past the trash cans. When I got onto Selma Avenue, which was quiet and tree-lined, there was a man outside a house pruning his roses, but no cars.

My heart was pounding and I made myself breathe slowly. I nodded to the man with the roses and kept walking down Selma. I told myself it was silly to be afraid: No one was following me. They had no reason to follow me. I tossed my hair, wishing it would move in one glossy, curvy mass, and then the black sedan came around the corner ahead and cruised slowly toward me. I felt a cold flush, as if ice water had been pumped through my veins.

I looked back to the rose man, but he had gone inside his house. I gripped my books to keep my hands from shaking, and I kept walking as the black car drove toward me, ridiculously slowly. As it passed, I kept my chin very high and slid a glance sideways. In the car were two men in dark suits. The one closest to me, in the passenger seat, had hair so short he looked like a soldier, and he was watching me. There were two dark, brimmed hats on the backseat. I didn't know any man who wore a hat.

I kept walking, and the black car stopped and idled at the curb. I turned on Vista, my own street, and when I thought I was out of sight, I ran for the house, fumbling for my key. My parents were at work and wouldn't be home yet. I dropped the key and picked it up off the sidewalk as the black sedan turned onto Vista, and then I got inside and slammed the door and slid the chain.

"Hello?" I called to the empty house, just in case. No one answered.

I dropped my books and ran to the back door, which led out to the patio, and I made sure the door was locked. Sometimes we were careless about that door because it led to the hedged-in garden, not to the street, but the bolt was thrown, so the house had been locked all day. I looked out the front window and saw the sedan parked by the curb at the end of the block, waiting. I closed the curtains and turned on the lights in the kitchen, my hands still shaking. The kitchen was the room where I felt safest, because it was where I sat every night with my parents, doing homework while they cooked, listening to them talk.

I told myself it was fine, it was probably in my mind. It was my imagination taking over. I made myself a peanut butter and honey sandwich and started doing my algebra homework. Each problem was like a puzzle, and it helped take my mind off the men who might or might not be sitting in their black car on the corner of our street, behind the curtains I was determined not to open.

At six o'clock, I was deep in a hunt for the value of x when I heard the door open and hit the end of the chain hard. My heart started to race again. I'd managed to pretend that the men weren't really after me, but here they were, breaking in.

"What *is* this?" a man's angry voice said.

Then I realized the voice was more annoyed than angry, and then I realized it was my father's. "Janie?" he called, more alarmed now than annoyed. "Are you here? What's going on?"

☤

We walked that night to Musso and Frank's, which was my favorite restaurant, but it didn't feel like a treat. My parents tried to pretend everything was just fine, but we took back alleys, and they watched the corners at every street. My father walked so fast that my mother and I had to walk double-time just to keep up.

We took a booth, and I ordered the thin pancakes called flannel cakes for dinner. I wanted my parents to object and make me order chicken and vegetables—I wanted things to be normal—but they didn't even notice.

"So who *are* those men in the car?" I asked.

My mother sighed. "They're U.S. marshals," she said. "From Washington. The government."

That didn't make any sense. "What do they want?"

"We've been wanting to tell you, Janie," she said. She always got right to the point, but now she was dancing around whatever she was trying to say. "We have news, and we think it's good news. We're—well, we're thinking we'll all move to London."

I stared at her.

"It will be an adventure," she said.

I looked at my father. "What did you do?" I asked.

"Nothing!" he said, too loudly. A woman at another table looked at us.

"Davis," my mother said.

"But I *haven't* done anything! This is all so ridiculous!"

A waiter brought water glasses to the table, and my mother smiled up at him. When he was gone, she said, "I don't know if you remember Katie Lardner."

"Only from birthday parties," I said, slumped in the booth. I was being what my mother called *a real pill*, and I knew it, but I didn't want to move to London. I liked my friends, and I liked my school. I liked junior lifesaving at the beach, and trips to Santa Barbara, and oranges growing in the front yard. I liked everything except being followed by men from Washington for whatever my parents had done.

"The Lardners moved to Mexico," my mother said, "because her father became a target. It became impossible for him to work here."

"No," I said. "They moved because her father was a Communist." Then the floor of Musso and Frank's seemed to open beneath me. "Oh, *no*! Are you *Communists*?"

Both my parents glanced around to see if anyone was listening. Then my father leaned forward and spoke in a low voice that wouldn't carry.

"We believe in the Constitution, Janie," he said. "And we've been put on a list of people they're watching. That's why they're watching you, when it has nothing to do with you. And I will not have them following my *child*." He thumped the table, and his voice had started to rise again.

"Davis," my mother said.

"I won't, Marjorie," he said.

"I don't even understand what Communism *is*," I said.

My father sighed. "The idea," he said, in his low voice, "is that people should share resources, and own everything communally, so there aren't wildly rich people who have everything and desperately poor people who have nothing. That's the idea. It's just hard to get it to work. The trouble right now is that the U.S. government—or at least something called the House Committee on Un-American Activities—has gotten so paranoid about the *idea*, as if it's a contagious disease, that they're going after innocent people who may hold the idea, or have held it in the past. It isn't fair, or rational, or constitutional."

I was determined not to cry, and wiped my nose with my napkin. "Can I at least finish the semester here?"

He sighed. "Those men want to make us appear in court, under oath," he said. "We could answer for ourselves, but they would ask us to testify about our friends, and we can't do that. We've heard they'll confiscate passports soon so people can't leave the country. So we have to go right away."

"When?"

"This week."

"This *week*?"

My mother broke in. "There's someone we've worked with before," she said. "Olivia Wolff. She already moved to London, to produce a television show about Robin Hood. She wants us to work on it, which is—Janie, it's an amazing opportunity. It'll be like living in a Jane Austen novel."

"You mean I'll get married at the end?" I asked. "I'm fourteen."

"Janie."

"And Jane Austen was *from* there, she wasn't American. I'll be so out of place!"

"Janie, please," my mother said. "This is a great chance that Olivia's giving us. We don't have a choice."

"*I* don't have a choice. *You* had a choice, and you got on that list!"

"We didn't choose to be on the list," my father said.

"So how'd you get on it?"

"By believing in freedom of speech. By having faith in the First Amendment!"

The waiter came and slid our plates in front of us. "Flannel cakes for the little lady," he said.

I gave him a weak smile.

My father stared at my stack of pancakes, with the pat of real butter melting on top. "That's what you ordered for *dinner?*"

"She can have whatever she wants," my mother said.

I glared at my father in defiance, but when I took a forkful of my last thin, golden, delicious Musso and Frank's flannel cakes for a long time—maybe forever—they tasted like sawdust, and I made a face. My father couldn't resist the joke.

"You look like you're eating real flannel," he said, smiling. "Pajamas with syrup."

"Very funny," I said.

"Look, kiddo," he said. "If we can't laugh together, we're not going to make it through this thing."

I swallowed the sawdust. "Don't call me kiddo," I said.

CHAPTER 2

The Apothecary

I t's safe to say I was not graceful about the move to London. I was no witty, patient, adaptable Jane Austen. And if I was anything like Katharine Hepburn, it was in the scenes where she's being a giant pest. I cried in the taxi all the way to the airport, past the churning oil rigs on La Cienega. I cried on the first airplane I'd ever been on, which should have been exciting, and *was* exciting—all those tiny buildings below—but I wasn't going to give my parents the satisfaction of knowing that I was enjoying it.

At Heathrow Airport in London, there was a framed picture of the brand-new Queen Elizabeth II on the wall.

"She's not that much older than you are," my mother said. "And she's been through a war, and her father's dead, and now she has to be queen, poor thing."

"See?" my father said. "Your life could be worse."

I looked at the picture of the young queen. We had escaped ahead of the U.S. marshals, locking up the house and packing only the things we could carry. My parents were going to be writing for the BBC under fake names—*fake names*, when my mother wouldn't even put yellow food coloring in margarine! We were living like criminals or spies. Although I was angry, standing there looking at the plucky young queen's portrait, I allowed myself to think that my mother was right, and it might be an adventure.

But February in London crushed those hopes. We took a taxi through streets that were still bomb-scarred and desolate, seven years after the war's end, to a tiny third-floor flat on St. George's Street in Primrose Hill. Across the street was a haberdasher—my father said he was like a tailor—standing outside his shop with his hands behind his back and a look on his face as if no one would ever come in.

Our new landlady, Mrs. Parrish, took off her apron and patted a wild cloud of hair to show us around. She said the gas water heater over the kitchen sink was broken, and we would have to heat pots of water on the stove.

The kitchen was along one side of the living room, no bigger than a closet, and could be closed away just like a closet. The rooms were freezing and the walls seemed damp. The brown wallpaper was water-stained near the ceiling.

We must have looked dismayed, because the distracted Mrs. Parrish suddenly focused on us. She was *not* going to let some spoiled Americans fail to appreciate their good fortune. "You're lucky to get the place, you know," she said.

"Of course," my mother said quickly. "We're very grateful."

"People are queuing up for a flat like this, with its own lavatory, and separate bedrooms, and a working telephone line. But the BBC asked to hold it, specially." It was clear that we did not deserve such a bounty, when her countrymen, who had lost so much, were still going without private bathrooms.

"We're very grateful," my mother repeated.

"Do you have your ration cards for the marketing?"

"Not yet," my mother said.

"You'll need those," the landlady said. "And you'll find that the butcher sells out first thing in the morning, ration cards or no." She lowered her voice. "I can sell you some eggs, if you like. They're hard to get, but I know someone with hens."

"That would be very nice."

Mrs. Parrish showed us where to put penny coins into the gas heater in the wall, to make it work. We didn't have any English pennies, but said we would get some.

"Mark you," she said, brushing dust from the heater off

her hands, "it doesn't do much. Apart from eat up pennies. You'll want your hot water bottles for the beds."

"We don't have hot water bottles," my mother said.

"Try the apothecary," the landlady said. "Round the corner, on Regent's Park. He'll have pennies, too."

And she left us alone.

℞

My mother started investigating the closet kitchen, and my father and I put on every warm thing we had, which wasn't much, to go find the apothecary, which my father said was like a pharmacy. The sky over St. George's Street was gray, and the buildings were gray, and people wore gray. It sounds like a cliché, but it was true. Going from Los Angeles to London in 1952 was like leaving a Technicolor movie and walking into a black-and-white one.

Round the corner on Regent's Park Road, just as the landlady said, we came to a storefront with two bay windows full of glass bottles. A painted sign over one window said **APOTHECARY**, and one over the other window said **ESTABLISHED 1871**. My father pushed the paned glass door open and held it for me. The shop had a strange smell, musty and herbal and metallic all at once. Behind the counter was a wall of jars. A balding man on a wheeled ladder, halfway up the wall, pulled a jar down. He seemed not to have noticed us, but then he spoke. "I'll just be a moment," he said.

He carefully climbed down the ladder with the jar in one hand, set it on the counter, and looked up at us, ready for our needs. He had wire-rimmed glasses and the air of someone who didn't rush things, who paid close attention to each particular task before moving on to the next.

"We're looking for three hot water bottles," my father told him.

"Of course."

"And how about some chocolate bars?"

The apothecary shook his head. "We have them sometimes. Not often, since the war."

"Since the *war*?" my father said, and I could see him calculating: twelve years without a steady supply of chocolate. He looked a little faint. I wondered if he could get a prescription for chocolate from a doctor. Then I could have some, too.

"Come back again," the apothecary said, seeing his dismay. "We may have some soon."

"Okay," my father said. "We'd better get some aspirin, too." I could tell he was embarrassed by his undisguised need for candy, and he always made jokes when he was embarrassed. I could feel one coming. "And how about something for my daughter, to cure homesickness?"

"*Dad*," I said.

The apothecary looked at me. "You're American?"

I nodded.

"And you've moved here to a cold flat with cold bedrooms that need hot water bottles?"

I nodded again, and the apothecary guided the ladder along the back wall on its metal wheels.

"I was joking," my father said.

"But you *are* homesick?" the apothecary asked, over his shoulder.

"Well—yes," I said.

He climbed the ladder and chose two jars, tucking one beneath his arm to climb down. At the counter, he unscrewed the lids and measured two different powders, one yellow and one brown, into a small glass jar. "The brown is aspen, the yellow is honeysuckle," he said. To my father, he said, "Neither will hurt her." To me, he said, "Put about a dram of each—do you know how much a dram is? About a teaspoon of each in a glass of water. It won't take effect right away, but it might make you feel better. And it might not. People have different constitutions."

"We really don't—" my father said.

"It's free of charge," the apothecary said. "It's for the young lady." Then he rang up the hot water bottles and the bottle of aspirin.

"Thank you," I said.

"You'll want some pennies, too, for the wall heater," he said, handing me our change in a fistful of big brown coins that clinked, rather than jingled, into my hand.

BENJAMIN, PIP, AND JANIE ARE THROWN INTO A
DESPERATE CHASE AROUND THE WORLD IN THE
SECOND BOOK OF THE APOTHECARY SERIES,

THE APPRENTICES

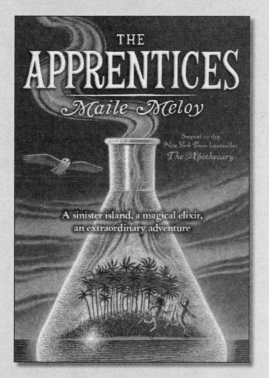

"[A] magical romp."
—*Family Circle*

"*The Apprentices* is thrilling! . . . This book is even better
than *The Apothecary*, and I didn't think that was possible."
—Ann Patchett, *New York Times* bestselling
author of *State of Wonder*